The Malthusian Catastrophe

A Novel

Ernesto Robles

Loyal Dog Publishing - New York

Loyal Dog Publishing

First Edition, November 2009.

This is a work of fiction. All of the characters and events
are a product of the author's imagination and all names,
businesses, places, and incidents are used fictitiously.

This book should not be sold without its cover.
Cover inspired by Andrew Meara.
Cover Designed by Loyal Dog Publishing
Bethesda Fountain, New York City.

Published by
Loyal Dog Publishing
Park West Finance Station
Post Office Box 21022
New York, NY 10025

ISBN 10: 0615335527
ISBN 13: 978-0-615-33552-0

Acknowledgements

I would like to thank my editors, Kristin Kearns and Kirstin Peterson. A special thanks goes out to Jean Fontana for her support and contributions towards the development and production of this book. Everything good found herein should be attributed to them. Everything else is my fault.

I would also like to thank every person who struggled through the first drafts and gave (mostly) constructive feedback. In no particular order (except subconsciously I guess) Andrew Meara, Richard Spivack, Hilary Hochberg, Gary Harris, Michael Johnson, Cindy Godell, Emily Stowe and Sam Johnson. I owe you guys dinner.

For My Mom

The
Malthusian
Catastrophe

Prologue

New York. The Seventh Year. September.

"My God! They are going to destroy everything." Caroline stood in the living room, with both hands covering her mouth, watching the events unfold on television. Mrs. Klein sat on the couch with little Gregor by her side. Just a few feet away, two well-armed guards in dark suits peered out of the floor-to-ceiling window of the fifty-first-floor apartment. They could see the chaos in the distance. The riots had begun earlier in the day. Now night was approaching.

"Don't worry, Gregor, we'll be fine here." Mrs. Klein held his tiny hand. Gregor was young, but he could sense the fear in the room.

That morning, one day after the announcement was made, the natural order of the city collapsed. Many people were too afraid to leave their homes to go to work. Several countries declared a bank holiday until further notice. The stock markets opened briefly, only to be closed by the authorities after panic trading commenced. By noon, it was reported that businesses were no longer taking credit for transactions. A run on ATMs ensued. By 2 p.m., all of the cash had been withdrawn from the machines. No one knew when they would be replenished. By 3 p.m., the stores that had remained open were sold out of inventory. Opportunists brought out what they could from their homes and sold it on the streets for ten times what it would have cost the day before. By 4 p.m., almost everyone with a car had left the city. No one was picking up the hitchhikers desperate to get out. By 5 p.m., the Governor had declared martial law. Everyone had to remain indoors after sunset.

The looting started around 6 p.m. The National Guard was called in to maintain order, but they were hours away. By 7 p.m., all ground transportation came to a standstill. All stores were closed. Every channel on television was broadcasting the news. Much of the information coming through was contradictory. There were more rumors than facts. One fact was indisputable: a catastrophe was unfolding.

"Why are they doing this?" Mrs. Klein stared at the television. Throngs of looters lit ablaze any car that remained parked on the street. Almost every large window within throwing distance of a sidewalk was broken. The rioters were now only a few blocks away.

"Let them eat cake" was all that Caroline could say.

"What's that, my dear?" Mrs. Klein asked.

"That's what they told them. 'Let them eat cake.' Everyone should have seen this coming. It's ironic that the one thing that couldn't possibly hurt them would cause this."

Boston. The First Year. May.

"So it's not Wall Street," Caroline said, digging through the closet for Michael's suitcase. "It's still a very good job." Their apartment could barely accommodate the belongings of one person, let alone a couple. Caroline had to navigate piles of papers and textbooks in order to move the suitcase onto the bed. There were cheaper places to live in Boston, but they had decided to sacrifice comfort for the quaint brownstone buildings and tree-lined streets of the Back Bay.

"Yeah, a very good job as a vitamin salesman." Michael considered which of his two presentable ties to wear with the only good suit he owned. The interview was the following afternoon, but he had decided to take the train down to New York a day early. Aseso Nutraceuticals had offered to put him up in a hotel for the night.

"Come on, Michael. You're not going door to door. You'll be a distribution manager. Moving products around the world."

"I think I'll go with a standard white shirt. What do you think?" Michael held up two shirts, a white and a blue. He could not believe that he'd left his position as a senior logistics manager at the world's largest online retailer to enter one of the top business schools in the country, only to end up interviewing with a company that sold herbal supplements.

"Michael, if you want to land a job, you're going to have to at least pretend to care."

"I do care," Michael said. He didn't. Not really. Not about this particular job. But it was late in his final semester of business school and he still did not have an offer. He had no choice but to go after any available opportunity.

He could not have picked a worse year to enter the job market. The ongoing recession had decimated investment banking and management consulting positions. Caroline had left her hometown of Seattle to follow Michael across the country and support his dream of a career on Wall Street. While she'd worked to pay the bills, Michael had incurred more than a hundred thousand dollars in debt for an M.B.A. from MIT.

And now he was applying for a position he could have performed blindfolded, and definitely without a graduate degree.

Still, even though it wasn't Wall Street, at least the Aseso job was in New York; and it would pay enough for them to live there.

Michael laid the white shirt in his suitcase. "I will say one thing about Aseso. I don't know much about herbal supplements, but I do know about sales," he said. "And Sinsen definitely sells." Aseso claimed that its one and only product, Sinsen, a root based herbal supplement, promoted good health by improving the immune system. Michael had finally managed to purchase a bottle, after calling more than twenty drug stores that were sold out.

He put on his favorite baseball cap and zipped up the suitcase. "I probably won't even get the job, but at least I'll get a free trip to New York."

"Be positive, Michael! If they do hire you, we can move and get an apartment that we can actually move around in. Plus, you could do a lot worse than being the head of distribution for a fast-growing company. Anyway, they must be doing something right. I just found out that my friend Beth—you know, the one I work with at the shelter—takes Sinsen. Did I tell you? And she swears by it. She thinks it makes her look younger."

"Babe, I've met Beth. The opinion of a flighty twenty-something isn't going to make me feel any better. I swear by saw palmetto to prevent hair loss, but that doesn't mean I want to go to work for a saw palmetto distributor."

"You are not losing your hair, sweetie."

"That's because I'm taking saw palmetto."

"Right. If you say so." Caroline denied Michael's hair loss the same way she denied that she was going prematurely gray. At twenty-nine, she was so pretty that no one noticed. She was the envy of Michael's friends.

Michael kissed her. She pulled back and looked into his eyes. "Michael, I have three things to say to you. One, I love you. Two, go knock 'em dead. Three, Beth is thirty-four."

Michael spent the first hour of the train ride to New York with his head resting on the window, staring at the New England countryside as it flew past.

"Coffee, sir?"

He looked up. A pleasant-looking blonde woman in her late forties was standing behind the sort of cart he was accustomed to seeing on airplanes.

"Uh, sure. How much?" Michael had never ridden in the first-class section of a train before. He hadn't realized that they served refreshments.

"No charge." She unlatched the tray table next to his and set down a napkin, a cup of coffee, and two creamers. "I also have the Wall Street Journal or USA Today."

"No, I'm fine, thank you."

"I'll just set this right here for you. It's a long ride." She placed the Wall Street Journal on the empty seat beside him.

Michael added one of the creamers to his coffee and glanced at the paper she'd left. One of the front-page articles was on Aseso. It was as if they'd not only paid for his travel and hotel, but personally selected the reading material for the trip as well.

Michael was familiar with most of the information in the article from the research he'd done on the company. The piece focused on Aseso's founders. Dr. David Oaks—undergraduate in philosophy and mathematics at the University of Chicago, Ph.D. in biology at Stanford, former research scientist at the National Institutes of Health (NIH) —had cofounded Aseso in China seven years earlier with Dr. Toshiro Tanaka, a wealthy Japanese doctor-turned-businessman who'd made his fortune selling cheap generic pharmaceuticals throughout Asia in the nineties. Apparently the Sinsen craze had started in China among the new wealthy class. Sinsen was made from the root of an Astragalus plant, which some believed to have anti-aging properties. The plant had been used in Chinese medicine for thousands of years, so it was easy for people in China to believe it might work. After a slow start, Aseso had become the market leader in Astragalus extract supplements. The first incarnation of its product, simply called Astragalus Extract, did not catch the public's attention. But after a name change (to Sinsen) and the emergence of a persistent and widespread rumor that the substance stopped aging, sales soared. From what Michael could discern, the founders of Aseso were great marketers, if nothing else.

A quick glance at the company's website had informed Michael that Aseso had operations in Nanning, China, and in Barbados, with corporate headquarters in New York.

A familiar ring told Michael that he was receiving a call. He half-stood to dig his cell phone out of his front pocket. The caller ID revealed that it was Joon, a friend from business school.

"What's up, man?"

"What up, homey?" Joon was part of a group that Caroline affectionately called the CKC, short for Cool Korean Crowd, a group of affluent Korean-Americans at MIT that took the "work hard, play hard" motto to the extreme. Michael played poker with the group every Thursday night. He invariably came home poorer than he had left.

"I'm on a train down to New York for the Aseso interview."

"You got to watch yourself, dawg." Members of the CKC fancied themselves a bit more "street" than their upper-middle-class background would suggest. Caroline always wondered why Michael's friends spoke as if they were on a cable network reality show.

"Why, what's up?"

"I finally spoke with my uncle in Hong Kong." Since Joon had influential and well-connected relatives throughout Asia, Michael had asked him to get the inside scoop on Aseso. "He didn't know much about the company other than their product is flying off the shelves because some people believe it's a miracle drug. But he did say that one of the founders, Dr. Tanaka, has a shady past."

"What's so shady about it?"

"Back in the nineties Tanaka bribed officials in a few Southeast Asian countries to have their governments buy his pharmaceuticals for their state-run health programs."

"Huh. What happened to him after that?"

"That's the interesting part. Nothing. Somehow he was able to keep out of jail while everyone associated with him went down."

"Is that it?"

"Isn't that enough?"

Michael was underwhelmed by this revelation. Joon had a tendency toward the overdramatic, and New York in the twenty-first century seemed a universe away from Asia in the nineties. In any case, he certainly was not going to ask his prospective employer about the official company policy on corruption during the interview.

"Thanks, man. Are we still on for poker Thursday?"

"We're on. My place, 8 p.m. sharp."

Michael ended the call, returned his cell phone to his pocket, and slouched in his seat. He'd been hoping Joon would give him some insights into the company, something to make the job more desirable—or at least more interesting. But face it, he thought: Aseso might have been featured in the Wall Street Journal, but it wasn't Wall Street. It wasn't anything like what he'd envisioned for himself.

Things had always come easy for Michael Jeffs. School, sports, making friends, girls. He'd grown up in a town just outside of Dallas. Michael's father had provided a comfortable living for his wife and three children by working hard at the automotive shop he had inherited from Michael's grandfather. In high school, Michael had excelled at both academics and sports. His father had hoped he would take the football scholarship he was offered by the University of Texas. Instead, he accepted a swimming scholarship to U.C. Berkeley. At the time, California seemed like it was on the other side of the world. At Berkeley, Michael studied operations research and industrial engineering. Upon graduation, he took a job in Seattle with the operations division of the biggest retailer on the Internet. He quickly rose through the ranks and became a senior manager in the company, responsible for the procurement and distribution of thousands of products from all over the globe. His stock options grew more valuable throughout the years. Although the options would never generate a tremendous amount of money, owning them got Michael into the habit of following the stock price and, by extension, the stock market in general. His interest in financial markets quickly became an obsession. He was hooked. He wanted a career change. He wanted Wall Street. His research informed him that the most direct path to landing a job on Wall Street was through graduating from one of a few select business schools. From that moment on, getting into business school was his second job.

The singles scene in Seattle was small enough for a girl like Caroline Bové to be noticed and mentioned continuously among the bachelors within the professional set. She was a couple of years younger than Michael. A University of Washington graduate, she had studied art history and wanted to become a photographer. She created wonderfully artistic photographs of urban settings. In her spare time, Caroline volunteered at a homeless shelter.

Although Michael was not very interested in politics, he considered himself a Republican. There were few Republicans at Berkeley and even fewer among his friends in Seattle. He'd never thought he would end up with a politically active Democrat. But Caroline was the kind of woman that would drive most men to amend their political position for the chance to go out with her once. She was tall and thin, with long dark hair, and she had a smile Michael couldn't get out of his head for weeks after they met.

And to top it off, she was passionate about sports.

When Michael received his acceptance letter to MIT's business school less than a year after they'd met, Caroline immediately agreed to move with him to Boston. He thought he was positioned to have it all. He would get a job on Wall Street and one day marry the girl of his dreams.

Now, the worst recession since the 1930s had changed everything. Wall Street jobs were almost impossible to find, as financial institutions crumbled and bankers were laid off. Michael's business school debt was as large as most Americans' mortgages. He'd given up a great job to follow his dream. More importantly, Caroline had given up everything to follow him.

The passing landscape lulled him into a dreamless sleep. He woke up to the conductor's announcement: "Next stop, Penn Station."

New York.

Michael's spirits lifted as his taxi headed north on Avenue of the Americas. Dizzyingly tall buildings, throngs of people, hot dog vendors on every corner, endless traffic. He was back in New York. He'd fallen in love with the city six years before, during a vacation with his college friends. New York was the most alive city Michael had ever experienced: it was an endless surge of stimulation. The energy was everywhere. Choices were limitless and so, it seemed at the time, were the opportunities.

As the cab pulled up in front of the hotel, a doorman hastened to open Michael's door. "Welcome to the Suffolk Hotel."

Michael stepped out of the cab and made his way to the trunk to retrieve his suitcase.

"Don't worry about that, sir." A bellhop appeared from nowhere and transferred the bag to a cart. "Is this all the luggage you have?"

"Yeah, that's it," Michael said. He paid for the cab, tipping a dollar. He hoped it was enough; he never took cabs in Boston.

He made his way to the reception desk, noticing quite a few older men sitting in the lobby with much younger-looking women. A pretty, petite blonde greeted him at the reception desk.

"Aseso Nutraceuticals made the reservation for me. My name is Michael Jeffs."

She quickly brought up the reservation. "Your account is being taken care of, including any incidentals. If you will just follow this gentleman, he will show you to your room."

Michael followed the gentleman, an assistant manager named Mark who wore a plain black suit, across the lobby. The bellhop with Michael's suitcase was close behind. They took the elevator to the top floor. Michael was shown into a suite overlooking Central Park.

Michael gave a dollar to Mark, who left with the bellhop, and made his way to the floor-to-ceiling window. It was still light enough to see across upper Manhattan. The Upper East Side to the right and Upper West Side to the left banked a large lake of green foliage. Although it was getting late, Central Park was full of families, joggers and cyclists, vendors of all sorts, and couples walking hand in hand. Michael's apprehension about working for an herbal supplement company began to disappear.

He took out his cell phone and called Caroline. "You should see this place. I can see all of Central Park from the living room."

"Living room?"

"Yeah, they have me in a suite. It has two bathrooms. It's three times the size of our apartment. I wish you were here."

"I wish I were there, too."

"Once I get this job, we'll move down here, and you and I can see Central Park every day."

"I like the sound of that. So maybe health supplements aren't so boring after all?"

"Oh, they're boring," Michael said. "But a view like this would more than make up for it."

Boston.

After hanging up with Michael, Caroline spent an hour cleaning the apartment. While rearranging the closet, which seemed to have exploded its contents onto the bedroom floor, she came across a box of odds and ends that reminded her of their time back in Seattle. The memories were bittersweet. As much as Caroline missed Seattle and her friends back home, their dream had always been to move to New York. As she tidied up the rest of the apartment, she remained hopeful that this time Michael would get an offer, and they would soon begin the next chapter of their life together.

Realizing that she was running slightly behind, Caroline jumped in the shower before changing for dinner. She put her hair in a ponytail, completing her ensemble of skinny jeans, plain white t-shirt, black cardigan, and classic ballet flats. Within minutes she had made it to Newbury Street. She loved this neighborhood. Victorian brownstones, set just off the tree-lined sidewalks, were lit from within. She could see families preparing dinner tables that, sadly, appeared to be the same size as their bedroom.

Beth was already waiting when Caroline arrived at her favorite neighborhood restaurant. Caroline made it a habit to socialize with her friends on Sunday nights, giving Michael the apartment to host his study groups with other students who lived in the area.

"Sorry I'm late, Beth." Caroline was rarely on time. Her busy schedule of helping Michael, working at the shelter, practicing her photography, keeping up a disciplined exercise regime, and performing other volunteer activities kept her miles away from punctuality.

Beth smiled. "Don't tell me. You came across a homeless person and had to stop to help them."

"I know, I'm sorry. I was helping Michael get ready for his trip and fell a bit behind in my day." Caroline sat down and, with a little hop, moved her seat closer to the table.

"That's right, I forgot your boyfriend is interviewing with the maker of Sinsen."

"I hope he gets it. I know he would be perfect for the job."

"That would be great, Caroline," Beth said. "I love Sinsen and you would be able to get it for free."

"Tell me again how you came to learn about Sinsen." Caroline wanted to be reassured that the job with Aseso would be a good move for Michael.

"I've had the same yoga instructor, Olivia, for years. She's fantastic. In addition to yoga, she is really into eastern and herbal medicine. She learned that a major herbal supplement craze started around Sinsen in Asia. Apparently, it has all these great medicinal properties. So when they finally started selling it here about three years ago, I started taking it."

"I know you think it makes you look younger, but what exactly is it supposed to be good for?"

"Well, I started taking it because Olivia told me it would help prevent me from getting sick. It is supposedly good for your immune system. But a lot of people really believe it keeps them young. I don't think I've aged in three years."

"Don't you think that is because you work out and eat right? Or because you have good genes?" Caroline tried to be supportive of Sinsen in front of Michael, hoping to get him excited about the job opportunity; but outside of his presence, she was a skeptic.

"Maybe, but I am telling you, a lot of people believe it stops aging."

"You know, Michael bought a bottle. I looked at it, and all it said was that it's a root extract of some Chinese plant, and that it promotes good health."

"Yeah, I'm not sure why that is. It's all been word of mouth, but some say that it works better than the other products out there that actually do claim to be anti-aging."

"What other products?"

"You know, the ones that claim to have the same stuff found in red wine."

"And you think Sinsen works better than the others?"

"I'm hooked on it."

"Weren't you also hooked on flax seed oil for a while? And then you went through a ginseng phase and tried to get all your friends to try it."

"Yeah but this is different. Last year I stopped taking Sinsen for about six months because it was starting to get expensive. I tried substituting it with other herbs, but they didn't seem to have the same effect. So I got back on Sinsen. All I know is that I feel great. Plus, they constantly sell out of it, so somebody's buying it."

"All right, all right, enough with the Sinsen commercial. Now, speaking of red wine..." Caroline said, opening the wine list.

5

New York.

After settling into his suite at the Suffolk, Michael went to meet his old college friend for drinks. On his way, he again felt the electricity in the air. Horse-drawn carriages were filled with tourists taking photographs of his hotel. Attractive women of debatable purpose smiled at him. He smiled back. The night was warm, and everyone he passed on his way to Fifth Avenue seemed in good spirits.

Michael's first visit to New York was with a group of five college friends that included his college swim team friend Brad Johnson, who'd grown up near the city. Brad had taken great pride in showing the town to Michael and the others. Restaurants, clubs, shops, museums, sporting events, and parties: all of these things cost money, and Brad seemed to have no trouble affording them. He'd graduated with honors in economics and had been very successful in on-campus interviews with investment banks. His first couple of years on the job were hard, commuting every day from his upper-middle-class home in Glen Rock, New Jersey, and working hundred-hour weeks. The hard work paid off, though, and he'd been one of the few analysts in his bank to be promoted to associate. His new position came with a salary that afforded him the luxury of a one-bedroom apartment in a doorman building on Manhattan's Upper East Side. By the time he was thirty, he was a managing director, and the owner of a two-bedroom apartment in Manhattan and a weekend home in the Hamptons.

Michael had always been somewhat envious of Brad. Even in college, Brad had been the most well-traveled and financially secure of all his friends. Brad had also been the strongest swimmer on the relay team. He was known within the group as the Golden Boy. But all his talent and hard work couldn't protect him from the collapse of his bank due to bad investments and even worse decision making by the bank's upper management. Now even Brad was looking for a new job on Wall Street.

Within minutes, Michael had arrived at one of Brad's favorite watering holes, the Whiskey Bar, at the bottom of what was once the Piazza Hotel, a New York institution now converted to condominiums. When Michael walked in, Brad was already halfway through a Scotch on the rocks.

"Don't you know you're supposed to drink Scotch neat?" Michael tried to impress upon Brad one of the many social skills he had picked up while in business school.

"It's a warm night," Brad said, standing to shake Michael's hand. "I needed something to cool me down." He stood a couple of inches taller than Michael. Although historically the better athlete, Brad had now put on some weight and was filling out his clothes much more than before.

Brad ordered a round of single-malt Scotch and asked that the nut bowl be replenished.

"So what are you doing these days?" Michael asked. "Any progress on the job front?"

"I have a few things lined up. I had an interview with Bearing Brothers last week."

"I hear they're a pretty good shop." They were not just pretty good. They were unquestionably the best. Michael had tried and failed to land an on-campus interview with them.

"That would be my first choice. There are a lot of bankers on the Street looking for jobs, so I'd be lucky to get it. Anyway, let's talk about you. How's Caroline?"

"She's still working at the homeless shelter and doing her photography. And looking forward to moving here if I ever get a job."

"How do you feel about your chances at Aseso?"

"Fine, I guess. But it's not Wall Street, you know? I worked my ass off the last two years for a Wall Street job."

"Careful what you wish for, buddy. Banking is dead."

"Yeah, but it seems like I wasted two years and a lot of money to get a degree I might not even use."

"Dude, what are you talking about? Everyone on Wall Street is falling over themselves to get a ten-second audience with David Oaks. Aseso is the hot company right now."

"Really? An herbal supplement distributor? What's so hot about them?"

"Every stupid little company that claims to have an anti-aging product is banging on doors up and down Wall Street, wanting cash. Meanwhile, those Aseso guys don't do shit. They don't talk to investors. They don't run marketing campaigns. They don't even label their product as an anti-aging supplement, even though that is why people buy it. They just let people believe the rumors. Anyone who doesn't need to advertise must have something going for them."

"Yeah, I read about that in the Wall Street Journal. The anti-aging stuff. People believe that?"

"Are you kidding me? You can't find Sinsen in a store here to save your life. People drive miles out of the city to stock up on it."

Michael took another sip of his drink. It was going to his head. They were drinking quickly. Brad finished off his Scotch and leaned forward. "Listen, David Oaks is killing it. I could make a fortune as his banker. If you do get the job, just make sure you get me in there before the bubble bursts."

Michael didn't know what to think of Brad's aggressive attitude. He had a lot of questions regarding the business side of the industry. Who were the investors? How big was the industry? Who were the major players? But at that moment he had just one fundamental question. "So, do you believe all this anti-aging stuff really works?"

"Hell, no!" Brad chuckled as though the answer were obvious. "At the end of the day, David Oaks is just a snake oil salesman with a nice suit and an impressive resume."

The Next Day.

"Good morning, Mr. Jeffs. This is your courtesy wake-up call."

Michael looked at the clock beside his bed: seven a.m. "Thank you."

"You're welcome. Have a very nice day."

Michael had one drink too many to have a very nice day. He wished he had not had that last Scotch the night before. Brad always made him drink more than he otherwise would have. Michael walked over to the window and drew open the curtains to reveal a beautiful morning in New York. The sky over Central Park was as brilliantly blue as the trees were invitingly green. He needed to secure this job. Brad's take on Aseso, combined with actually being in the city, had substantially increased his enthusiasm for the position.

He did not have to be at Aseso's offices until one o'clock, so he thought he'd put a few luxuries on Aseso's tab. He ordered room service and a copy of the Wall Street Journal. While the hotel kitchen prepared his breakfast, he took a torrential shower in the aqua marble tub—a few grades above the tiny stall he was used to. He opened every little bottle at his disposal and shaved while wrapped in a terrycloth robe. He was weighing himself for the first time in years when room service arrived.

He signed the bill and sat down to the most decadent breakfast he had eaten in a long time: a spinach-and-goat-cheese omelet with a side of chicken sausage, wheat toast, a bowl of fruit, grapefruit juice, and coffee. Flipping through his newspaper, he learned that the Commerce Department had disclosed another consecutive quarter of lower GDP and a continued decrease in housing sales, while the Labor Department had announced a post-World War II record for unemployment. The economic situation elsewhere in the world was not any better. The only good economic news to be found in the newspaper was that the growing nutraceutical industry was, unlike the rest of the economy, actually creating jobs.

He decided to take a walk in Central Park to digest his four-course breakfast and clear his head for the interview. It was ten o'clock by the time he made it to the zoo. The temperature had risen to a comfortable seventy degrees, and it felt even warmer in the sun. Children holding pink cotton candy ran past him. Some people wore sweaters or coats, while others wore t-shirts or light dresses. The seasons were changing. The trees lining the promenade at the entrance to the zoo were alive with birds and squirrels.

He was pleased when his phone rang and it was Caroline. "Morning, babe. What do you think about Central Park for a back yard?"

"They're closing the shelter," Caroline said.

"What? Why?"

"It ran out of money. The largest sponsor was a community church that's having its own problems, and the biggest donors were local banks that have cut back on donations. Even the rich individual donors aren't giving any more."

"Hang on. They can't do that. The shelter's been there for over twenty years. It wins awards every year."

"Well, my last day is Friday. I don't know how some of my co-workers are going to survive, let alone the homeless people we help."

All of Michael's lingering doubts about wanting the job with Aseso vanished. Forget Wall Street. At this point, any job was a dream job.

Aseso's main office was located on a quiet, cobblestoned, tree-lined street in the lower western part of Manhattan known as SoHo. The buildings were old, but the new glass entrances suggested an interior restoration. Small boutique clothing stores and coffee shops peppered a mostly residential neighborhood. The few office buildings he saw reminded him of converted spaces back in Seattle.

The elevator was as modern as the lobby of the otherwise historic building. Aseso occupied the third and the fourth floors. Stepping out of the elevator, Michael was immediately impressed by the modern décor. The reception desk was flanked by a glass-walled conference room, and to his right, exposed brick walls were decorated with framed black-and-white photographs.

His dark suit stood out amid the jeans and khakis that seemed to be the norm in the office. Even the receptionist wore denim and a simple white blouse. Michael took a seat on the leather couch and picked up a magazine that he hadn't seen before. It featured David Oaks on the cover. Aseso really was everywhere these days.

"Hello, Michael." An attractive redhead approached. "I'm Heather Hannigan, Head of Human Resources."

Michael laid down the magazine, thinking that they should not have hired a Head of Human Resources named Heather Hannigan, and followed her past the receptionist's desk and down a long hallway. As they walked, she gave him an overview of the afternoon.

"You'll first be meeting with Brian King, our CFO. Then you'll meet with Margaret Bixley, who's in charge of our processing facility in Boca Raton. Finally, you will meet David Oaks, our CEO."

"What about Toshiro Tanaka?" Michael asked, hoping to impress her with his knowledge of the company's founders.

"Dr. Tanaka lives in Barbados. He rarely comes to New York," Heather said. "If you come to work for us," she added, "you'll visit him there."

The meetings with Brian and Margaret were brief and involved very few questions; mostly, Michael listened as they outlined Aseso's structure and goals. Brian explained that the company was preparing for heavy expansion and was ready to invest in infrastructure for both production and distribution.

Margaret informed him that they were going to completely change the way in which Sinsen was distributed. By the end of the year, customers would be able to obtain Sinsen only by ordering it from the Aseso website. The product would be shipped directly to customers from the processing and bottling center in Florida. It would no longer be available in stores, and all intermediary distributers would be cut out. Michael's role would involve coordinating sales with the logistics department, managing shipments of Astragalus root extract from Barbados to the processing center in Florida, and then overseeing shipments of the finished product to end customers throughout the world.

The position involved more responsibility than Michael had anticipated. Given the new business model Aseso was adopting, the role of managing direct sales, warehousing, and shipping was more suited to a chief operating officer than a distribution manager. Michael was surprised to learn that Aseso had its own bottling and processing center; this was in sharp contrast to what he would have expected from a company of this size. Newer, smaller companies usually wanted to outsource that function, since it was inefficient to maintain such a large infrastructure for small production volumes. A stand-alone processing center in Florida would be warranted only if the company were increasing its sales exponentially. Despite all the hype, he doubted that could be the case. He also thought Aseso should use many independent distributors, which would be more cost effective and would expand the national sales presence. But an interview wasn't the time to voice his concerns.

After he'd finished with Margaret, Michael made his way upstairs to see David Oaks. Now feeling a bit more comfortable, he took the time to look around, and noticed that there were very few cubicles. Most employees, including those who seemed to be the most junior, had their own offices. This was unheard of in New York. His friends who'd managed to get jobs in some of the most prestigious Wall Street banks complained of having to work all day in small cubicles, despite earning hundreds of thousands of dollars a year.

David was on the phone. His corner office looked out onto treetops. Simple and elegant, the office had just enough furniture for a small meeting. The confidence in David's voice, his full but slightly graying hair, his casual but clearly expensive clothes, and his athletic build confirmed the impression Michael had formed from the magazines. A small bar displayed bottles of Balvenie Scotch that Michael had seen before but never tasted. The desk was large, but empty except for the phone; a computer, its monitor dark, sat on a smaller desk against the wall.

David got off the phone and waved Michael to the couch; he himself took a seat in a large leather chair on the other side of the coffee table. "Michael. Thanks for coming down here from Boston."

"Thanks for bringing me down. I've enjoyed meeting your staff."

David got right to the point. "I sent recruiters around the country to interview students at the best business schools, but we only invited one from Boston to come down here. Why do you think that is?"

"I have no idea."

"It's because all of the Harvard kids already had job offers."

Michael was stunned. David's face remained completely emotionless. Michael stared back. So it was true: somehow, he'd ended up on the lowest rung of the business ladder. The office was dead quiet.

David let out a small laugh. "I'm just kidding. I hate those guys. No, the reason is that you have just the background I'm looking for. You have experience in managing the volume of business that I anticipate doing in a couple of years. This position is not for someone who is going to learn on the job, and we don't have a training program. I want bright young talent with a lot of experience to come on board." He smiled. "I just have one question for you."

"Sure." Michael tried to recover from the shock that lingered from David's little joke. As a world expert in online retail operations and logistics, he was sure he could answer any question David could possibly ask.

"What would you do differently if you learned right now that you had one thousand years to live?"

"What would I do? How do you mean?"

"How would you approach life? What would you do differently tomorrow than you had planned on this morning?"

Michael was applying for a job in business development and logistics. He had come prepared to talk about operating initiatives and financial modeling, not philosophical what-ifs. "I guess I wouldn't do anything differently," he finally replied.

"You would," David said. "You would."

New York. June.

B y the time Michael and Caroline arrived at their new apartment building, it was two p.m. The cool morning had turned into a very warm afternoon. Trees in full leaf provided shade from the bright sun; the sky was a pale blue with almost no clouds. The sidewalks were swarming with joggers, window shoppers, and new parents pushing strollers.

The neighborhood was not unlike the one they were leaving behind. They'd chosen the Upper West Side for its proximity to parks, museums, and restaurants. Once again they'd settled on a smaller apartment than they could have had in other parts of the city, although this one was considerably larger than their last. The comforts and quaintness of the neighborhood would more than make up for lack of space.

"I can't believe we're finally here," Caroline said. A moving truck was parked in front of the Aveline, a beautiful seven-story red stone apartment building located in the heart of the neighborhood. It was one block away from the Museum of Natural History and Central Park. Movers in matching blue t-shirts were busy unloading the boxes.

"I can't believe they hired me." Michael still couldn't understand why they'd zeroed in on him; the interview had been more of a welcome wagon than an actual job audition. Aseso had coordinated the entire moving process, including locating an apartment, hiring movers, and putting Michael and Caroline up in at a local hotel the night before the movers arrived. They were receiving the royal treatment. Caroline had told Michael she didn't believe a Wall Street firm would have been so generous.

By eight o'clock, boxes on top of boxes filled the living room, leaving just enough room to squeeze into the bedroom, which was filled with its own clutter. They decided that there was either not much left to do or too much to do to bother starting. Either way, it was a beautiful night and they needed dinner.

At the elevator they ran into their neighbors, a couple that looked like an older version of Michael and Caroline. They introduced themselves as Laura and Matt. "And this is little Robby," Laura said, pointing to the contents of her stroller.

"How old is he?" Caroline asked, smiling at the baby.

"One month," Laura replied, sounding surprised by her own answer.

The elevator arrived and they crowded in. "I can't believe how time passes," Laura said. "We've been here for six years, since Matt finished his residency. The only person I know who has been here longer is Mrs. Klein. She's been here for thirty years! She lives in the rent-controlled apartment down the hall."

"I heard she only pays seven hundred a month," Matt said. New York City had established rent control in the 1940s to confront the housing shortage after World War II. Since then, other programs had come into effect, creating a multi-tiered system of apartments, many of which were rent-regulated in some way.

"It's great to see people moving in," Laura said. "It seems like most people in this neighborhood are moving out. With so many layoffs, people can't afford to live here anymore."

Michael felt luckier than ever to have a job. But how long would Aseso last? They were selling a fashionable nutritional supplement at a time when consumers were drastically cutting back on spending.

The elevator doors slid open. Michael asked for dining tips, and Matt recommended Barney's, up the block on 83rd Street. "It's pretty good food, and they have a fun crowd on Saturday night," Laura said as they parted ways.

The crowd at Barney's was plentiful, if not exactly fun. The hostess's prediction of a ten- to fifteen-minute wait was a gross underestimation. After more than half an hour at the bar, Michael and Caroline decided to have their bartender serve them dinner instead of waiting for a table. Eating at a crowded bar had been their Saturday-night tradition in Boston.

The food was worth the wait, and the prices didn't induce the same sticker shock as New York rents. Michael ordered a bottle of wine that, prior to accepting the job with Aseso, he could never have afforded. The meal ended with a couple more cocktails; by the time they made their way home, they had managed to spend three hours at the bar.

They strolled down Columbus Avenue, taking in the neighborhood. It was late. It had started to drizzle. The lack of pedestrians made the empty storefronts more apparent. "I read that the city is witnessing the highest retail space vacancy rate since the early eighties," Michael said, hand in hand with Caroline. "The economy keeps getting worse."

"Don't worry about that tonight," Caroline said. "Things will change." She swung Michael's hand playfully.

New York. The Next Day.

The 3 train was more crowded than Boston's red line had ever been. Michael stood pressed up against three other people and had to fold his paper and read it square by square.

The tourist season had started early. The U.S. dollar had fallen as a result of the historic amount of government spending needed to bail out failing corporations and stimulate consumer spending. Europeans had come to shop. New York was on sale.

The walk from the subway to the office was just long enough for Michael to take in a bit of early morning sunshine. It was a beautiful early summer day. Aseso's building looked fresh and hopeful. On the third floor, he met with Heather, who gave him a folder and went through its contents with him. In addition to the health benefits, 401k, corporate credit cards, and key to the building, he was entitled to monthly transfer tickets to pay for his daily transportation to work, as well as a per diem for meals eaten at the office when he stayed late. Also contained in the folder were reimbursement forms for travel expenses.

"There is only one form that I'll need you to sign and leave with me now." Heather pulled out a two-page document entitled "Nondisclosure and Noncompetition Agreement."

"This stipulates that you will keep confidential any information you may obtain here with respect to both business and technological processes. It further stipulates that you will not work for any competitor for a period of five years, should you leave Aseso for any reason."

"Fine by me." Michael took the pen she handed him. If he left Aseso, it would be either because he found a Wall Street job or because Aseso failed; he wouldn't be leaving to work for another health supplement company.

Michael's office, to his surprise, was located on the fourth floor, on the opposite end from David's. Like the other offices he'd seen, it had one exposed brick wall; the other walls were glass. A large plant made the otherwise functional room look welcoming. A wireless keyboard and mouse accompanied two large flat-screen monitors on the large metal desk. A rather complicated-looking phone completed the sparse setup.

Heather left him to get settled in, and he wasted no time in filling out the forms. While he was trying to decide among the various health insurance plans, the system administrator arrived. Sandeep was around Michael's height and age but much thinner, with dark eyes and complexion and a barely noticeable Hindi accent. He gave Michael a fifteen-minute introduction to the computer system and set him up with a login to the network, an email account, and a standard smart phone. "My contact information is already programmed into your phone. Feel free to contact me any time, day or night, with any IT questions. David expects all of the staff to be available twenty-four hours a day."

After Sandeep was convinced that Michael understood the office technology, he left him to finish the paperwork. Michael skimmed the product literature that Heather had included in his employee packet. The company brochures suggested that Sinsen promoted good overall health; that claim was followed by a footnote stating that it had not been validated by the Food and Drug Administration. They certainly weren't making any sensational claims. But regardless of what was on the label, it was clear that people believed Sinsen worked. The expensive office furniture, generous benefits, high salaries, and sold-out shelves indicated that money was coming in.

Once Michael had returned the paperwork, Heather introduced him to the rest of the staff. To Michael's surprise, the introductions included his very own assistant, Jason, a young, good-looking kid with longish blond hair. So Michael had his own office on the executive floor, plus an assistant. Everyone seemed very friendly, as well as professional. All the employees were attractive, fashionably dressed, and in good shape. Michael was becoming more impressed with the company as the day progressed.

In the afternoon, he met with David. Once again, the CEO was on the phone. This time he was more casually dressed, in jeans and a button-down white shirt. He wore a stainless steel diving watch and rimless glasses.

Just like before, Michael was waved in and to the sofa. "Welcome, Michael," David said, hanging up the phone. "You have a big project in front of you. We are changing the way we do things around here."

"I'm ready to tackle it." Michael had been part of the internal build-out of the distribution system back in Seattle. He had experience working with shippers, Internet service providers, and warehousing facilities. This project would be small in comparison.

"I assume you met Jason."

"Yes. He seems like a smart guy."

"Well, he left a good job in Chicago to come work here, so how smart could he be?" David paused to let his sarcasm sink in. "But now that he is here, we'll take advantage of his skill set. He's young but has double the experience you would expect. He's used to working eighty to a hundred hours a week, so don't be afraid to abuse him."

David explained that the seeds for the Astragalus plants were first engineered eight years ago in a laboratory in Laos. Once the company had developed the new plant, it had leased land in Nanning, China, planted the seeds, and built a processing facility. That facility was used to support the Asian market.

Two years after Sinsen was introduced in Asia, David and Dr. Tanaka decided to enter the U.S. market. They leased land from farmers in Barbados, grew the plants, and shipped Astragalus root extract to the U.S. for processing and distribution. Although Sinsen had been in the U.S. for only three years, it had been available in Asia for five years, and consumers there were hooked.

On this side of the world, the Aseso facility in Florida received the root extract from Barbados and manufactured the herbal supplement. Then an outsourced distribution company picked it up and sold it to drugstores or online retailers.

"Sounds like a very efficient, low-cost way to do things," Michael said. "Why would you want to change it?"

"The problem is that we are incredibly popular in Asia and less well known here. People have come to the U.S. to buy up all of the product from distributors and retail outlets so that they can sell it at inflated prices back in Hong Kong—making it impossible for U.S. consumers to get hold of it."

"Sounds like a high-class problem."

"I didn't set up a headquarters in New York only to have all of our product be rerouted back to Asia. And the problem is only going to get worse. If we are going to establish a growing market here in the U.S., we need to get control of the whole process, seeds in the ground to pills in the mouth."

"I assume you aren't going to open up any retail stores, which means you will have to set up a whole new marketing department and an online ordering system."

"Forget about the marketing. The customers will come to us." David made it sound self-evident. "What you have to do is set up the whole logistics infrastructure. I want to track the seeds from Nanning to the plantations in Barbados to the facility in Florida to the individual customers who order from us directly. We will ship to real people with real addresses. No P.O. boxes. A two-bottle limit per address. Nanning will take care of Asia. We'll take care of the U.S., and then Europe from here."

"This all seems feasible. I just have a few questions."

"Shoot."

"What's the real difference between Sinsen and other herbal supplements?"

"We developed a new genetically engineered plant that has more beneficial medicinal properties. Most companies use an extract from an Astragalus variant that has been used in Chinese medicine for thousands of years."

"But given that people back in Asia will pay anything for Sinsen, couldn't thieves simply steal your plants and grow a plantation of their own?"

"For sure, they are going to steal some. The plantation owners we subcontract have their own security, but over the two years it takes to grow the plants, you would expect some thieves to be successful. We employ a technique known as Genetic Use Restriction Technology. V-GURT. Our plants produce seeds that, in turn, produce sterile plants. The thieves will have stolen plants of limited use."

"That sounds like a brilliant technology. Did you come up with that, as well?"

"No. V-GURT is used by many agricultural companies that produce seeds for farmers all over the world. The companies' proprietary seeds yield plants that are immune to diseases and insects. They use V-GURT technology so that their customers can't simply plant new generations from the seeds of the first crop. V-GURT ensures that farmers have to buy seeds every season."

"Last question." Michael knew he might be treading on thin ice now, but his curiosity had gotten the best of him. "I've read all the new buzz about Sinsen, and I also know there are other companies offering anti-aging products. Why don't you label Sinsen as an anti-aging supplement? You could really get the attention of investors, and you could charge whatever you wanted for it here in America."

David laughed. "Do you really think that Sinsen keeps people from getting older?"

Michael felt ridiculous.

"A good Bible salesman doesn't need God to exist," David said, sitting back in his chair.

New York. Later That Day.

The senior staff started leaving the office at around six-thirty. By seven, even the junior employees were leaving, so Michael thought it was safe to call it a day. They seemed to be overstaffed for the amount of work that needed to be done. Perhaps it was part of the build-out that David had spoken about. Michael had spent the afternoon getting to know Jason and beginning the planning process. He'd accomplished surprisingly little, but he was sure he could create a solid outline by the end of the week.

As he walked out of the office, the night cleaning crew was walking in. All his business school friends who had managed to get investment banking jobs would still have another four hours left in their workday. They'd eat dinner at their cubicles. And here he was, leaving at a decent hour, having spent the afternoon in his own private office. On his way to the subway station, he walked by sidewalk cafes filling up with fashionistas who seemed more interested in the people at the surrounding tables than those at their own. Just before he entered the subway station he noticed a billboard sign advertising an anti-aging supplement produced by a new company, Reversetrol.

The train was not as crowded as it had been during the morning commute. Those who worked the nine-to-five schedule had already been home for a few hours, and the workaholics were just now starting the second part of their day. He was sharing the subway car with a wide variety of people. Young and old, rich and poor, Americans and foreigners. One of them was of particular interest to Michael. A tall, gray-haired man in an expensive yet faded suit, which he must have bought years ago, stood on the opposite side of the subway car. He looked exhausted. Not from that particular day's work, but from many years of days just like it. Michael wondered what he would be doing with his own life by the time he reached that age.

When he walked into the apartment, Caroline was busy collapsing the last of the boxes. The apartment had been transformed into a livable space, complete with plants and drapes.

"The place looks great!" Michael said.

"How was your first day?"

"Get dressed and I'll tell you all about it over dinner."

"Thank God," Caroline said. "I didn't have time to buy groceries." She abandoned the boxes and ran into the bedroom to change. Michael set his briefcase down and admired his new home, no longer camouflaged in clutter.

They picked a seafood restaurant with outside seating, just around the corner from their apartment. The sun had not completely set. People were taking advantage of the warm night to stroll around the neighborhood. Michael ordered as soon as they sat down, without even bothering to look at the menu. Within minutes, the waitress brought out a plate of fried calamari and two cold beers.

Caroline squeezed lemon onto their appetizer. "Tell me about your day."

"Couldn't have gone better. I have my own office and my own assistant."

"Your own assistant? You wouldn't have had that on Wall Street. What are the people like?"

"Laid back but motivated. They look like they could all be in a fashion magazine."

"There was an article about the founder in the paper today. What's his name? David?"

"David Oaks. He's quite the character, with a good sense of humor. He's convinced that one day everyone is going to be using Sinsen, and Aseso is going be a huge company."

"Here's hoping," Caroline said, clinking her beer against his.

"But the thing is, he seems to think everything will work out without any marketing effort. I don't know how he thinks anything is going to happen that way." Michael thought about the billboard he had spotted on his way to the subway station advertising a competitor.

"Well, something seems to be happening. I walked by the drugstore today. Just out of curiosity, I looked at the herbal supplement section. I didn't see Sinsen, so I asked the pharmacist. He told me that they've been sold out for months and are on a waiting list with the distributor."

Michael shook his head. "He's not going to get any."

"Why do you say that?"

"Apparently, the distributors are selling most of the shipments to people who sell it back in Asia. It's becoming impossible to get it here because people in Hong Kong are willing to pay ten times the retail price."

"I also went online and tried to get some from websites. They were sold out as well."

"Wow. I should hire you as my researcher."

Caroline laughed. "I needed something to do when I got sick of unpacking."

Michael sat back, glowing in his new role. Here he was, having an after-work dinner he would have reserved for a special occasion months before.

"So how's Beth going to get Sinsen in the future?" Caroline asked. "She takes it every day. From what I can see, a lot of people do."

"David's asked me to put together a new distribution plan. People will have to become subscribers through our website, and we'll ship directly to them."

"Are you going to raise prices?"

"I hadn't thought about that yet. But we'll probably have to. Of course, as an Aseso employee, I'll always have access to it."

"Beth could barely afford it when she had a job. Now, with the shelter closed down, it'll be even harder."

"Good point. We should reward our existing customers." Fortified by a cold beer, an expensive appetizer, a job in Manhattan, and Caroline sitting beside him, Michael was prepared to begin establishing company policies right away. His mind raced with the possibilities. An hour before, he had been glad to leave the office at a decent hour; now he couldn't wait to get to work the next day.

Before going to bed that night, Michael decided to take one of the Sinsen pills he had bought in Boston. He already took saw palmetto; it wouldn't hurt to add another supplement to his regimen as a sign of his faith in his new employer.

11

The Next Day.

When Caroline woke up, Michael had already left for the office. She vaguely remembered him getting up, getting ready, and kissing her goodbye. She wandered into the kitchen to make herself a cup of coffee. She'd opened two cabinets before she remembered that she didn't have any. In fact, the kitchen was bare.

She skipped her shower and morning email ritual in favor of getting dressed and finding coffee. An elderly lady stood by the elevator. Her hunched posture made her look shorter than she really was. She wore a prim suit that looked too warm for the weather, and her makeup seemed a bit heavy for eight a.m.

Caroline introduced herself. It took the woman a moment to respond. "I'm Ruth Klein."

"My boyfriend, Michael, and I just moved in on Saturday," Caroline said.

Mrs. Klein smiled. After a pause she said, "It's very nice to meet you. You'll like the building. I've been here for thirty years, you know."

The elevator opened and they entered.

"Yes, Laura told me that you have been here a long time. You must have seen a lot of changes over the years."

Caroline gathered that the delays in Mrs. Klein's responses were due to age; it seemed to take a while for Caroline's words to register in the older woman's ears.

"Oh, my. I don't recognize this neighborhood anymore. It was a nice place, then it got worse, then it got better. Now it seems like it is getting worse again." She paused. Caroline waited, sensing that Mrs. Klein had more to say. "Things are getting so expensive. I have a fixed income, and it's barely enough to cover my expenses."

The elevator doors slid open and Mrs. Klein stepped out, arranging her face in a smile. Caroline said goodbye and was down the street by the time Mrs. Klein had made it to the front door of the building.

It was another beautiful day. The birds were particularly vocal. Double-parked delivery trucks lined the avenue, finishing their morning rounds. Commuters making a late start hurried by on their way to the subway. Caroline admired the new mothers, much less hurried, pushing strollers while sipping coffee. Caroline asked one of them where she'd bought her coffee and was directed a few blocks up and over, to a place on Amsterdam Avenue that, the woman said, had the best bagels and lox in the city.

FRED'S DELICATESSEN: SERVING THE PEOPLE OF NEW YORK SINCE 1921. When she arrived at the store, Caroline wondered how much of a service it was to charge the people of New York a small fortune for a cup of coffee and a bagel with lox. Not wanting to waste the day, she ordered her breakfast to go and headed for Central Park. She was a little disoriented and ended up walking north instead of east. Within a couple of blocks, the neighborhood transformed from a predominantly white neighborhood, where most people seemed to have some place to go, to an ethnic neighborhood, where most people were standing around.

She asked for directions and redirected herself toward the park. On her way, she passed a homeless shelter that reminded her of the one she'd worked for in Boston. Within a few minutes she was at Central Park West, and things looked familiar again. Walking along the avenue she noticed an advertisement on the side of a bus stop for a new anti-aging product by a company she had never heard of, Carotegen.

Soon, she found the perfect bench, underneath a large tree against a stone wall on a busy corner. It was an ideal spot from which to observe people entering and exiting the park. Across the street, uniformed doormen stood underneath the awnings of expensive apartment buildings, greeting residents. At the building directly across from her, Caroline counted seven chauffeured black town cars in ten minutes. A double-decker bus drove by, and the tourists sitting on top looked down at her as if a New Yorker in Central Park was as fascinating as a lion in a zoo.

Caroline thought it interesting that the corner of 86th Street and Central Park West was so desirable that tour buses showed it off, while only a few blocks away, a completely different neighborhood existed, crammed with subsidized housing. Some of the richest and poorest people in America lived only a few blocks away from each other in what seemed like near-perfect harmony.

In the time it took to finish her overpriced bagel, Caroline decided that she couldn't put up with many idle mornings like this one, pleasant though it was. She threw away her wrapper and coffee cup and made her way back to the shelter she'd come across earlier.

She knocked on the door, but no one answered. She knocked again and then walked in. Almost none of the furniture matched. Concrete walls were covered by announcement boards and stains of various shades. The floor was also made of concrete, and it was cracked in several places. Peeling paint revealed several layers of old, poorly done refurbishments. Women sat at tables as their children drew on newspapers with crayons. On a door across the room, a handmade sign said "Office."

An African-American woman in her early fifties sat behind a desk, studying a piece of paper. "Can I help you?" she asked, without looking up.

Caroline walked toward the desk and extended her hand. "My name is Caroline. I was wondering if there were any volunteer opportunities here."

"Hello. I'm Christine Johnson." This response was considerably more friendly. Christine set down the piece of paper, took Caroline's hand in both of hers, and held it for a moment. "I'm sorry. For a moment there I thought you were more bad news."

"Bad news?"

"Never mind. Please sit down."

Caroline explained that she had worked at a similar shelter in Boston for almost two years. "It catered to single mothers and provided meals and temporary housing. My job was to coordinate local government programs to help the mothers find employment, housing, and education. It was very successful, but it had to close recently due to lack of funding."

"We're very familiar with lack of funding here," Christine said. "We are always looking for new volunteers. With your experience, I am sure you'll be very helpful. Let me give you a tour."

Christine escorted Caroline through the complex. The shelter had three floors. The first floor acted as the dining center and combination recreation and education room. The tables were used for eating during mealtimes. During the evenings, the room served as a classroom for training programs. The basement contained a large kitchen as well as a playroom for the children. The sleeping quarters were located on the second floor. According to Christine, there was never an empty bed at night.

"Like your shelter in Boston, we specialize in helping single mothers. However, given the hard economic times in the community, we offer a free meal to anyone who shows up here between noon and one, any day of the week. Lately, the line for lunch has been getting longer and longer."

"What do you need help with?" Caroline asked.

"I'm interested in what you did back in Boston. We are very understaffed here, and working with the city can be such a nightmare. They're short on staff as well, and it's all so political. Unless you have connections, it's impossible to get any help from them. We receive money as part of a state program, but most of the funds for free meals and training sessions comes from donations and volunteers."

"I don't have any connections, but I'm not shy. Back in Boston, I had to go down to City Hall and knock on a few doors to introduce myself. I can be very persistent," Caroline said.

"Wonderful. Before you commit yourself here, why don't you help out with lunch today, so you can see exactly what you're getting yourself into?"

Caroline agreed to return at noon. She passed the time grocery shopping, answering emails, and reading newspapers online. By eleven-thirty, she'd absorbed enough of the news and decided to head back early.

A block away from the shelter, she could already see the line as it wrapped around the building and down the street. It was a longer line than she had ever seen in Boston.

12

Barbados. August.

The early morning flight down to Bridgetown from JFK was almost five hours long. Michael didn't mind. He had once been upgraded on a crowded domestic flight. International first class, he now learned, was altogether different. The seats were much bigger, reclined to a near-horizontal position, and allowed him to control the lights, call button, and leg rests from a control panel on the armrest. The preflight drink, hot towels, warm nuts in a ceramic dish, and menu with a wine list were all new to Michael. He watched a movie and played chess on his personal entertainment system. The hours flew by.

David had been impressed with the new online-based distribution plan Michael had put together. An ordering system was to be built into the existing Aseso website, requiring customers to register with personal information. This would give David an understanding of the demographic makeup of his customers, as well as total control over the distribution. The plan also involved estimating how many bottles of Sinsen could be produced from the plants growing in Barbados. Over the next few months, Michael would fine-tune the entire process so that David would know exactly how many new customers could be accommodated each year. To put the plan in motion, Michael had been sent down to Barbados to meet Dr. Tanaka and take a tour of the Astragalus plantation.

As the plane approached the airport, a tropical landscape came into view. White beaches hugged the shoreline. A swath of palm trees came up close to the water. Strange tree-like rock formations rose out of the surf as though a forest of coral were sprouting. As they touched down, the ocean view was replaced by buildings nestled within a vast mountain jungle.

After clearing customs, Michael was met by a young, thin man in a suit, holding a sign with Michael's name on it. He introduced himself as Lawrence, Michael's personal driver during his stay on the island. The terminal was full of tourists and a few businessmen. Booths offering tourist information lined the wall near the exit. As he followed Lawrence out of the airport, Michael was caught off guard by a wall of humidity. The air was slightly suffocating, hot even in the shade.

The road to Bridgetown cut through the jungle. Michael stared out the window of the SUV as approaching cars sped past on the right. As a former colony, now a commonwealth country, Barbados kept many of its traditional British practices.

"First time in Barbados, Mr. Jeffs?"

"Yes. But please call me Michael."

"Bridgetown is located in the parish of St. Michael." Lawrence's accent was strong, but he was articulate enough that Michael had no trouble understanding.

"Are you from Bridgetown?"

"No, Michael, I am from St. Lucia. I came here for university."

"What are you studying?"

"I am a graduate student in economics at the University of the West Indies. It is located in Cave Hill, just up the road from your hotel."

"Is this your summer job?"

"This is my job throughout the year. I work to pay for school."

"What will you do with your degree?"

"I would like to be a professor or perhaps work for a bank. I am very flexible." Lawrence's answer revealed his humility.

At the hotel, the staff stood outside, waiting to greet them. A beautiful oceanfront resort, the Rocky Lane was the only five-star hotel on the island. Tropical gardens featuring white marble fountains were the hotel's signature. Past the swimming pool and lounge area, the light blue ocean was clearly visible.

"If it is OK with you, Michael, I will pick you up tonight at eight to take you to dinner with Dr. Tanaka," Lawrence said, opening the back of the SUV to take out Michael's luggage.

"That will be fine. Thanks, Lawrence."

Lawrence handed over the luggage to the bellhops, who escorted Michael to one of the reception desks. After being seated and served a welcoming mimosa, he was checked in and escorted to his room on the second floor. Michael wished Caroline were there to share the marble bathroom's double vanity and the canopied king bed. From his balcony, he had an unobstructed view of the resort's grounds and the beach beyond.

Michael couldn't help wondering how long a startup herbal supplement company could afford to spend this kind of money. Over the past two weeks, he'd learned that Aseso had retained the best accounting and law firms in the world. Every employee had an impressive resume. The fringe benefits were well above market. His salary—adjusted for actual work hours—was the highest in his graduating class. Aseso was making money, but for how long? The herbal supplement craze could easily go the way of the dot-com boom, and David wasn't investing any of the company's money in marketing.

Michael put his doubts aside as he changed into his swimming shorts and made his way to the beach. He was determined to enjoy it while it lasted.

After spending a good part of the afternoon on the beach, Michael returned to his hotel room to catch up on the news and review the work-related materials he brought with him. He'd managed to dig up only a few articles on Dr. Tanaka. Most of the press focused on David, although Michael had learned from his coworkers that the two were considered equals within the company. He'd also learned that some of his coworkers feared Dr. Tanaka; it seemed the man had little patience for employees who did not meet his standards. Firings had been commonplace during the early days of the New York office.

Michael walked down to the lobby a few minutes early and found Lawrence already waiting. Other drivers seemed to be waiting for their clients as well. Apparently, being chauffeured around the island was common among guests of the Rocky Lane. Michael realized that he had no concept of island attire. He was slightly overdressed, and obviously an American.

On the way to the restaurant, Lawrence described the local culture and a bit of the history of Barbados. His accent was becoming more familiar. They headed down Highway 7 toward St. Lawrence Gap, located in the parish of Christchurch, a lively mile-long stretch of beach known to the locals simply as The Gap. It was almost dark, and the nightlife was beginning. Familiar reggae songs streamed out of bars and restaurants as tourists streamed in.

After a fifteen-minute drive, they arrived at the restaurant. Lawrence stopped the car and told Michael that the hostess would know who he was.

"Where will you be?" Michael asked. He felt guilty knowing that Lawrence had to drive him around and wasn't even invited to the dinner.

"Don't worry, Michael. I'll be waiting for you here. Enjoy your dinner." Lawrence remained seated, and Michael got out of the car.

The restaurant was full of tourists and wealthy locals. As Lawrence had predicted, the hostess knew to expect him. She escorted him to a table, asked him if he wanted something to drink, and informed him that Dr. Tanaka would arrive shortly. The restaurant was decorated more formally than those he'd passed during the drive. It would have looked more like a New York restaurant than one on a tropical island if it weren't for the view of the water and the pearly pink beach, which was unmistakably Caribbean.

Just after the waitress brought him a bottle of Banks, a locally brewed beer, Dr. Tanaka arrived. He was a Japanese man of solid build in his sixties. Wearing dark brown loafers, tan linen pants, and an un-tucked short-sleeve white shirt, he looked comfortable in his island surroundings. The stainless steel rims of his glasses matched the pen clipped to his shirt pocket and his watch. Michael stood to shake his hand.

"Welcome to Barbados, Michael."

"Nice to meet you, sir."

Dr. Tanaka held Michael's hand for a moment longer than Michael thought necessary. Finally, he let go and took his seat. "I see you're drinking one of the local beers." He had a slight British accent.

"I like to try new things when I travel."

"When you get to my age, you stop trying new things. You just hope to live long enough to keep enjoying the things you have come to love. However, if David's magic potion works as well as everyone claims it does, I might just live long enough to try more new things. Isn't that right?" He laughed. Michael laughed too, unsure how to read Dr. Tanaka's tone.

Dr. Tanaka motioned the waitress over. She was a local girl, beautiful and ethereal, with short hair and a slight frame.

"What can I get for you tonight, Dr. Tanaka?"

"Unless they've stopped making gin and tonics here, I'll have one of those. My friend is probably ready for another beer."

He turned his attention back to Michael. "David tells me good things about you. He shared with me the plans you have developed for our new corporate distribution strategy. But plans are one thing, Michael. Action is something altogether different."

Michael had expected to get through another beer before beginning the business portion of the evening. "I'm very confident that we can implement the new plan," he said, feeling as if he were being interviewed for the job he already had.

"The gentleman that previously held your position was confident as well. It was not his lack of confidence that resulted in his termination."

After a short pause, Michael finally asked, "So why was he terminated?"

"Because he did not share our vision," Dr. Tanaka replied. "Do you share our vision, Michael?"

"I'm sure I share your vision." Michael forced a smile. He had no clue what Dr. Tanaka's vision was.

"In that case, I suspect you will hold on to your position for quite some time. Now, let's order some dinner, and then you can tell me all about your new plan."

The next day, Lawrence drove Michael to the Astragalus plantation, located about an hour inland. Dr. Tanaka was waiting with Clifford, the plantation manager. After the introductions were made, Michael was given a tour of the plantation in an open-air Jeep. Although the island of Barbados was relatively flat, the interior rose, forming hills and valleys. What had not been cut down for agricultural purposes retained its native jungle look and feel.

Michael rode in the back seat with Dr. Tanaka. Clifford sat up front with the driver. The road was dusty and uneven. It was only nine in the morning but already oppressively hot; the interior of the island did not benefit from the comforting sea breeze. Michael was surprised to see so many soldiers guarding the fields. The soldiers smiled as the Jeep passed, waving with the hand not occupied by the machine gun. More surprising was the holstered pistol that their car's driver had on his armrest.

Clifford explained that the seeds shipped to him from Nanning had been planted in a different field every six months for the last two years. They would begin harvesting plants within the next couple of weeks, and then every six months after that. All of the extract would be trucked to a port on the island and then shipped to Florida, where the manufacture of the herbal supplement pills would take place.

"I look forward to working with you, Michael." Clifford, unsure of the hierarchy at the headquarters in New York, assumed that Michael was senior to him in rank.

"I look forward to working with you, as well. Feel free to call me should you ever need anything." Michael wanted to appear as enthusiastic as possible in front of Dr. Tanaka.

"Clifford runs a tight ship here," Dr. Tanaka interrupted. "He knows more about this plantation than anybody. He also knows how to crack a whip to get things done. There should be more whip cracking in New York."

"I'll do my best," Michael responded, unsure how to answer.

"I have no doubt you will."

Michael wanted to steer the conversation toward a more productive subject. "Why weren't all the fields seeded in the beginning?" He would have thought that Aseso would want to produce as much as possible, as soon as possible.

"David and I set up the seed-producing facility in Nanning seven years ago. Originally, it was only designed to produce enough plants to supply the Asian markets. Sinsen is now sold in every major market in the world, yet we have not expanded our seed-production capabilities." Dr. Tanaka seemed annoyed by his own explanation. "Producing the genetically engineered plants and generating seeds is time intensive. My son, Clive, who is in charge of the facility, produces as much as he can given the facility's capabilities. We plant seeds here as quickly as we receive them, which is not quickly enough. We shall soon remedy that."

After the tour, the Jeep made its way back to the plantation house. Silence fell, and Michael could hear the bumpiness of the road that he'd felt on the drive in. A dust trail stretched behind them. Michael had to hold on to the strap above him to keep from being tossed around in his seat. The plantation was a world away from the office in Manhattan. Despite Dr. Tanaka's cantankerousness, he still felt that he'd landed the easiest job on earth. Given the limited volume of seeds available, and the minimum two-year period for growing the plants, there was simply not enough product to meet the growing demand. By his estimation, the Nanning facility would have to produce ten times as much to catch up to the demand that would exist by the end of this year alone. All of the inventory could be sold in advance to customers, and he would simply ship the product as it became available. There would be no reason to worry about trying to attract new customers, since there would be nothing available to sell them.

Still, it didn't seem to be entirely smooth sailing. Michael sensed tension between David and Dr. Tanaka. Dr. Tanaka's reference the previous night to David's "magic potion," and his irritation at how slowly the seeds were being produced, made it clear that the two men weren't entirely on the same page. Dr. Tanaka seemed as comfortable on a tropical island, away from the media attention, as David felt in the spotlight in New York. Michael was beginning to understand their roles. David was the genius inventor and personality of the company, while Dr. Tanaka supplied the money and political connections behind its operations. Dr. Tanaka held the title of Chairman of the Board, while David's business card read Chief Executive Officer. In theory, Dr. Tanaka was David's boss, but to the world, the company was entirely David's.

13

"Did you have a good meeting with your colleagues, Michael?" Lawrence asked, doing his best to avoid rocks and potholes as they drove away from the plantation.

"It went well. I finally have a clear picture of the operations here."

"Excellent. Hopefully your company will prosper and bring more business to the island."

"Do you know much about the company?"

"They say they use the plants to improve health and longevity."

"Do people around here believe the plants work in improving longevity?"

"The people around here don't care if it works or not. As long as the Americans and Europeans believe it works, it will bring more jobs."

"What do you think?"

"They pay me to drive, not to think." Lawrence smiled in the rearview mirror as he steered onto the smooth, paved road to Bridgetown.

"You must have some opinion. Don't worry; I won't share it with anyone."

"I hope it does work, Michael. People should live long, happy lives. Now, if you could only invent a pill to make them happy." Lawrence laughed, and Michael laughed with him.

"I'll have to get my guys back in New York to work on that. Anyway, where are you taking me on my last night in Barbados?"

"Anywhere you want to go, Michael. Anywhere you want to go."

"Show me how the locals live."

"You got it," Lawrence said. He dropped Michael off at the hotel; he'd pick him up again at seven, to have dinner with his university friends. There would be just enough time for Michael to take another swim in the ocean. After a quick change into shorts and a t-shirt, Michael made his way to the beach. There, an army of hotel staff descended with a beach chair, beer on ice, and an umbrella to shade him from the sun.

Michael treaded water just a few feet out from where the waves were breaking, looking back at the tropical landscape and the sprawling resort. Only a few months earlier his savings had been dwindling, his debt accumulating, Caroline worrying that they'd never get out of their tiny Boston apartment. Now he was travelling first class to the Caribbean. But the old question returned: how long could this last? A pack of children splashed toward him, and Michael decided a cold beer was in order.

Once he'd showered and dressed in jeans, a white t-shirt, and his favorite Cal Berkeley baseball cap, he made a quick call to Caroline.

"You'd love it down here. I'm watching the sunset right now." Michael stood on his balcony. The bright yellow sun had turned to fire-orange on the horizon.

"I wish I could be there," Caroline said.

"Next time. I've spent most of my time in meetings, anyway. Dr. Tanaka seems to have more aggressive plans for Aseso than David does. I had dinner with him last night. I like him, but I'm glad I don't have to have dinner with him again. He's a bit intense."

"What are you doing tonight?"

"I'm going out with my driver and some of his friends."

Caroline was quiet for a moment. "Well," she said, "I put in a full day at the shelter. Christine is letting me help her run it. It's not quite Barbados, but I had a great time."

"Good," Michael said. "I can't wait to hear how it went. What are you doing tonight?"

"Believe it or not, I'm having dinner with Mrs. Klein. She seems lonely, so I offered to take her out. But I want to tell you more about the shelter. I've got a lot of ideas for improving it." Caroline seamed as eager to share what was going on in her life as she was to hear about Michael's trip. "They're really low on funding."

Michael glanced at his watch. "Babe, tell me all about it when I get home. I've got to go meet Lawrence. He said he'd come at seven, and he's always on time."

"Oh, OK," said Caroline. "Have fun. Love you."

"Love you, too."

Lawrence was waiting, as Michael had predicted. He was dressed in a more casual outfit than before. Michael didn't see the white SUV he'd grown accustomed to.

"Where's the car?"

"If you want to know how the locals live, Michael, you must move as the locals do."

"Sounds good. Which car is yours?"

Lawrence laughed and pointed to an old, slightly rusted motorcycle.

Michael welcomed the chance to completely immerse himself in the local culture. They navigated the streets of Bridgetown on Lawrence's bike. Within minutes they were out of the tourist section. The cars became older, the houses more modest. The streets narrowed and filled with playing children.

After a brief ride, they came to an outdoor restaurant. People filled the benches. The kitchen, located in the back, was the only enclosed space, and even that was sheltered by just a tin roof held up by steel pipes. Caribbean music filled the air. Locals milled about, trying to find a place to sit down. The menu was a wooden board covered in handwriting.

Lawrence and Michael made their way through the crowd to a group of young men drinking the now-familiar local beer. Michael sat down beside a man who introduced himself as Robert.

The mood was festive, and Michael had to raise his voice to be heard. "What's good here?" He asked.

"You have to try the fish fry, Michael. It is the best on the island." Robert's smile was as genuine as Lawrence's.

The group ordered more beers and several orders of the restaurant's famous fish fry. Michael was surprised at how good it tasted, given the modest means by which it had been prepared. Lawrence explained that this group of friends gathered frequently to catch up on the latest gossip. Robert, in particular, was impressed that Michael had graduated from MIT. He was writing his Ph.D. dissertation on the economics of Caribbean islands, and when Michael asked for a tutorial on the economics of Barbados, Robert was happy to oblige.

"We are, like many other Caribbean countries, dependent on hard currency activities, such as agricultural exports and tourism. We are a net capital goods importer. We import our oil, cars, and capital equipment. These things need to be paid for in American dollars. To get dollars we must sell things to the rest of the world, or else we must get the rest of the world to visit Barbados and spend their dollars here."

"What does Barbados sell?" Michael was slightly embarrassed not to know the economics of the country where his new employer was doing so much of its business. He usually prided himself on his research skills. He would have to make sure the easy pace of the New York office didn't make him lazy.

"Traditionally, we have been a sugar cane exporter. As such, our wealth is subject to the fluctuations of international sugar cane prices. If prices go down, our exports are not worth as much in U.S. dollars and we have less money to buy things such as medicines and computers. This is why everyone is very excited about your company."

"Why is that?"

Robert set down his beer, leaving his hands free to gesticulate. He might as well have been standing in front of a blackboard. "Countries like Barbados that sell agricultural products and compete for tourists will never get rich. There will always be competition, and that competition will keep prices down. However, if your company can produce what people believe it is producing, Barbados will become famous. Your boss, Dr. Tanaka, pays the farmers here twice as much as they would get from planting sugar cane. The soldiers up there make more money in one day guarding those fields than they would in a week working for the government."

"What do the government officials think about all this?" Between Dr. Tanaka, Lawrence, and Robert, Michael had heard more about Sinsen's anti-aging potential—or the lack of it—than he'd ever heard from David.

"They are the happiest of everyone. It is said that the two things in life you cannot avoid are death and taxes. Dr. Tanaka might try to avoid death, but here in Barbados, you have to pay your taxes." Everyone laughed, as if in on a joke that Michael might or might not understand.

At that moment it became clear to him that everyone on the island was on Dr. Tanaka's payroll—and his was the newest name on the list.

14

New York. August.

When Caroline had asked Mrs. Klein to go out to dinner — her treat — the older woman had jumped at the opportunity. Caroline knew that Mrs. Klein had not been to a restaurant in years. It was obvious that with her limited means, Mrs. Klein could not afford to spend money on anything but the most basic necessities.

Mrs. Klein had confided to Caroline that when she was much younger, she and her husband had run a fabric supply business that catered to the textile industry in SoHo. That industry had vanished during Manhattan's transformation in the seventies. Her husband's subsequent death left Mrs. Klein heartbroken and financially devastated. Now in her eighties, she still lived in the same rent-controlled apartment; this was the only way she was able to remain in the city where she had lived all her life.

Caroline took Mrs. Klein to a popular restaurant on West 71st Street — the same place where Mrs. Klein and her husband dined years ago whenever they went to Lincoln Center. It was Mrs. Klein's recommendation, and Caroline was happy to oblige.

"What did you say your husband does for a living?" Mrs. Klein sat across the table from Caroline. She was wearing what appeared to be her best summer dress, a classic mint green shell with white trim that had the look of careful preservation.

"Oh, we're not married yet. We're waiting until things settle down a bit with Michael's job. He works for a company called Aseso. They produce a health supplement." Caroline was also wearing a dress that evening, which was rare for her.

"A health supplement? Like a vitamin?"

"Kind of like a vitamin. Some people think it stops aging, if you can believe that."

"Why would anyone want to stop aging?"

"I guess people want to be young forever." Caroline broke off some bread from the loaf in the basket. The restaurant was full of festive patrons. She was looking forward to her dinner.

"What is the point of staying young when everyone you love moves on?"

"I'm not sure. Michael thinks it would be foolish not to stay young if you had the choice."

"You can tell Michael what this old lady thinks. Some people are young and some are old. Some are rich and some are poor. Tall, short, fat, skinny. Life is meant to be lived and then passed on to a younger generation. It is what God intended."

"I agree with you," Caroline said. "I'm looking forward to growing old with Michael, having children and grandchildren."

"Of course you are. Everyone should want that."

"Do you have children?"

"No. We wanted to start a family, but the business got in the way. My husband always told me that once the business grew large enough, we could afford to buy a spacious apartment and have lots of children." Mrs. Klein's eyes watered slightly. "Don't you let Michael put things off for too long."

"I won't," Caroline said, picking up the menu. She wondered exactly how long was too long.

The next morning was unseasonably cold, with drizzle and wind. It felt like autumn. Some people held up umbrellas as they walked along Columbus Avenue. Caroline avoided stepping in puddles as she made her way to Central Park for a long walk; her new camera, which had taken a large chunk out of her savings, dangled from her neck. It had been her welcome-to-New-York gift to herself. She was determined to pursue her own interests and goals.

Joggers, undeterred by the weather, filled the running path around the Central Park Reservoir. A dog walker holding five leashes fought to prevent her clients' pets from chasing down squirrels.

Caroline's phone rang. She answered it, although she didn't recognize the number's western Massachusetts area code.

"Caroline, it's Beth."

"Beth! It's great to hear from you!" Caroline was elated to hear a familiar voice. She had met many people in New York but had not yet made any close friends. "How are you?"

"I'm fine. I moved back in with my parents for a bit, trying to decide what I want to do next."

"So the frustration of social work finally got to you?" Caroline said. "What are you thinking of doing?"

"I might go back to school. There's a pretty good M.F.A. program at the local college here. It might be a good time to get serious about my writing. We'll see." Beth never liked to talk much about her writing. "What about you? How's life in the Big Apple?"

Caroline walked onto the bridal path to avoid a clump of joggers running toward her. "It's great. I love it here." Love was probably too strong a word, but she wanted to seem upbeat. "I'm working at a homeless shelter and concentrating on photography."

"That's great. You really have the talent, and you should use it. How's Michael?"

"He's doing really well. He loves his new job. Right now he's in Barbados on business – the lucky dog. He comes back today."

"I still can't believe Michael got a job with Aseso. That's a really big deal."

"Yeah. I know. Maybe too big."

"Why do you say that?"

"Things are changing. He's really caught up in his job. He doesn't have the energy to talk about anything else." Caroline found an empty bench underneath a large elm tree and sat down.

"I'm sure it will be very rewarding in the end," Beth said.

"I'm not so sure I care about a big reward. We came here to start our lives together. I know I encouraged him to take this job, but sometimes I feel like he's so consumed with it that he doesn't have time for anything else."

"Like what?"

"He was going to join a swimming club and we were going to start taking cooking classes together. But he just doesn't have time."

"I'm sure everything will work out, Caroline. He's a great guy, and he's crazy about you. This is just a phase he's going through because he's starting something new. Guys get all wrapped up in themselves. Besides, since both of you are taking Sinsen, you'll have plenty of time to figure things out."

"I'm not taking Sinsen."

There was a pause. "What?"

"I don't take it. I don't believe in it," Caroline said.

"You don't believe in using it, or you don't believe it works?"

"Either. Neither. I don't know. People have become so obsessed that I think even if they did stay young longer, they would just die from the stress anyway. All I want is to grow old with someone and have a normal life."

"I want to grow old with someone, too; I just don't want to get any older before I find that someone."

They both laughed. Beth's statement had a certain logic to it.

"So you aren't seeing anyone?" Caroline asked.

"Are you kidding? In this podunk town? No, first I'll figure myself out, and then I'll be ready to meet someone. Listen, Caroline, can I ask you a huge favor?"

"Sure. Anything."

"Since I lost my job, I really haven't been able to afford Sinsen. Besides, you can't get it around here. I know you think it's stupid...but do you think Michael could get me some?"

PART TWO

THE SECOND YEAR

15

New York. The Second Year. August.

"You know what the problem with women is?" David sat with two friends at his favorite table at New Amsterdam House, a trendy private drinking club where the only thing more outrageous than the drink prices was the membership fee. "When you break up with women, they only seem to remember all the good things they've ever done for you and all the bad things you've ever done to them."

"I think the problem with your women, David, is that they're so young they haven't fully developed memory yet." Craig was David's partner in crime in the downtown social scene. As a remarkably good-looking retired bachelor in his early forties, he made an effective companion.

"I don't know why you dropped Shannon. That girl causes traffic accidents. It should be unlawful to be that good looking." Eric was a successful restaurateur who, by his own admission, had married far too young.

"Speaking of illegally attractive women, where are we going after this?" Craig finished his drink and looked for the waiter.

"Look around. There's plenty here," Eric said.

"All these chicks are bought and paid for. I'd like to find someone who is going to put up a little resistance." Given Craig's employment status, chasing down girls was the only real challenge in his life.

"Let's have one more drink here, and then we can head over to an after-party I know about." David signaled the waiter to bring over three more glasses of Balvenie.

The drinks came in less than a minute, and Craig lifted his glass to toast David's "newly available" status. "Here's to having

David back in action," he announced. Craig hit the other glasses with his own slightly harder than was strictly necessary.

"Now that you are back in action, David, are you staying in town for a while? You've been doing a lot of traveling." Eric took out a handkerchief to blot at the Scotch that had spilled on his hand as a result of Craig's enthusiastic toasting.

"No. I'm heading to Norway in two days. I'm trying to get the government to put in a large order. They're thinking about supplying Sinsen to their citizens as part of their healthcare program."

"I thought you hated working with governments."

"I hate working with intrusive governments. I'll sell to anyone, anywhere, as long as I'm not told how much I can sell or at what price. I don't want Big Brother looking over my shoulder, interfering in my business."

"You know, David, you really take that University of Chicago libertarian free-market bullshit too seriously," Craig said.

"You know, Craig, if you actually had a job like the rest of us, you might take an interest in something other than chasing girls around."

"Speaking of working, who actually *does* any of that at Aseso, you know, while you're off having dinner in Oslo?"

"I've got this great kid, Michael, running my operations."

"A kid, huh?" Craig smirked. "So you like your employees as young as you like your women?"

"He knows how to get the job done, but he doesn't really know what he wants. People with too much moral fortitude are of no use to me."

"Keep 'em guessing?" Craig lifted his glass for another toast.

"Keep 'em guessing."

16

September. Sunday.

"Michael, wake up." Caroline was shaking him. He pulled the comforter up to his chin and turned his back to her.

"Five more minutes." Michael cherished his weekend mornings and used them to catch up on sleep. He'd been averaging less than six hours a night. A year after starting at Aseso, he was considered the highest-level employee. He supervised every aspect of the production process, which was now completely automated. He'd gotten rid of all third-party distributors; orders were taken exclusively through the website he managed, and everything shipped from the facility that he oversaw. He traveled constantly to Florida and Barbados, managing the company's logistics. All new projects taken on by any department had to be cleared by both him and David.

"It's ten o'clock, Michael. I think you'll want to read this."

"What is it?" He did not move, but this time his response was slightly more articulate.

"Look at this front-page article in the Times."

Michael rolled over and sat up, and Caroline propped a pillow behind him. He took the paper obediently and looked myopically at the main headline: U.S. SINKS FURTHER INTO ECONOMIC RECESSION.

"The economy sucks, I know," Michael said. "That's not news. It's definitely not worth waking me up for." He slid down beneath the covers.

"No, Mr. Cranky. The article on Aseso."

He groped for his glasses and sat up again, this time with less help from Caroline. The article began with a stock overview of the baby boomer generation. Born in the decade after World War II, the boomers had lived through one of history's longest economic booms and had relied on investments in homes and 401ks to preserve their lifestyle throughout their retirement years. The recent economic crisis had radically changed the generation's outlook for retirement. It was clear that many would have to continue working well into their sixties and seventies. Social Security and Medicare, coupled with what remained of their savings, would not be enough.

These individuals were now looking for ways to extend their productive lives – not out of a desire to enjoy more leisure time, but out of necessity, just to pay the bills. As a group, they'd always been obsessed with preserving their youth, but now, in addition to exercising and adopting healthy diets, they'd begun taking vitamins and herbal supplements obsessively. Consumption of Astragalus extract, once considered a fad with a small cult following, was now a national phenomenon that had been fully adopted by the mainstream.

Sales of nutritional supplements had soared over the last few years, the article continued, but now there was one clear leader in the category: Astragalus extract. People not only believed that they could live healthier lives, but with Astragalus, they also believed they could actually extend life. Three manufacturers of the extract – Aseso, Reversetrol, and Carotegen – owned versions of the plant that had been genetically engineered to have highly targeted effects on human beings. Other manufacturers simply used a naturally-grown variety that was native to Northern China. Since the natural version of the plant had been used in eastern medicine for over a thousand years without dramatic results, it was not believed to have the revolutionary effects of the three industry leaders' products.

The article went on to mention a study recently published in the American Journal of Aging and Society by Dr. Joanna Hochberg, a sociologist from the University of Wisconsin who studied the behavior of baby boomers. In the study, Dr. Hochberg noted her own admittedly anecdotal observation that people who took Astragalus extract actually did look younger than their peers who did not. She cited this observation only in a small footnote, but it had been enough to get the media's attention. Michael remembered the media frenzy that had ensued when the story broke. Although no rigorous scientific studies had attempted to measure the extract's efficacy in preventing aging, the comment in Dr. Hochberg's report had been enough to ignite a nationwide craze.

The Times article ended by noting that two of the three leading Astragalus supplement companies had filed for patents for their genetically engineered plants. Only Aseso had opted not to, preferring instead to keep its technology a trade secret. Since all three of the companies were private, there was little public information that could be used to estimate the amount of Astragalus extract being sold or the number of people taking it. The Times writer's casual observations, however, led him to conclude that demand had reached the level of millions of people.

"This is great!" Michael was excited to see what he now referred to as "my company" appearing as the subject of a front-page article.

"Do you know much about the other companies? I didn't know they had the same version of the extract as Aseso."

"I know they have their own versions. David knows the founders of both those companies. They all worked together at NIH before he left to start Aseso."

His phone rang. It was Brad, who'd secured a managing director position with Bearing Brothers & Co. not long after Michael's Aseso interview. For weeks, Brad had been harassing Michael to get him a meeting with David to talk about going public and other potential investment banking opportunities. Landing such a meeting would make Brad a star in the eyes of his new bosses.

"Hey, buddy, have you seen the paper?"

"Yeah, I just read it." Michael tried to contain his excitement. For years he had been envious of Brad's success. Now he was an important player in a company that was part of a national phenomenon.

"You have got to get me a meeting with David Oaks. All of the shops on Wall Street are going to be banging on his door. I hear Carotegen is having a beauty pageant this week and Reversetrol is talking to strategic buyers." So Carotegen's board was having various investment banks make proposals to manage an initial public offering – it was going to go public! The banks would be falling all over themselves to impress the company with how successfully they could pull off the IPO – all trying to win the "beauty pageant" and be chosen as the lead underwriter. Reversetrol, by contrast, was looking for a larger company that had a strategic interest in acquiring it. Both companies were taking major steps to expand their influence in the market.

"Brad, I've told you before. David doesn't want to talk to anyone. He likes to keep quiet about the company."

"Well, he likes to keep pretty public about himself."

"Those are two different things," Michael said.

David was a brilliant workaholic, but he took full advantage of the luxury that Aseso's fortune could provide. He was a fixture on the New York social scene. A known epicure and oenophile, he frequented the finest restaurants in New York and thought beautiful women were a perfect complement to his dining experiences. His image had been elevated when the gossip magazines had revealed that he was dating a famous model while in the process of buying one of the most expensive apartments in the history of Manhattan real estate.

"The guy is in every copy of People magazine. He might have enough cash to buy big apartments and fancy dinners, but I'm pretty sure he doesn't have anywhere near what's needed to grow his business to meet demand. Your competition is doing the smart thing. They're raising capital and expanding. Within a year, they're going steal all your market share, leaving Aseso with less than a mention in the history category of Trivial Pursuit." Brad's tone had lost its enthusiasm and grown slightly aggressive.

"Look, Brad. I'll talk to David on Monday. I'll share your concerns, but I can't promise he'll listen."

"Okay, buddy. Just get me in there before the vultures come calling."

"I'll keep you posted," Michael said. "By the way, one of the models that he's been dating came into the office the other day. She was smoking hot!"

"Is that right, Michael?" Caroline had just come in with a cup of coffee.

"Okay then, Brad. I'll talk to you later." Michael hung up the phone and prepared for some minor damage control.

17

Monday.

Michael left for the office early. He knew that the Times article would make for a busy Monday. The subway was less crowded at seven in the morning than it would be at eight, when he usually started his commute. He heard several people discussing the article, asking each other whether they were taking supplements, debating whether they worked. It was like the Monday after the Super Bowl; the article was all anyone could talk about.

My brother and his wife have been taking Sinsen for some time. They look great.

I take Carotegen's product. Sinsen is so much more expensive. Who can afford it?

Yeah, I'm gonna start taking Reversetrol; it's cheaper than the other two. It's all the same stuff anyway. isn't it?

When Michael arrived at Aseso, Jason was already at his desk.

"Is David here yet?" Michael asked.

"No, but the phones have been ringing off the hook. We've got really slow server speeds from the overload of hits on the website. Also, Dr. Tanaka called. He wants to know how much inventory we have in Boca Raton and how long we can keep growing before we run out of product. I told him you would call him back with that. Also...."

"Good to see my men in here bright and early," David said, sauntering into the office.

"Looks like we're going to get pretty busy," Michael said, holding up the Times.

David grabbed the paper from Michael. He glanced at it and handed it back. "What do you know? It looks like my former colleagues are keeping themselves occupied."

"You don't seem too concerned about the competition," Michael said, remembering Brad's comments. He'd grown accustomed to David's nonchalance, but he'd expected a little more reaction than this.

"Those guys didn't know what they were doing back at NIH; I doubt things have changed. The ones who should be concerned are their customers. Keep up the good work, gentlemen, and don't worry about what you read in the press."

Dr. Tanaka did not share David's come-what-may attitude toward the article. He'd already left four messages on David's voice mail.

They'd known each other for years, but David had never called Dr. Tanaka anything but Dr. Tanaka. Nothing else seemed to fit. Dr. Tanaka was a man with a single mission. Governments, people, and land were all necessary tools in his plan to secure his place in history. He was happy to let David be the figurehead for the company, as long as the company grew to satisfy his vision.

But, of course, Aseso would not have existed without David. He'd spent years as a researcher at NIH before he decided to leave and start his own biotech company. Two other members of his NIH team had left not long afterwards, forming what would become Aseso's largest competitors: Carotegen and Reversetrol. Now they were back in his life. The three of them had once competed vigorously in the lab; now they were competing in the marketplace.

Dr. Tanaka's son, Clive, was the one who had convinced his father to invest in Aseso. Since then, the two men had developed a symbiotic relationship. David was happy to let Dr. Tanaka fly around the world, doing the dirty work and building the company, while he played the role of media darling, secure in the knowledge that he was responsible for Sinsen's creation. He had a vision of his own, and he knew how to handle the press. Celebrities wanted to be associated with him, and that only added to Aseso's luster. For David, it was all good.

When Dr. Tanaka called for the fifth time, David was just entering his office. "Good morning, Dr. Tanaka. How are you today?"

"Today? Today I am concerned, David. I have a copy of the New York Times here. Frankly, I am tired of staying quiet. We have to grow this company now, before our competition grows."

"Our competition is not our concern. Those guys are selling placebos. Eventually, the world will realize it."

"We should not wait for the world to realize it. We must tell the world."

"We have to be very careful here, Dr. Tanaka. I suggest that we stick to the plan."

"How much inventory do we have right now in Florida?" Dr. Tanaka's voice was becoming louder.

"It's hard to say. Michael has the exact numbers. But I suspect, given our current levels of production and inventory, that we can grow our customer base by fifty percent next year."

"That's unacceptable. We need to prepare for faster growth, even if our plan did not anticipate it coming so soon. David, we have to take advantage of this opportunity. I understand that Michael has a contact at Bearing Brothers. I want you to set up a meeting with him."

"Investors right now would require more information than we're prepared to give them," David said. "I suggest we triple our prices instead. From what I see, even if we do that, we'll sell out pretty soon. That will bring in enough cash to accelerate our plan by a year."

Dr. Tanaka was quiet. David had learned to wait out his silences. Finally, Dr. Tanaka said, "I am traveling to Haiti tomorrow to negotiate with some plantation owners. I'll call Clive and tell him to increase seed production for new plantings in six weeks."

"Good. I'll tell Michael to implement the new pricing scheme at the end of this month."

"How much have you told him?"

"Not much."

"He is becoming very important to the company. You rely on him too much. If he should ever leave...."

"He won't leave. You worry too much. Everything is under control."

"David, we need to start thinking about buying land now, before the secret gets out."

"Dr. Tanaka, if we act too aggressively now, the secret will get out."

To celebrate their three-year anniversary of living together, Michael and Caroline had made a dinner reservation at Barney's, the restaurant where they'd eaten the night they moved into their apartment. Behind schedule in leaving the office, Michael decided to take a taxi instead of the subway, but he ran into traffic on the West Side Highway. He arrived fifteen minutes late. Caroline was at the bar drinking a beer. A second beer perspired beside hers.

"Hey, gorgeous! Is this for me?" He kissed her and picked up the untouched pint.

"No, I bought it for the cute guy who was sitting here. He's in the bathroom right now. He's going to be really upset when he sees you drinking his beer."

"Damn. I guess I'll have to kick his ass when he comes back. Sorry I'm late. Traffic was a nightmare."

"How was work?"

"An even bigger nightmare. Everyone and their mother decided to call us today. Journalists, bankers, lawyers. We had more hits on our website in the last two days than we've had in the last two months."

"What did David say about the article?"

"He said it's time to raise prices. We're going to start charging three times as much."

"Isn't he worried that people will just turn to your competitors?"

"As usual, all he thinks about is our product. He seems to believe Sinsen is going to keep selling itself."

"Well, is he at least going to change the label on the bottle?"

"He didn't mention anything about that." Michael took a sip of his beer. He'd have to drink it fast. It was already getting warm. "Besides, I think he wants to avoid the whole FDA approval headache."

"Michael." Caroline traced small designs in the condensation on her glass. "What if it really does stop aging? I mean, you've been taking it for a year. That means you'd be younger than me soon if it works."

"Take it with me, then."

"I'm serious. What if it does work? You're looking pretty good, even with the stress of a new job in New York. You don't look any older to me."

"If it does work, then it's pretty stupid of Aseso to keep labeling Sinsen as simply a health supplement, don't you think?"

"True," Caroline said. "But you did mention that FDA approval is a pain. Maybe that would require people to get prescriptions, too."

"I guess, but here's a question for you," Michael said, not sure how to address Caroline's point. "Astragalus has been used in Asia for thousands of years, right?"

Caroline nodded.

"So if it keeps you from aging, why are there so many dead Chinese people?"

Caroline laughed and leaned back before realizing that there was no back to her bar stool. She seemed willing to let the subject shift. "So did you talk to him about a meeting with Brad?"

"I mentioned it to him, but he still doesn't want any outside investors. I have to admit that I don't understand it. We're making a fortune now, but it won't be enough to substantially grow the company. We'd need to build a facility in Europe and expand the one in Asia to meet the demand in those markets. The biggest cost will be lots of new plantations. Barbados isn't big enough. We'll have to find other countries."

"Well, while you guys are making money," Caroline said suddenly, "the shelter is really suffering."

"Why, what's going on?" Michael realized that he had been ignoring her life. He'd been too wrapped up in his own job's issues.

"We turn away people all the time. Mothers who come to us looking for a place to stay. People who show up for lunch. We can't accommodate them. Our established donors aren't giving as much anymore. Many of the local businesses that supported us are suffering or even closed down. It's exactly what happened in Boston. I can't believe it's happening again. Though the way things have deteriorated, I guess I shouldn't be surprised."

"You want me to talk to David?"

Caroline brightened. "Would you?"

"Of course. Anything for you."

"I've felt hesitant to ask. There's always some new development with Aseso. There hasn't seemed to be a good time." She leaned back and took a big sip of beer. He could see how relieved she was.

"I always want to know what's going on with you, even if I'm busy. I'm not the kind of guy who ignores his girlfriend." Michael thought to himself. Am I? He quickly reached for Caroline's shoulder and gave it a squeeze. "What else is new?" he said. "How's your photography class going?"

Caroline had begun to take her nascent photography career more seriously. She was enrolled in a night class at New York University called Creating The Photo Essay, and she had been going out regularly to take photographs. On their first date, she'd told Michael she wanted to be an urban landscape photographer, but she had never found her perspective in Boston.

"It's going well, but for a bad reason," Caroline said.

"What do you mean?"

"A few weeks ago, I wanted to pick up some flowers from the florist near the grocery store. And you know what? It's closed. There was a 'For Rent' sign in the window."

"I guess people don't consider flowers to be essential when they're short on cash," Michael said.

"Apparently there's a lot that people don't consider to be essential. There were two other closed businesses on that one block."

Caroline told Michael that after the trip to the florist, she'd become much more aware of the way the urban landscape was changing around her. There were shuttered businesses everywhere. People were looking through garbage on every other street corner. High-end restaurants – places where they hadn't been able to get a reservation when they first moved to the city – were now advertising two-for-one entrée specials.

"I used to think I'd take these beautiful photos of skyscrapers and bridges. The kind you find framed in camera shops. But how will that help anything? We don't need more beautiful photos. People need to see the decay of urban America. After all these years of prosperity, look where we are."

Their dinner arrived: plates of lobster risotto and steak au poivre. In the context of their conversation, their meals seemed frivolous.

"I want to show you something. I printed this today." Caroline reached into her bag and pulled out a black-and-white photo of a disheveled homeless man sleeping in front of a storefront. "This store is where I bought my first bagel in New York. I told you about it; it had the most expensive bagels I've ever bought. Now look."

The store's sign read FRED'S DELICATESSEN: SERVING THE PEOPLE OF NEW YORK SINCE 1921. Underneath the store another sign hung in the window: FOR RENT.

18

The Following Thursday.

Michael slept with his arms wrapped around Caroline. The room was completely dark, and quiet except for the ticking of the alarm clock on the nightstand. When his cell phone rang, he incorporated it into the dream he was having. He was back in Texas, running through the high school parking lot, and the bell rang, indicating that he was late for his final exam in physics. If he failed physics, he would not graduate. He ran through the familiar halls of his high school, but each door he opened was the wrong one. Minutes raced by. He opened door after door, desperate to find the classroom where the exam was taking place without him.

At last, he realized that he'd taken his final physics exam more than a decade ago. Then he began to comprehend that someone was calling him at four in the morning. The number registered as "Unknown" on his caller ID.

"Hello," he said, trying not to sound fully asleep.

"Michael, hello Michael." The voice on the other end sounded continents away, but Michael could hear the excitement.

The connection seemed to cut out. "Yes? Hello? This is Michael. Hello?"

"Yes, Michael, it's Clifford. Can you hear me?"

"Yes, Clifford. I can hear you." It took Michael a moment to place the name. Clifford. The plantation manager in Barbados. Michael had met him several times, but they'd never had much of a conversation.

"Michael, the shipment scheduled for Florida tomorrow has been stolen from a warehouse here at the port."

"What? What do you mean, stolen?" Any shipment bound for Florida would weigh several tons. After the plants were harvested, the roots were separated and cleaned at the Barbados plantation. Then they were trucked to the port at Bridgetown, where they were packaged into containers and stored at a warehouse for shipping to Miami. Once in Florida, they were trucked to the facility in Boca Raton, where the extract was processed, put into capsules, and bottled.

"Probably pirates, Michael."

"Pirates?"

"Pirates!" Clifford spoke louder to cut through the static. "Pirates have been stealing from ships in the Caribbean. They came in last night in boats. They took the guards by surprise. They shot and killed one of them and tied up the rest. They somehow moved the containers onto their boats, and then they left. One of the guards freed himself and called the police."

"Have you spoken to Dr. Tanaka?" Michael tried to tone down the panic in his voice. By this time Caroline was awake. She'd turned on the light and was propped up on her elbow, hanging on every word Michael was saying.

"No, Michael. Dr. Tanaka is in Haiti. I can't reach him."

"Where are you right now?"

"I'm at the warehouse at the port. The chief of police is here, and some of the military. No one can explain this. These were very professional pirates, Michael!"

"Okay. Keep trying to contact Dr. Tanaka. I'll speak to David first thing in the morning."

Michael hung up the phone and looked at Caroline. All the possible implications of the theft competed for his attention. He had anticipated that people might try to steal some plants, but stealing an entire shipment from an armed warehouse was a disaster on a much grander scale than he'd thought possible.

"What happened, Michael? Is everything okay?"

"They stole the shipment from the warehouse in Barbados."

"Who did?"

"Clifford called them pirates, but these people came on shore. They must have known what they were looking for. It takes special equipment and know-how to move those multi-ton containers."

"Pirates? Did they steal it for ransom?"

"I don't know. I'm not sure."

"I'm going to make coffee," Caroline said.

Michael got out of bed and powered up his computer while Caroline went to put on the coffee. He swiveled in the chair, waiting for the desktop files to appear on the monitor. It was a slow process.

The pirates had to have known a lot about what was in the warehouse. Could someone on the inside have been involved – someone who worked at the warehouse?

He connected to the office network and brought up his inventory spreadsheet and projections. This theft would really set them back. He studied the page with his fist to his mouth, running through the projections over and over.

Since Michael had implemented his new distribution plan, many more American customers had been able to obtain Sinsen. When these new customers told their friends about it, the growth in demand became exponential. Compared to the easy availability of the other Astragalus extract supplements, the limited supply of Sinsen made it that much more desirable to a certain type of customer. And after the article in the Times, Sinsen had become the year's "it" drug. Hundreds of thousands of potential Sinsen devotees logged onto Aseso's website each month, only to see that the supplement had once again sold out.

In quiet moments, Michael allowed himself to worry about what would happen if studies concluded that Sinsen did not, in fact, prevent aging. He would lose his prestigious high paying job. But at the moment, there were more pressing concerns.

Caroline came in from the kitchen with two cups of coffee. She set them down by Michael's keyboard and rested her hand on his shoulder. "What are you looking at?"

It took him a moment to collect his thoughts. "Supply. I think our current customers will be okay, but we won't be able to take on any new ones."

"Aseso has insurance for this kind of thing, doesn't it?"

"It's not just the money. The company has a responsibility to its customers. They depend on us for their health," Michael said.

"But can't people just get Astragalus extract from somewhere else? One of those other companies?"

"Yeah, but obviously our customers think that Sinsen works better, or they wouldn't pay as much as they do for it. The other guys are much cheaper. It's become a sort of religion. People are obsessed with us."

Caroline sat down on the bed with her coffee mug. "Michael, what do you believe?"

"It doesn't matter. I'm not paid for my opinion. My job is to make sure new customer orders are filled, and this means they won't be."

"What you just said – about people depending on the company for their health – it sounds like you believe Sinsen really is special," Caroline said, seemingly to herself. She paused, then came back to the moment. "The theft is not your fault," she said. "Don't beat yourself up. You'll just grow more plants and hire more security guards."

Michael definitely wasn't ready to call David yet. He wanted to hear back from Clifford first, and he wanted to try to formulate a plan for how to move forward.

But he'd only taken his first sip of coffee when his phone beeped. It was a text message from David.

JUST HEARD FROM TANAKA ABOUT SITUATION IN BRIDGETOWN. MEET AT OFFICE AT 7 AM.

Given how early it was, Michael had the subway car almost to himself. He was able to take a seat in an empty row and look over

- 77 -

the projections he'd printed out in preparation for his meeting. But he couldn't give them his full attention.

On his trips to Barbados, he'd met many of the security guards Aseso employed; he wondered which one of them had been killed. Could the competition be so sinister as to plot something like this? Did someone know something about Sinsen that he didn't?

The fourth floor hallway was empty. As he walked toward David's office, he could hear Dr. Tanaka's voice over the speaker phone. David stood behind his desk with his hands in his pockets.

"Michael just arrived," David announced, waving Michael in.

"Michael, what does this mean for our ability to meet our orders?" Dr. Tanaka demanded, skipping even the barest of pleasantries.

"We'll be fine for our existing customers, but we won't be able to sign up new ones."

"Michael, I've secured vast new tracts of land throughout Haiti. The next seed shipment out of Nanning can be sent to a warehouse here in Port-au-Prince. Adjust our website to announce that no new customers will be accepted for the time being. David, don't let this distract you. Continue with your trip to Portugal. We need to push forward and establish the European facility. I am on my way to Africa after this. I will meet with several governments there to secure even more tracts of land."

"That's fine, Dr. Tanaka," David said. "But I'm more worried about our current customers at the moment. I don't see any choice but to pay a ransom if the pirates demand one. We need to get that shipment back."

"When do the authorities believe the pirates will ask for a ransom?" Michael asked.

Dr. Tanaka didn't bother answering. "I'm not so sure pirates did this, David. Most pirates use small vessels to take over ships at sea. It's a pretty elementary maritime procedure. Whoever did this was fairly sophisticated and had the necessary equipment to execute it." He paused. "Not to mention the fact that for this to happen while I was away on business would be too great a coincidence."

Michael's anxiety gradually gave way to an odd sense of anticipation. Piracy, ransom, eternal youth. Even if all the anti-aging claims turned out to be false, he was participating in one of the most exciting periods in history. What would be next?

"Who do you think did it, then?" David's face was red, his tone more angry than curious.

"I don't know, but I am not going to wait around for a ransom note to find out."

19

Ghana. The Following Monday.

D r. Tanaka's house in Bridgetown was next door to the residence of a South African gentleman named Dirk Hertzog; retired Colonel Dirk Hertzog. Although originally from Cape Town, he had served in the Dutch military, as was not uncommon among Afrikaners. After leaving the army, he'd joined an Australian-based private security force known as Black Falcon. Black Falcon's clients included many multinational corporations with interests in places like Iraq, Nigeria, and the Philippines. Black Falcon provided these clients with "risk management services." Everyone knew this to mean paramilitary solutions to undesirable situations.

Dirk lived in Barbados, but most of his work took him to the neighboring countries of Venezuela and Colombia. He played bridge with Dr. Tanaka every week. Dr. Tanaka had never availed himself of Black Falcon's services; the far less costly local military had always been sufficient. But things had changed. Whoever stole the shipment from the port in Bridgetown was too sophisticated and knowledgeable about the local situation to have been a roving band of pirates. Dr. Tanaka needed to elevate the quality of his security personnel.

In the ransom note, that was sent two days after the incident via fax, the pirates demanded four million dollars in exchange for the return of the containers and an assurance that they would not commit such a theft again. Rather than handing the note over to the authorities, Dr. Tanaka gave it to Dirk for analysis. He asked the local officials to give Dirk and his team full cooperation. Several days later, Dirk called Dr. Tanaka with his findings.

"I hope you have some good news for me, Colonel." Dr. Tanaka had been in a meeting when the call came through. He'd been escorted from the conference room of his hotel in Ghana to a private phone booth just off the lobby.

"In my line of work, news is rarely good."

"Is there any chance that we can get the shipment back without paying the ransom?"

"The ransom note is a wild goose chase," Dirk said. "It is meant to distract you and the police by focusing your attention on potential suspects in the Caribbean. By now the thieves are halfway to Singapore with the shipment. They have no intention of returning it."

"How do you know that?"

"I have a colleague in Hong Kong who has learned that an importer has been contacting distributors claiming he will soon have large amounts of Sinsen to sell them."

"You believe this is our stolen shipment?"

"Yes. My colleague did a bit of surveillance work. He gained access to some e-mails the importer had been sending to a warehouse in Singapore. That warehouse is expecting a shipment that should clear customs next week. That shipment originated from Miami."

"Miami? What does Miami have to do with us?"

"We looked into the shipment from Miami. It left with a cargo of chicory root extract, another herbal supplement."

"I hope you have more convincing evidence than what you have told me so far."

"Here is the most plausible scenario. Some very clever black market dealers in Hong Kong ordered a shipment of raw chicory root extract from Miami to be processed and bottled in Singapore and sent to Hong Kong for distribution. Soon after the ship left Miami, it dumped its contents into the sea, sailed for Barbados, executed the theft there, and headed off to Singapore. Once the Astragalus root is in Singapore, it will be repackaged and shipped off to black market dealers, to be sold throughout the region. "

"Very clever. What proof do you have?"

"That scenario is possible only if there was help from someone who knew exactly when and how the Astragalus root would be delivered to the warehouse in Bridgetown. That person also knew when you would be traveling, leaving him in charge of the operations in Barbados. You have a rat in your house, my friend."

"Clifford? Are you saying it's Clifford?"

"We suspected early on that whoever did this had some local help. We have been monitoring Clifford. He has been very careful about not sending e-mails or making calls, but yesterday he made a day trip to Antigua. It so happens that we have an operative stationed there. He followed Clifford to a bank in the capital city. Clifford told your staff at the plantation that he would be visiting his sick mother for a couple of days."

"Go on."

"His mother does not live in Antigua."

"I see." Dr. Tanaka leaned against the wall. The telephone room was no larger than a closet, and he suddenly felt trapped. "How do you suggest we move forward?"

"We will work with the authorities in Singapore. When the shipment attempts to clear customs, our colleagues will be there to greet it. If it turns out to be your Astragalus root instead of chicory, the culprits will be arrested. We'll inform the authorities in Hong Kong to round up the thieves' associates there as well."

"Good work, Colonel."

"There is one last concern, my friend. I am told by one of my colleagues that the men Clifford is working with have no intention of letting Clifford live. Now that his usefulness is over, he has become a liability to these men. Clifford went to Antigua to find out why the money that had been wired to him there was frozen. Freezing accounts is a tactic used to lure people to the island. They don't usually make it back off."

"Are you sure that's why he went?"

"We've seen this before. Promises of unimaginable wealth are made. Money is transferred but then frozen. Instructions are transmitted: go to Antigua to iron out the problem. Then, during the stay on the island, one of their people ties up the loose end."

"I see. Where is Clifford now?"

"He is still in Antigua, but he is scheduled to return here tomorrow. If we don't intervene, I doubt that he will make it through the night."

"And if we do intervene?"

"The thieves on the ships might get word that their mission has been compromised. They could very well turn the ship to another port or dump the cargo for fear of getting caught. It is a big ocean."

"That it is."

"The only way to catch them is to wait until they arrive in Singapore in a few days. What would you like us to do?"

Silence.

Dr. Tanaka gripped the phone tightly. He found himself holding his breath.

Dirk, on the other end, registered the silence.

"Understood."

20

New York. October.

The leaves in Central Park had begun to turn to fall colors. Humidity gave way to cooler, drier air. Halloween decorations were hung in shop windows along Columbus Avenue – a welcome diversion from the growing number of FOR RENT signs. Michael's workload had lightened lately. A new shipment from Barbados was not expected for weeks, and they would not be able to sign up any new customers for months. For the first time in a year and a half, Michael could catch his breath.

After the stolen shipment had been recovered and the shock of Clifford's mysterious death had worn off, Michael had spoken to David about donating money to Caroline's shelter. Thanks to Aseso's generosity, the free meal program had grown to include lunch and dinner. In her spare time, Caroline documented the needy with her lens. She saw new faces at the shelter every week.

Everyone at the shelter knew that her boyfriend worked for Aseso; they were grateful for his contributions and thought of both of them as lifesavers. Now, as Caroline told her friends, what the pair needed was a relationship saver.

Michael decided it was time for a long-awaited vacation. They rented a car and spent the weekend in a cabin in northern

Connecticut. The cabin was surrounded by towering trees, their leaves red and gold, and with the windows open, they could hear the gentle sound of cascading water from a nearby stream. During the day they hiked on state park trails. At night they cooked dinner together and ate beside the stone fireplace. Caroline showed Michael the photos she had developed. "They're amazing," Michael said. It was true: he was stunned by how good they were. Caroline had really captured the mood of a city that had lost its economic footing. He couldn't believe he had never realized how talented she was.

He had no trouble refraining from talk of Aseso. For the first time in months, he and Caroline were sharing quality time together rather than simply coexisting. The ride back to the city on Sunday was a visual delight. Although they'd only driven a couple of hours north of New York, the fall season was in full swing throughout New England. Autumn leaves covered the country roads. They stopped to pick apples and bought pies to take home. Closer to the city, they stopped at a roadside pumpkin patch to pick out an artfully carved jack-o'-lantern.

They picked up a movie after dropping off the car and arrived back at the apartment just as darkness fell. The getaway hadn't been long enough. "I wish time wouldn't pass so quickly," Caroline said, placing their jack-o'-lantern on the dining room table. Michael turned on the television news to catch up on the world they'd forgotten over the last two days. A familiar face recapped the weekend's events. Further job cuts were announced at major corporations; problems in the Middle East continued unabated; another member of Congress resigned in disgrace. At Caroline's urging, Michael changed the channel to the sports network.

They ordered Thai food from their favorite restaurant and, for dessert, ate slices of the apple pie they'd bought. They finished the evening with the movie and a bottle of wine.

"We're very lucky, Michael." Caroline wrapped herself around Michael in bed.

"We are," Michael said. "We are very lucky."

As Michael walked into the office on Monday morning, he sensed a buzz in the air. Staff huddled around Jason's cubicle as he read aloud from the Wall Street Journal. Michael felt a twinge of guilt; after his relaxing weekend, he hadn't been able to bring himself to open the paper this morning.

He stopped short to listen as Jason read that Reversetrol had been purchased by one of the largest pharmaceutical companies in America for more than two billion dollars. The article also mentioned rumors on Wall Street that Carotegen was planning an initial public offering of its shares.

Jason stopped reading when a junior staff member feigned a cough to alert him to Michael's presence. "Oh. Hey, Michael."

"Don't let me stop you. Continue reading."

Jason hesitated.

"Go on," Michael said. "We need to know what our competitors are doing."

"Okay." Jason skimmed the paper to find his place. "'Millions are spent on nutritional supplements, which take the form of vitamins, minerals, fatty acids, amino acids, and botanicals. This last category has seen the largest growth in terms of sales. As baby boomers enter their retirement years, they look for new health-enhancing and anti-aging products. The most popular of these products is Astragalus extract. Three companies dominate this category.'"

He glanced at Michael, who nodded for him to continue. He was as interested as anyone. "'Aseso was the first to come out with an extract from a genetically engineered plant. Its product, known as Sinsen, is perceived as best in breed and commands a much higher price. Reversetrol was second, announcing its genetically engineered version two years ago. It leads in terms of market share. In sharp contrast to Aseso's strategy of limiting the amount of product available for purchase, Reversetrol has flooded the market with a cheaper version of Sinsen and acquired more customers. With its acquisition, it will have the resources to further expand its operations.

"'The third company, Carotegen, although just over a year old, has quickly gained market share by offering its version of

Astragalus as a sports drink powder that also contains the daily requirements of vitamins and minerals. Industry analysts estimate that nearly fifteen percent of the U.S. and ten percent of the rest of the developed world are now taking some version of an anti-aging supplement on a daily basis. Some people claim that these products actually reverse aging. The scientific community discounts any of these claims and attributes Astragalus users' healthful looks to diet and exercise. A few scientists support the theory behind the claims but call for clinical trials to validate the supplement's efficacy. Only time will tell whether Reversetrol is worth its lofty sale price.'" Jason set the paper down, and everyone looked to Michael for a reaction.

"Has David seen this?" Michael asked.

"I don't know. He's not here. He left for Europe over the weekend."

David had been traveling abroad more and more frequently to promote Sinsen – a practice he avoided in the U.S. He gave frequent interviews on European television, lectured at conferences, and met with various heads of state. His social status had only increased. He was named one of the most eligible bachelors in America by several popular gossip magazines. Michael appreciated the trust David placed in his capabilities, but at the moment he didn't feel all that capable. He asked Jason if he could borrow his copy of the Wall Street Journal and escaped with it to his office.

The article bothered Michael. Sinsen was the most expensive product on the market, making Aseso incredibly profitable. But they hadn't had enough inventory to sign up a meaningful amount of new customers. The other companies were signing up new customers daily. Dr. Tanaka frequently expressed his frustration at the increase in competition. Only David seemed confident in the company's position.

Michael sat in front of his computer, having failed to reach either David or Dr. Tanaka. The phone rang constantly. Michael let all the calls go to voicemail. The company had been receiving daily offers from investors and distributors wanting to take part in the action. People from around the world had been calling to voice their frustration at being unable to sign up as customers. Reporters were undoubtedly calling today to get a reaction from Aseso about the latest market developments. Michael was beginning to grow tired of the media. He was always expected to know everything, to have a reaction.

Finally a call came through from a name he recognized. He punched the speakerphone button and sat back in his chair.

"What's up, Brad?"

"I'll tell you what's not up: Aseso's sales. The competition is going to eat your lunch while your CEO does the international talk show circuit." Brad had become increasingly obsessed with Aseso. He called Michael weekly, pleading with him to let Bearing Brothers help Aseso obtain financing to help grow the company. If Michael stopped reading the papers altogether, he would have no problem keeping abreast of Aseso's developments. He could just call Brad.

"I've told you before, buddy. We're not interested in talking to outside investors." It was the standard answer. Michael hadn't mentioned Brad to David in some time.

"It's all very cool and sexy that you guys were the first to come up with this stuff, but now the big boys are getting into the game. Reversetrol is going to have unlimited access to capital. Unless you guys make a major move, it's going to be over for you by this time next year."

"Why do you say that?"

"Come on, Michael. Didn't you read the paper today? The cat's out of the bag. All three of the founders worked at NIH together. Now everyone knows that both Reversetrol and Carotegen have the same stuff as you guys."

"No, Brad. They all worked at NIH, but that doesn't mean the products are the same. David developed the second generation of Sinsen after he left NIH. Who knows what the other guys have? If people didn't think our stuff works better, they wouldn't pay up for it."

"They pay up for it for the same reason people pay up for designer jeans. It's a cool brand. But brands come and go. I don't know if the Astragalus thing works or not, but I do know that after Carotegen does their IPO, they're going to flood the market with advertising. They are going to promote the hell out of their shit while you guys lag behind as the small niche player. Come on, Michael. Get me in there. If Carotegen can go public, so can you."

"I don't know what to tell you. David doesn't want to make a major move right now."

All Michael could do was voice the company's official position. He had been concerned about the competition for months, but although David left him in charge of the office, he didn't give him any power over policy. Brad sounded defeated, but he finally accepted Michael's answer. Michael knew he'd be calling again next week.

Michael hung up the phone and stared at the Wall Street Journal. Up to this point, all three companies had funded themselves using private investors. Their capacity to grow had been limited. Now that the large pharmaceutical companies and the public equity markets were interested, it was a whole new ball game.

Botanical products had been around for years, with customers spending hard-earned cash on the promise of youth, but this time it was different. Three scientists who had worked together in the same government lab had each started a company to sell potential immortality. The technology was unproven, but investors were willing to spend millions of dollars in hopes of great returns. Many companies had offered to invest in Aseso and help it grow. With new funding, Aseso could build laboratories around the world to produce new seeds instead of being limited to what was generated in Nanning. Many more plantations could be purchased. Warehouse facilities in Europe and Asia could be built. It was frustrating that Aseso was not taking advantage of these opportunities.

On the other hand, if it turned out that Sinsen and the other products on the market had no more anti-aging properties than a multivitamin, customers' hopes and dreams would be devastated. It would all have been a fraud, and Michael would be out of a job – in the best-case scenario.

But was this really his responsibility? Consumers and investors believed what they chose to believe. That was what Brad had been telling him for over a year. It didn't matter whether Sinsen worked or not. All that mattered was that people thought it did and were willing to pay for it. Michael was simply satisfying market demand. This was a business. And business ran on money.

When the phone rang again, Michael was prepared to let it go to voicemail. But it was Brad again. "Listen, Michael. How about this: no outside investors. I have a plan for how to get you guys new money without selling any ownership in your company."

This, Michael thought, was something David could not possibly say no to.

"All right, Brad. I want to hear a little more first. But I'll definitely see what I can do."

21

November.

As soon as he got off the phone with Brad, Michael sent a fax to Dr. Tanaka, who had been in Africa for the past week to meet with government officials and business leaders. Knowing that Dr. Tanaka might be difficult to reach, Michael waited anxiously by his phone.

Dr. Tanaka's African negotiations were proving to be a challenge. Many African plantation owners were eager to plant Aseso's seeds on land traditionally used for cocoa, coffee, and sugar cane. Aseso was offering very attractive prices to lease this land. However, given the many years it took to cultivate Astragalus plants, the owners required payments up front. Although the total revenues generated from the plants would be more than twice what they could make with traditional crops, the owners were afraid the demand for Sinsen might suddenly vanish, leaving Aseso unable to pay for the harvest. The military governments also wanted timely payments in exchange for providing the security necessary to prevent a repeat of what had happened in Barbados.

Although Aseso had been incredibly successful, the company did not have enough money to pay in advance for the millions of acres it needed. Aseso's ambitions were of oceanic proportions; the plan would require upfront payments of hundreds of millions of dollars to several countries in Africa. Dr. Tanaka was a wealthy man, but his personal fortune was measured in the tens of millions, not the hundreds. Aseso's business model was considered too speculative for it to secure bank loans that large. Successful pharmaceutical companies and equity investors were the only source of capital available to Aseso, but accepting their money would require the co-founders to give up partial ownership and possibly even control. This was something neither David nor Dr. Tanaka was willing to do.

The constraints resulting from Aseso's lack of investment capital were a constant source of frustration to Dr. Tanaka, who wished to expand Aseso's planting capacity as quickly as possible.

That day, Dr. Tanaka had dined with a wealthy businessman in Accra, Ghana, who afterwards had dropped him off at his hotel. They shook hands and assured each other of the prosperous business they would conduct in the near future. The businessman retreated into his limousine as Dr. Tanaka walked toward the hotel entrance. Dr. Tanaka would return to Barbados that evening. As he headed for the elevator, the concierge rushed over with a fax.

"This came for you an hour ago, sir."

"Thank you." Dr. Tanaka took the folded piece of paper. "Can you please arrange for a car to take me to the airport in one hour?"

"Certainly, sir."

The elevator arrived. Dr. Tanaka stepped inside, pressed the button for the twelfth floor, and unfolded the paper. It was from Michael: a page copied from the Wall Street Journal.

He called Michael as soon as he was inside his hotel room. The packing would have to wait.

Michael knew from the international caller ID that it would be one of his two bosses.

"Michael, this is Dr. Tanaka."

"Did you get my fax?"

"Yes, I most certainly did get your fax. Where is David? I told him this would happen. I told him we would find ourselves at a competitive disadvantage." His tone, though quiet, was one of anger and frustration.

"David's in London. I just spoke with him. He doesn't believe these developments pose a real threat."

"And why is that? We are falling behind in the industry that we created! We need to do something soon."

"My friend Brad, at Bearing Brothers, thinks he can get us funding without having to sell any part of the company."

"Good. We need new ideas. Tell your friend to meet us in London in two days, and contact David. Let him know that I will be in London tomorrow. I want you to fly there as well. We will all meet with your friend."

"Will do." Michael knew Brad would travel to the North Pole on a moment's notice for an opportunity to do business with Aseso.

Michael had spent a good deal of time supporting the sometimes contradictory activities of his two bosses. There were times when he felt overwhelmed. At the moment, though, he felt empowered. This was his meeting. He was directing the activities of his bosses. He was going to London. Michael instructed his assistant Jason to contact David and inform him of the plan.

Then he called Brad. "You're on, buddy. They want you in London in two days."

"You're kidding."

"This better be a really fucking good meeting, Brad."

"It will be, it will be. Thanks, dude. I'll fly out tomorrow. I'll get our London guys to help put together the presentation. You won't be disappointed."

"I better not be," Michael said, putting his feet up on his desk. He could definitely get used to calling the shots.

Michael took a flight to Heathrow that night. His first-class seat offered a fully reclining bed, but by the time he had finished with dinner service, there were only four hours left in the flight. With the time difference, he would land at eight a.m. local time. Jet lag was inescapable.

After clearing customs, he took a cab to his hotel. London was very different from New York. The buildings were much older, the streets much narrower. Michael noticed how clean the sidewalks were, in contrast to the gritty concrete of Manhattan. And the taxis, instead of modern yellow sedans, had the look of 1940s station wagons that were either black or completely painted over with brand logos in eye-popping colors. His cab navigated the streets of the West End, along Hyde Park, to his hotel.

A note was waiting for him. David was staying at the same hotel and wanted to meet for lunch. Michael was escorted to his room by the bellhop, to whom he handed a 10-pound tip. The bellhop thanked him profusely and left the room.

Michael opened the curtains to let in some light. His room had a nice view of Hyde Park. Not quite as large or full of trees as Central Park, but uniquely beautiful. Wooden benches lined gravel pathways. Weeping willows lent magic to the landscape. One of these days, he thought, he'd have to bring Caroline with him on a business trip. He was always leaving for pleasant destinations in a hurry; there never seemed to be time to plan for a companion.

He closed the curtains and laid down for a nap.

David was already waiting in the lobby when Michael stepped out of the elevator. Michael had expected London attire to be more formal; he'd worn slacks, a white button-down shirt, and a blue blazer. David was standing there in jeans, a black t-shirt, and a dark brown leather jacket.

"First time in London, Michael?"

"Yes. I can't wait to see more of it, now that I'm slightly awake."

"Great. Let's go see one of its best inventions."

"What's that?"

"The gastropub."

They made their way through the confusing streets of Notting Hill and arrived at the Westbourne. As David explained, it was one of London's more popular gastropubs, a combination of high-end cuisine and casual alehouse ambience. Pot-roasted pheasant and herb-infused whole fish were on the menu, but everything had to be ordered at the bar. Long benches were available for communal seating. David recommended that Michael try a Tetley's Bitter to get the full pub experience.

"So your friend Brad will finally get his opportunity to meet with us." David rotated his plate to have the whole fish closer to him.

"I think he has some pretty good ideas," Michael said. "We've just about hit a plateau. If we don't grow our capacity, we'll be left in the dust in terms of market share."

"I'm all for growing the company, Michael, but we have to be careful. Dr. Tanaka is making both friends and enemies. It is incredibly important that we associate ourselves with the right people."

Michael wasn't entirely sure what kind of enemies David was referring to, but now didn't seem like the best time to ask. "I understand. But aren't you concerned that Carotegen and Reversetrol are going to take our customers?"

"They aren't going to take our customers; we are going to take theirs. They're spending millions of dollars in marketing campaigns so that we don't have to. Once everyone believes in the concept, the better mousetrap will sell itself."

"And you're sure ours is better?" Michael recalled Brad's observation that all three founders had started out at the same NIH lab. And on a more basic level, did David really believe that any of the three products prevented aging?

"Michael, cream always rises to the top. Now why don't you go to the bar and get us a couple more pints?"

The next day, David and Michael met Dr. Tanaka in the lobby of Bearing Brothers' London office. The three of them took the elevator upstairs and were shown to a glass-encased conference room furnished with a long, dark mahogany table and several wide-screen TVs.

Brad, dressed in a dark blue pinstripe suit, strode in and introduced himself to David and Dr. Tanaka. He thanked Michael for setting up the meeting.

"I've been looking forward to this for some time," Brad said, with a bit too much excitement in his voice.

"Well, then, I expect we won't be disappointed," Dr. Tanaka replied in his typically surly manner.

Coffee arrived and Brad, taking his cue from Dr. Tanaka's game face, took a seat and started his presentation. He turned on one of the wide-screens, narrating an introduction to the bank and its long list of qualifications, neatly outlined in a stock PowerPoint presentation.

Michael took notes, trying to conceal his nervous energy. Dr. Tanaka asked a few pointed questions about the bank while David sat quietly reading e-mails on his touch screen phone. Finally, Brad came to the point of the presentation. He stood and walked over to the screen.

"Gentlemen, we understand your position. Your competition is taking actions to raise capital that will enable them to capture this exploding market. They have decided to sell themselves entirely to other companies, or to sell pieces of themselves to the equity markets. We have come up with a way for you to obtain cash without having to give away equity. We will get your customers to give you the money."

Brad paused for emphasis. David looked up. Brad had his attention. "Here is the idea: your customers are incredibly loyal. They think that Sinsen is the fountain of youth."

"Hold on," David said. "We're not saying anything about the fountain of youth."

"It doesn't matter," Brad continued. "They'll do anything to keep taking it. The first you should do is change your business model and sign up your existing customers to long-term contracts – like the ones mobile phone companies use, but without the option to cancel before the contract ends. These contracts will obligate each customer to pay you every month for Sinsen for the term of the contract.

"Now, here's the most important part. We have investors who are ready to pay you a lump sum to buy these customer contracts from you. The lump sum will be at a discount to the total monetary value of the contracts. You'll get the money up front, and the investors will get an annuity. We'll calculate the annuity so that the investors will earn a decent return on their money."

David broke in. "Brad, this is intriguing, but isn't it the same type of thing banks did with subprime mortgages a few years ago?" He straightened in his seat. "As I recall, it didn't work out so well for those institutions, which are now defunct. Given that investors got burned with mortgage-backed bonds before, why would they want to buy our bonds?"

"The mistake that investors made with those collateralized debt obligations—CDOs—was in believing that people would do everything they could to not walk away from their homes during financial hardship. In a financial crisis, people might walk away from their homes. But I doubt they will walk away from their lives."

"How soon could you put this into place?" Dr. Tanaka's tone revealed increased enthusiasm.

"Just give us the word and we'll start drafting the documents." Brad left the final image of the presentation, Aseso's logo plastered across the globe, on the screen and sauntered back to the conference table.

"How big could the deal be?" Dr. Tanaka asked.

"Oh, I don't know." Brad took a seat, practically smirking. "A billion dollars is a nice round number."

The next day, David took the high-speed train down to Paris to continue with his public relations tour. Dr. Tanaka returned to his home in Barbados. Michael and Brad flew back to New York together.

"So, do you think your guys are going to go for it?" Brad asked Michael. He took a sip of his Scotch at the bar on the second level of the jumbo jet. Brad's confidence had slipped a notch as the waiting began. Dr. Tanaka had promised to get back to Brad with a decision, and it was clear that Brad was going to have trouble sleeping until he heard. A deal of this size would more than make Brad's budget for the year and earn over forty million dollars in fees for his firm.

"Not sure." Michael had opted for a martini. "But if we want to keep growing, we have to do something."

Michael was starting to get nervous. His worlds had begun to collide. Brad needed the deal to make his career. Caroline needed the donations to keep the shelter going. Just two days ago, Michael's mother had called him. She wanted a few bottles of Sinsen for herself and her friends. Expectations from Aseso's customers seemed unrealistically high.

Michael needed to deliver success not only for his employer, but for everyone else in his life as well.

22

December.

Since his presentation in London, Brad had called Michael every day, sniffing around for an update. David and Dr. Tanaka hadn't made any decisions. Every day the response was the same: nothing yet.

"I think Dr. Tanaka and Brad are right." Michael found himself pressing David on the issue over lunch at their favorite café in SoHo. "We should do a deal now and go after the market share we're giving up."

"Yeah? Why's that?"

"To expand our capacity and grow like Reversetrol and Carotegen."

"Our capacity is limited by the seeds we can produce in Nanning, a technical dilemma that no one but Clive and myself seems to either understand or appreciate. Dr. Tanaka just wants the money to go play real-world Monopoly in Africa. If he's not careful, he's going to end up on the jail square of the board. Brad just wants to do the transaction so he can get written up in The Daily Deal. He'd sell his girlfriend if he thought it would help him get promoted."

"Don't you want the money?"

"We'll need money soon enough, but not before I can do a deal without anyone asking too many questions."

"How soon is that?"

David smiled as he set his fork down. "Did I ever tell you the story about the big bull and the little bull?"

"No, I don't think so."

"A big bull and a little bull are sitting on top of a hill overlooking a large field of heifers. The little bull looks up to the big bull and says, 'I have an idea. Why don't we run down there and fuck one of those heifers.' The big bull looks down at the little bull and says, 'I have a better idea. Why don't we walk down there and fuck 'em all.'"

"That's a funny story," Michael laughed.

"Tell your buddy Brad to stop being such a little bull."

Brad found the story less than funny. Michael understood Brad's sense of urgency. Senior management at Bearing Brothers was putting pressure on him to secure the contract with Aseso. Carotegen had successfully conducted its IPO, using Bearing Brothers' biggest competitor. It had been a celebrated deal, putting the supplement company's value at over twenty billion dollars. The sale of Reversetrol months earlier had been managed by yet another competing bank. Bearing Brothers had chosen its horse in Aseso, making itself off limits to any of Aseso's competitors who might want to do a deal. That choice was now being seriously questioned by Brad's superiors. The economy showed no signs of recovery, and there was very little business in the financial world. At this point, a yes or no on the Aseso deal would make or break Bearing Brothers' year and Brad's career.

Still, Brad's obsession was starting to wear on Michael's nerves. When he saw Brad's number come up on his caller ID, he assumed it would be another "Hey, buddy, any word since yesterday?" call.

Michael didn't bother with a salutation. "Nothing new to report."

"This is huge, Michael. Something just came across the wire. The options action on Carotegen is crazy." Michael had never heard Brad so worked up before—which was saying something. He sat up straighter. Speculators had spent weeks waiting for Carotegen's stock prices to move dramatically. This could be exciting.

"What's going on?"

"Dude, this stock is ready to make a major move. Wait. Hold on. I just got an e-mail from a buddy of mine who works at a hedge fund." Brad's world moved at the speed of broadband. "He's hearing a rumor that Stanford University has been conducting a confidential study on telomerase activators. That means the stuff that's being sold by you guys, Reversetrol, and Carotegen. He says they're supposed to announce the findings within a few weeks. Someone leaked the study."

"What is the market predicating?"

"It looks like there are just as many bulls as there are bears. It could go either way."

"What does all of this mean for us?"

"It means that you guys should have done a deal when you had the chance." Brad's tone was ominous. "If this turns out badly, you and I are going to be looking for jobs."

"Look, Brad, there's a difference between us and the other guys. We never claimed to have an anti-aging product." Michael was beginning to see the method behind David's madness.

"No, dude, the real difference between you and the other guys is that they've already done deals and cashed out. Your company may be the one that avoids a fraud lawsuit, but so what? Who the fuck is going to invest in you now, when the study's results are about to be released? If the study shows no anti-aging efficacy, it's all over."

If Brad was right about the Stanford rumor, investors would hold off on investing in Aseso until the study came out. If the results were unfavorable to Aseso, Brad's deal, and therefore his budget for the year, would be dead. And Michael—Michael would forever be associated with a gimmicky company that had tried to make millions off the public's gullibility.

Until this moment, Michael had never been able to admit to himself that he, too, had finally bought into Aseso's anti-aging hype. He realized that he, like millions of Americans, badly wanted Sinsen to work. But his emotional investment had been made for completely different reasons.

"David's not worried," Michael said. His own words struck him as unconvincing. "He's got everything under control."

"You think so? What's he going to do about this?"

"I don't know."

"Didn't he get his Ph.D. at Stanford? Do you think he knew about the study?"

"I don't know." Michael's voice was getting fainter.

"Michael, I've got investors with one billion dollars waiting on the sidelines, ready to do a deal with you guys. I have to tell you, 'I don't know' is not going to instill a hell of a lot of confidence in them." Brad's voice grew stronger, as if feeding off of Michael's waning energy.

"David's in Europe. I'll get a hold of him. Tell your investors that we have absolute confidence in our product." It was the only thing to say. Ever since starting at Aseso, Michael had worried that they might be coasting on America's naiveté.

"All right, Michael. I'll keep our investors warm. Keep me informed if you guys hear anything."

"Will do." Michael hung up the phone and sat staring at his blank computer monitor. He'd been working on logistics for the next shipment from Haiti. Now his monitor was asleep.

His understanding had been that it would be another year before anyone could really begin measuring the aging of Aseso's customers. The majority of them had been taking Sinsen for less than two years. What conclusions could be drawn at this point? What sort of studies could be performed?

He hadn't been off the phone five minutes before Jason rushed into his office. "Big news!" he said.

Michael dropped his head into his hands. For once, he knew the news first. But he let Jason tell him: Stanford had been secretly conducting a telomerase-activator study with funding by the National Science Foundation, a federal agency in Washington. Although there was public awareness of most NSF studies, this one had been kept secret due to the enormous potential implications of the findings. It was not clear how word of the study had gotten out.

"It's on all the major networks," Jason said.

Michael's phone rang. It didn't stop ringing all afternoon. Customers wanted to be reassured. Reporters wanted a comment. Potential investors wanted to speak to someone with answers. Caroline wanted to know what he was thinking. His friends wanted to be in on the moment. His family wanted to know how he was doing.

It was real.

A little after four, Michael finally managed to contact David, who'd been skiing in France. Dr. Tanaka was in Africa again, negotiating with more governments, securing more tracts of land.

"Have you heard the news?" Michael asked. It occurred to him that he broke the news to his employers as often as Brad broke the news to him.

"Yeah, I'd heard that a couple of research teams were working on some studies." David was characteristically un-phased, and characteristically vague.

"More than 'some studies,'" Michael said. "This is huge. People have been calling nonstop, wanting a statement. What should we tell them?"

"Nothing. We stay the course. The finding will be what the finding will be."

"You want us to tell them nothing." Michael was sick of David's Zen philosophy. He wasn't at a new-age yoga retreat. He was trying to run a company. He took a deep breath so that he wouldn't say something he'd regret. "When will you be back?"

"Next week. Don't worry, Michael. Just keep doing your job. Everything is going to work out."

"Right," Michael said. "Thanks."

He pressed the phone's disengage button, then slammed down the receiver. He picked up both his stress balls and gave himself a minute to calm down. Then he put in a call to Brad, instructing him to tell the investors that Aseso had no comment other than that it stood by its products. After that, he called Caroline and asked her to meet him at Barney's for dinner.

A year earlier, patrons at Barney's had fought for a place at the bar. Now every seat in the restaurant was available. Michael was aware that he was straddling two different worlds. Aseso was making unprecedented amounts of money selling its product to the rich and hopeful. Meanwhile, the rest of society was suffering as the economy slowly deteriorated. Unlike most of the previous postwar recessions, this one had changed the cultural framework of America. It was now fashionable to be frugal. FOR RENT signs were everywhere. Stores were closed. Barney's, like many other restaurants, was empty.

"What do you think the study will reveal?" Caroline was clearly nervous. She could hardly manage a hello kiss before starting in with questions.

"Let me order a drink first," Michael said. Caroline had chosen two seats at the bar even though they could have had any table in the house. His beer arrived almost before he'd ordered it; the bartender could hear everything they said.

"There are a lot of smart scientists and investors who have put tons of resources into telomerase activators. I have to believe that it works. We get calls every day from people, thanking us for keeping them young."

"So you do believe it works?"

"I have to believe it works."

"You don't have to believe anything. Especially not what David tells you."

"That's just it. He doesn't tell me anything. He doesn't tell anybody anything."

"Maybe this is all just a mass delusion."

"So you're saying all the large pharmaceutical companies that call our office every day, wanting to give us billions so they can be part of Aseso, are wrong? They should know more than anyone."

"They've been wrong before."

"Fine. Are all of our customers who swear by Sinsen wrong, too? As well as the investors who can't wait to get a piece of us? They're all wrong?"

"I'm not saying anybody's right or wrong, but you can't just turn off your brain and rely on the beliefs of everybody else. You have to think for yourself."

"I hope for everyone's sake that the study shows this stuff works. All the people who have poured money into this industry, and the customers who take it every day, can't be wrong."

"If it turns out that it does work, the world is going to be a very different place."

"If it does turn out to work, will you start taking it?"

"Michael, I'm not taking it. I've told you a million times. I'm all for you working at Aseso, but I don't think you should mess with Mother Nature."

"This isn't messing with Mother Nature any more than penicillin is. We're not making people immortal; we're just making them live longer."

"How much longer?"

"I don't know. Nobody knows."

"That's my point," Caroline said. "Nobody knows much about all this. Millions of people are taking these pills every day, and it's only now that studies are being conducted? What if there are side effects? What if the long-term social costs are greater than the benefits? How could the government not have gotten involved earlier?"

Michael shrugged. "Like I keep saying, it's not technically a drug. It's a nutritional supplement. None of the anti-aging supplements have to get FDA approval because aging is not considered a disease."

"Of course it's not considered a disease. Old people aren't sick; they're just old. Mrs. Klein is a very nice old lady, and there is nothing wrong with her. I don't think the government should allow just anyone to take it."

"That would be pretty ironic." Michael stood to go to the restroom. "If the government allows people to smoke every day, which shortens their lives, they should allow people to take something that lengthens their lives."

"So just because mistakes were made with tobacco, no one should ever question any new health product? Not to mention the fact that companies at one time even made health claims about cigarettes." Caroline shook her head and sighed.

"Michael." She put a hand on his arm. "Here's what I'm really worried about. I've always been fine with you taking Sinsen as a health supplement, because neither of us thought it really worked. But now...I don't want a boyfriend who doesn't age. I don't want you to be thirty when I'm sixty."

"You're saying you want me to stop taking it?"

"I'm saying...I don't know. Go to the bathroom."

He went. When he returned, Caroline said, "What I want is for Sinsen not to work."

"Babe," Michael said, "that's out of our control."

23

The Third Year. January.

"I can't believe that no one from Aseso went to California for the press conference," Caroline said at breakfast. "It's not like you guys can't afford it."

Michael brought their cheese and egg white omelets to the table. The Stanford study results were set to be announced that afternoon. No one at Aseso anticipated doing any work before then, so he had time for a long breakfast at home.

"David wants everyone in New York for a meeting after the findings are announced. I've never seen anyone so cool. You'd think he'd gotten an advance report, but he says he has no idea what the findings will be. Even if it turns out favorably, though, it's going to be bad news for us."

"Why do say that? Aren't you hoping Sinsen works?" There was a hint of bitterness in Caroline's voice. Lately, she sounded that way whenever Sinsen arose in conversation—which was often. The once-secret study had been the center of the world's attention for the last few weeks. Scientists debated nightly whether it could prove anything conclusively, given the brief study period. Every major network had put together a documentary outlining the history of the three companies and the development of the worldwide Astragalus extract craze.

"All three companies now use a subscription-based model. So if you want to buy from any one of us, you have to sign up for at least a year. Our newest plantations won't be ready for harvest for another four months. That means everyone will rush to sign up with the other two companies."

"So why don't you have more plantations? It doesn't sound like the other companies have that problem."

"Everyone else's plants grow pretty much everywhere," Michael said. "The others were very aggressive in producing and planting as many seeds as possible. Our plants only grow in a very specific type of tropical soil."

Caroline nodded and cut into her omelet. Michael was having trouble eating. No matter what happened, their lives wouldn't be the same after today. If the Stanford study concluded that Astragalus extract had no anti-aging benefits, all three companies would surely collapse. If it confirmed that there were anti-aging properties, Aseso, along with the others, would become one of the most powerful companies in the world. And Michael, in turn, would become one of the world's most powerful businessmen.

After breakfast, Michael collected his briefcase and overcoat and asked Caroline to wish him luck.

"Luck," Caroline said quietly.

He kissed her goodbye and walked out the door. Mrs. Klein was waiting for the elevator.

"Michael, how nice to see you."

"Nice to see you too, Mrs. Klein." Actually, he wasn't happy. Mrs. Klein had a tendency to take fifteen minutes to say what could be said in three.

"I saw in the news that everyone is waiting to hear the results of the study your company conducted."

"We didn't conduct the study, Mrs. Klein, but the study is about us and a couple of other companies."

"Well, I've lived a long time, and I thought I'd seen everything when they sent men to the moon. Now they're saying people don't have to die."

"It's not that people won't die, but that they'll live longer." Michael kept pressing the elevator button, wondering what was taking so long.

"My grandmother once told me that young people shouldn't die, but old people have to die. Otherwise there won't be enough room for everyone."

"That is a very interesting thought, Mrs. Klein." It was time to give up on the elevator. "You know, I think I am going to take the stairs. I'm really running late." Michael opened the staircase door as he said goodbye. Within a couple of minutes he was on the street, looking for a cab.

Michael had begun taking taxis to work after returning from London. He was becoming accustomed to the good life—although, unlike David, he stuck to simple luxuries. No expensive real estate. No thousand-dollar dinners. But he had no problem hailing a cab. Not many people took taxis those days, and the subways were becoming unbearably crowded.

He read the Wall Street Journal as his cab made its way down the West Side Highway. Traffic was light. There was, unsurprisingly, a front-page article on the anticipated announcement. It was scheduled to take place at 4:30 p.m. Eastern Time, after the stock market had closed, in order to prevent nervous investors from sending stocks rocketing in either direction. Michael supposed that the university had agreed to this timing at the request of the stock exchanges. Heavy market activity was expected throughout the day as investors speculated on the outcome. On the opinion page, a famous economist warned of the potential social consequences of extended life spans: Hyperinflation. Overcrowding. Starvation.

When Michael arrived at Aseso, several news vans were parked outside. Reporters hovered around the entrance, checking sound levels on their microphones. Tourists took pictures of their friends standing in front of the building. Neighborhood residents and office workers stood across the street, observing the commotion. It seemed as though no one was working.

Michael got out of the cab and paused before making his way to the front door. This was his building. His company. His day.

He was in the center of it all. He wondered if the other two companies were receiving as much attention.

He walked quickly and deliberately toward the front door, expecting some harassment by the press. But no one stopped him or asked him any questions. No microphones were thrust into his face. He was a little disappointed. It was David they wanted. Michael was running the operations of the company, but the press did not care about logistics or shipping or procurement. They wanted a celebrity.

Just before entering the building, Michael did notice a tourist pointing a camera phone in his direction.

The Aseso office was a hive of activity. They had been on a months-long hiring spree and were running out of room for the new people. Most of the recent hires supported David's extensive public relations efforts. The company now had a new head of public relations, a head of charitable contributions, an in-house travel agent, an art designer, a staff researcher, a social coordinator, and a recruiter. All they were missing was an official marketing department. David had clearly been positioning the company for explosive growth.

This had better turn out the way he thinks it will, Michael thought, heading into his office. Whatever that might be.

The nonstop phone calls began earlier than usual. Michael couldn't even begin to keep up. He spent every minute on the phone, and still the messages multiplied. By noon, David had still not arrived at the office, and Michael needed to have him sign off on a few items before they could move forward. The Florida facility was having problems with some of its machinery and had been idle for the last two days. The company's servers were constantly going down as the volume of visitors to the website became unsupportable. Contracts with international shippers were expiring and needed to be renegotiated. Jason's sales estimates for the output of the new plantations had to be reviewed and then sent to Dr. Tanaka.

The work seemed overwhelming. Michael couldn't motivate himself to begin any of it. By 4:30, his workload would either double or become irrelevant. What he did between now and then would not make any difference.

He made a call of his own.

"Hello, Dad."

"How you doing, Mikey? You hanging in there?"

Michael's father's voice was comforting. They didn't speak often; Michael generally called him when he was especially anxious, or when talking to Caroline wasn't enough.

"I'm doing fine. Tired. There's a lot to do around here."

"I'll bet there is. We're watching the news here. I didn't go to work today. I don't want to miss this."

"Why don't you watch it for me and tell me what happens?"

His father laughed. "You and Caroline should go on a trip after today, regardless of what happens," he said.

"That's a good idea. We just might. Hey, have you been taking those Sinsen pills I've been sending you?"

"Every day. And you know, Michael, I think they're working. I looked in the mirror this morning and saw a boy of twelve." He laughed again.

Michael couldn't help laughing, too.

"How's Caroline holding up?" his father asked.

"She's...I don't know. She's not too thrilled with the anti-aging craze. I think she'd be happier if I were still selling books."

"When are you going to marry that girl?"

"One of these days, Dad. One of these days." David's name popped up on his caller ID. "Sorry, I've got to go. The boss is calling."

He switched to his other line. "David, where are you? A lot of people have been calling for you."

"I got a late start. Don't worry, I'll be in before the announcement. Listen, Michael, I want to change how we will accept new customers."

"Now? What kind of change? The study announcement is four hours away." Michael wondered if David derived special pleasure from requesting the unreasonable.

"My guess is that there's going to be a massive flood of visitors to our website. There is going to be panic in the streets if we tell them to come back later. Here's the plan: I want to create a waiting list for Sinsen. Anyone who isn't already a customer can sign up for the waiting list."

"What's the point of a waiting list? If we can't sign them up, they'll just go to one of the other guys right away." This had to be David's strangest request yet.

"I'm not so sure that's going to happen," David said. "Get Jason to start working on that now, so it'll be up by the time the conference starts. I'll see you in a couple of hours."

Michael glared at the dead phone. "Of course you don't think it will happen," he told it. "How could anything go wrong for you?" He hung up the receiver and went to convey David's orders.

24

Michael and Jason spent the afternoon working feverishly with the development and hosting company that maintained their website. Implementing the new waiting list database in real time was taxing the website firm's capabilities. It didn't help that the main developer was out sick that day, forcing junior staff members to make executive decisions that normally would require at least two senior managers' approval. Time flew by. The waiting list page consistently failed to load.

"How's everything going?" David asked, stepping into Michael's office. Michael was on the phone with a couple of the Web designers. Jason sat at the computer, trying to link their system with the newly created database.

"It's going." Michael held the phone away from his ear and feigned a cool demeanor. "We should have this up in about an hour." He had absolutely no idea when the new website would be up. Michael's can-do attitude was waning. It was three p.m.

"Great. That's what I wanted to hear." David looked as relaxed as he would have on any ordinary Friday afternoon. Meanwhile, it seemed that every phone not in active use was ringing endlessly. There was a line of employees outside David's office, waiting for him to get in. "Stop by my office before the press conference."

David walked away. Michael let out a long breath. He could feel a bead of sweat trickling down his face. He hadn't eaten anything since breakfast, but he was pretty sure that wasn't the reason for his nausea. This was the most important day in the company's history, and instead of planning accordingly, he was scrambling to implement something David could have asked him to do weeks before. Frustration and nervousness united to raise his stress level.

He realized that he was still holding the phone. He couldn't remember who was on the other end. "Hello?" he said. "Where were we?"

The Web designers sounded thoroughly peeved. Michael gave a few last instructions and hung up, turning his attention to Jason.

"Where we at?"

"This is going to take some time." Jason was visibly flustered.

"How much?"

"I don't know. I'm not sure if the problem is with our servers or theirs."

"Just get it done. You have one hour." Michael knew the demands he was making were as unreasonable as David's, and he wasn't surprised when Jason turned his back wordlessly.

At 4:20, Michael walked toward David's office. He was surprised to see Dr. Tanaka standing beside David, watching the large flat-screen hanging on the wall. It was tuned to MSNBC. A commentator was giving his opinion as to possible statements that could be made at any moment. The founders both turned as Michael approached.

"Dr. Tanaka. I didn't know you were going to be here." It was the first time Michael had ever seen him in New York.

"Michael. Good to see you. I hope everything is in order and we are ready to proceed." Dr. Tanaka was the most to-the-point man Michael had ever met.

"All set. We just finished making the changes. We have a page on the website where the public can input their information and be placed on a waiting list. That list will be automatically downloaded to our servers here."

"Good work, Michael," David said. "Did you wait until the last second to finish for dramatic effect?"

Michael didn't respond. He was exhausted from stress and in no mood for David's sarcasm.

"Michael, tell everyone to pile into the conference room in five minutes."

The energy in the conference room was electrifying. Aseso's staff now totaled nearly sixty. Those that could not fit in the room were standing in the hall outside, looking in through the glass walls. Dr. Tanaka and David sat near the windows, which afforded a view of the press waiting below in the street. Michael, from his position near the doorway, could see David chatting with some employees. There were some he'd never met before. David spent so much time travelling that he now allowed the department heads to hire new staff directly.

Dr. Tanaka seemed to have very little interest in any of the staff. He talked on his cell phone, glancing irritably at new employees when they laughed too loudly. On screen, the camera was focused on an empty podium as the commentary continued.

At 4:30 exactly, the television went silent as the head of the Stanford research team approached the podium. Aseso's staff went silent as well. Michael had instructed them to turn their phones to silent mode. The camera focused on a bearded man in his late fifties. Small facial features made his bald head even more pronounced. He wore a suit that he seemed uncomfortable wearing. As he prepared to speak, he fumbled through his coat pockets for his eyeglasses.

"Good afternoon, everyone. My name is Dr. Alexander Block. I am the lead researcher for the NSF-funded study entitled 'An Analysis of the Efficacy of Commercially Available Astragalus Extract Supplements in Preventing or Reversing the Effects of Aging.'

"The main objectives of the study were, first, to determine whether an extract from the root of the Astragalus plant, taken orally on a daily basis, acts as a telomerase activator in chromosomes, as measured by increased telomere length; and, secondly, whether there is evidence that Astragalus extract has measurable efficacy in halting the aging process."

He paused. "I understand that, in addition to the scientific press, representatives from the popular press are here as well, so I'll try to make the results clear to everyone. As background, the shortening of telomeres has been associated with increasing evidence of aging. Therefore, it is believed that a substance that is a telomerase activator might increase chromosome telomere length and, by extension—no pun intended" —a bit of polite laughter was audible as the scientists in the press conference audience got the joke— "have anti-aging effects."

Dr. Block appeared relieved to return to more familiar ground. "In the study, three hundred people new to Astragalus were given various forms of Astragalus extract on a daily basis. One hundred additional people in a control group were given a placebo. Before treatment began, the volunteers were given two biological tests. The first was a measurement of telomere length in their chromosome tips. The second was a determination of biological age through a series of physical, behavioral, and metabolic assessments, including blood cholesterol, triglycerides, glucose, and lung function. The volunteers of the study were divided into three groups of 100 each. Each group was given daily doses of the commercially available products offered by Reversetrol, Carotegen, and Aseso Nutraceuticals, for the period of one year. Then the two biological tests were repeated and the results compared to the measurements pre-treatment.

"Before I reveal our findings, I would like to state that this was a preliminary study." Dr. Block went on to emphasize that the findings were in no way conclusive. Michael could hardly sit still. Dr. Tanaka had closed his cell phone and was staring, tight-lipped, at the television. "Also," said Dr. Block, "to preserve the integrity of the research, we have not revealed any of our findings to the three companies whose products we tested... With that said, here are our findings."

David was still smiling, jiggling one foot almost imperceptibly. Dr. Block paused. He cleared his throat and said, "In the case of Reversetrol, we found both a measurable decrease in telomere length, and observable indications of aging."

The press room erupted in a roar of questions from the audience. At Aseso, the silence deepened. Faces stared blankly at the screen. Michael glanced over at David, who was leaning to one side in his chair, whispering in Dr. Tanaka's ear. Dr. Tanaka showed no expression; he just nodded slowly. Michael exhaled and forgot to inhale again until his body forced in a deep breath of air.

Dr. Block was waving his hands in the air, ostensibly to get everyone to sit down, although it looked more like he was trying to keep from drowning. It took another minute before the room was quiet enough for him to continue. "In the case of Carotegen, again, we found both a measurable decrease in telomere length, and observable indications of aging."

At Aseso, there were great sighs of disappointment. People looked around, stunned. Dr. Tanaka remained expressionless. David sat back in his chair and folded his arms. Michael felt numb.

This time there was very little reaction in the press room. Reporters could be heard talking amongst themselves. Dr. Block turned over some papers before continuing. "Finally, with respect to Sinsen, produced by Aseso Nutraceuticals, we found both no decrease in telomere length, and no observable indications of aging."

This time, the reactions at Aseso and the California press room were identical: dead silence. A sort of question mark hung in the air. Dr. Block said, "So there is no misunderstanding, we found, in those volunteers who took Sinsen daily for one year, no measurable indications of aging."

The press room and the Aseso office exploded into bedlam. Staff around David jumped out of their seats and patted him on the back as he stood up and began shaking hands. Everyone was talking at once. Dr. Tanaka stood up and whispered something to David, then buttoned his suit jacket and proceeded to make his way out of the conference room.

Jason rushed over to Michael and hugged him. Cell phones were turned on and immediately started ringing. Somehow, some of the reporters had made their way past security and were trying to enter the conference room. Close behind them, security guards were calling their superiors, requesting backup to contain the mob that was assembling in the building's lobby. Dr. Tanaka had already slipped away.

Michael stared at David, trying to make sense of what just happened. Voices echoed in his head. The noise inside the conference room was deafening. A reporter was tugging at his shoulder, but Michael wasn't in the mood to be grabbed at and questioned. While everyone was rejoicing around him he couldn't help but feel that something sinister had just taken place. He recalled David's instructions earlier in the day to make a last minute change to the website. David must have known this was going to happen. But what kind of person would hold back from telling the world about something so important? To have let so many people take the other products knowing they didn't work? Some of those people might have died and could have lived if David had just told them.

Michael could not make sense of it all. He finally realized that his cell phone was vibrating in his pocket.

"Caroline!" He was yelling, and he could barely hear himself. He began making his way out of the conference room and back to his office. Caroline was saying something.

"Hang on," he said. "I can't hear you." He rounded the corner and started walking down the hallway, past the reporters and the security guards escorting them out. As he looked back into the conference room, he caught David looking at him.

David winked at Michael and turned away. Michael ran up the internal staircase to the fourth floor. It was quiet there; everyone was still downstairs. "Caroline," he said, trying to catch his breath. "This is crazy. I never expected this."

"What does it mean?"

"I don't know." Michael stood at the top of the staircase, looking down at the chaos taking place below. "Maybe the study is wrong. I can't believe that David knew this would happen all along."

"Come home, Michael. Please." There was panic in Caroline's voice.

"OK. I'll get my bag from my office and leave right away."

"I love you, Michael."

"I love you, too. I'll be home soon."

He hung up and ran toward his office. A thousand scenarios raced through his head. He slowed down as he approached. Someone was standing by his desk, waiting for him.

"Come in, Michael," Dr. Tanaka said, as though it were his office, not Michael's. "We need to talk."

25

An uncomfortable combination of excitement, fear, and anger churned within Michael as he listened to Dr. Tanaka. Any statement about the efficacy of Sinsen had to originate with a third party, he explained. It would be too politically dangerous for Aseso to make a claim which the government could use against it. Having an institution like Stanford University reveal that Sinsen acted as an anti-aging drug was all part of the plan.

Carotegen and Reversetrol had outlived their usefulness. Their customers had already been conditioned to believe in the anti-aging concept. Aseso would remain quiet on the subject, letting the believers go on believing that it worked while allowing skeptics sufficient ambiguity to maintain their conviction that it didn't. This public uncertainty would keep the government at bay long enough for Aseso to become too politically and financially powerful to be stopped.

David and Dr. Tanaka were engaging in an elaborate strategy to buy time.

They had decided to keep everyone—including Michael—in the dark for fear of the secret getting out before it was publically announced by a government-funded scientific team. Now the world would come knocking on Aseso's door, and they had to be prepared.

They needed Michael's expertise now more than ever.

"Michael, I am not entirely convinced that you share our vision." Dr. Tanaka sat in Michael's chair with his legs crossed, one arm resting on the desk. Michael stood a few feet away, feeling ill at ease in his own office.

"I didn't know lying was part of the vision."

"When you play poker with your friends and you refrain from telling them what cards you have, it is not considered lying. It is considered playing the game. It is a nasty world out there, Michael. People would wish us harm if they knew which cards we were holding, and I am not in the habit of losing card games."

Michael felt more and more uncomfortable with this situation. "I need to go. I told my girlfriend I would go see her."

"Go see your girlfriend, Michael, but come back in a few hours. We need to finish this conversation tonight."

Michael grabbed his bag and left out of the rear of the building, avoiding the crowds and media that were now entirely blocking the main entrance. Once on the sidewalk, he ran toward Houston Street. It was Friday evening in SoHo. The streets were filled with tourists and young New Yorkers impatient to start their weekend in one of the area's many bars and restaurants. Each time he passed a group of people, Michael heard the same conversation.

Did you hear? One of the three works.

Do you think it's true?

What are you going to do? How can we get some?

Save your money, it's too early to tell. How can they know for sure? Just a one-year study?

It was the worst time of day to hail a cab. Unable to find an empty one, he ran into the subway station as a train approached. He swiped his subway card and ran onto the platform, barely making it into the car before the doors closed. His heart had already been racing. Now it was about to break free of his body. Sweat began to stream down his face. The same conversations continued in the subway car. No one knew who he was or that he could actually answer their questions. Michael thought: *Yes, it does work, and they knew it all along!*

After getting off at his stop, he had a two-block walk to his apartment. He couldn't wait to get there. He raced down the street, slowed down when he saw people staring at him, then raced again. When he reached his building, he stopped and fumbled for his keys.

Hands wet with sweat, he struggled to isolate the front door key. But the door opened before he could insert the key. Mrs. Klein stood in the doorway, startled.

"Thank you, Mrs. Klein," Michael said. He pushed open the door and ran past her. If Mrs. Klein responded, Michael did not hear her. Within seconds he was inside the elevator, frantically pressing the button to his floor. Michael had always thought that their elevator was the slowest in New York. That afternoon, it seemed to take an eternity. *C'mon c'mon c'mon*, Michael said to himself.

His life was going to change that night, one way or another.

"Are you sure they knew?" Caroline asked in disbelief.

"Yes. It was all part of their plan." Michael paced back and forth in the living room while Caroline sat on the sofa.

"You told me yourself there hadn't been any clinical trials. How could they know?"

"I don't know, Caroline. They just did."

"Michael, after the study was announced, they interviewed a few scientists on TV. They all said the same thing: it's too early to tell. Some people believe that the study is wrong and that there's no way Sinsen can work. I think you might be overreacting. "

"I am not overreacting. Dr. Tanaka told me himself. They knew all along."

"Did you know that the lead scientist on the study, that Dr. Block guy, was David's thesis advisor?"

"No. I mean, I knew David got his Ph.D. at Stanford, but...."

"Because of that, they're saying it's not an impartial study. I think David might be a much better marketer than you think he is. He still may have you fooled."

"Caroline, I am telling you, he knew." Michael was beginning to get irritated.

"OK, fine. Let's assume he did know. What are you going to do now?"

"I don't know. I can't just up and leave David now. All our customers depend on us."

"Who cares about David? He can just get somebody else to take your place. We can go back to Seattle. No one is going to think poorly of you for leaving now."

Her last statement cemented his desire to stay. All of Michael's insecurities, which had lain dormant for the last year, came raging back to life. Somebody else? Somebody else getting the glory for all of the work he had done? Somebody else getting the recognition? Going back to Seattle with his tail between his legs because he was too scared to play cards with the big boys? Aseso, the company the whole world was talking about, ran on a system that he had put into place. What did David do? He flew around the world dating models. What did Dr. Tanaka do? He was on permanent vacation in Barbados. Aseso wouldn't survive one day with somebody else! The two truly essential people in the company, he and Clive, never received the credit they deserved.

"I need to go back to the office." Michael stopped pacing and stood still for the first time since he'd entered the apartment.

"You don't have to go back, Michael. Think about it over the weekend. Call them Monday morning."

"I have to go now. Dr. Tanaka needs to talk to me tonight," Michael said. His newfound conviction felt good.

On the cab ride back downtown, Michael managed to convince himself that he was going to quit after all. Then he convinced himself that he would stay. He did this four times. Each decision came with an equally impassioned emotional justification. One moment, he thought that David and Dr. Tanaka together were the devil incarnate. The next, he could not have admired them more. He was going to go down there and have words. There needed to be an explanation for the actions of the company he ran.

When he arrived at the office, he had settled firmly on quitting. He could not work for a company that played with people's lives.

"Why didn't you tell me, David? Jesus Christ! Why didn't you tell the world? You fucking lied to me. Is this just a game to you?" Michael paced back and forth in David's office. He was taking the moral high ground thinking about how many of his extended family members, many of them with modest incomes, had squandered money on the other products believing they were the same. His aunt Eliza had just passed away. What did she take? Would she still be alive? All of the potential implications of David's deception were colliding in his head.

Deep down, however, he wanted to be sold on staying. He was enjoying his life and had never felt so important. Despite his anger at being deceived he admired their business acumen. These men were brilliant.

It was past seven. The rest of the staff had left for a restaurant that David had rented out to celebrate the results of the Stanford study. Dr. Tanaka sat quietly in the corner, preferring to let David do the persuading.

"Calm down, Michael." David poured three glasses of single malt Scotch from a bottle he kept in the corner bar.

Dr. Tanaka stood up and walked over to take his glass. "Is this the Sherry Oak seventeen-year-old?" he asked, sniffing the contents.

"No, it's the Port Wood twenty-one. I prefer the finish on this one. It's nuttier." David sniffed as well.

"Who gives a shit what year it is?" Michael exclaimed. He stopped pacing and stared at his bosses. "You guys are acting like you just closed a sale on a condo in Florida. You've been keeping the Holy Grail to yourselves!"

"That's not exactly true, Michael. Last time I checked, you could buy a bottle of the Holy Grail for ninety bucks on our website." David smiled. Dr. Tanaka took his seat again.

"We are dealing with people's lives here. " Michael was in no mood for David's humor. "You knew that Carotegen and Reversetrol didn't work. You let people believe they did...or could have...or whatever. Don't you have any sense of responsibility?"

"First of all, I didn't know for sure that the other products didn't work, since I've never tested them," David said. "It was possible—although unlikely—that they could have. Second, it is not incumbent upon me to tell other companies' customers whether the products they buy work or not. That should be up to independent analysts or the companies themselves. Since I am neither, I do not have that responsibility."

"What about a social responsibility?" Michael stood in front of David's desk. He glanced back at Dr. Tanaka, who was still sniffing his Scotch in between sips.

"Well, that's an interesting concept, isn't it? Social responsibility." David took another sip of his drink. "What do you think is the socially responsible thing to do here, Michael?"

"What you should have done was share what you knew."

"Why?"

"Why? Because you probably could have saved lives. People probably have...no, in fact, I am pretty sure that people have died during the last few years who could be alive today if they'd been taking Sinsen."

"I don't know whether or not that's true. On the other hand, I do think it's true that starving people around the world would have survived if people had just shared food with them. Where was the social responsibility there?"

"That's not the same thing."

"I think it is. People all around the world are dying because they can't get medicines or transplants or food. We don't have a shortage problem in this world; we have a distribution problem."

"That's my point. You could have told others about Sinsen and had them help make and sell it. You could have made a difference for people who are now dead." Michael watched as Dr. Tanaka stood and walked over to pour himself another glass of Scotch. He returned to his seat without saying a word.

"We will make a difference, Michael. Ultimately, we will use this for good. But we have to be careful. When the U.S. discovered how to construct a nuclear weapon during World War II, it didn't exactly share the blueprints with the world. There are similar potentially devastating consequences here."

He had a point. Michael relaxed a little, absorbing David's calm logic. "So what was the plan all along?"

"The plan was to grow Aseso to be powerful enough to make a difference. Reversetrol and Carotegen helped move up the calendar by helping develop the market. That wasn't part of the original plan but I'll take help where I can get it. They were useful for a time but that time is over. We still need to keep quiet. Let the world keep guessing. By the time there is no doubt we'll have established ourselves and then we can do as much social good as you want. It is not very effective to have the best intentions but with no way to act on them. It is too dangerous now to share the technology with others. We have to control the technology ourselves."

"How are we going to do that?"

"Over the last year, we've established a very lucrative arrangement with the Chinese government. It's in their interest to help keep our secret secure, to generate huge tax revenues from us in the future. They have no interest in making Sinsen available to their citizens, since they have too many to begin with. As long as the party elite get their subscriptions and the government gets its revenue, our technology will be safe."

The Chinese government. At this point, Michael was hardly even surprised. But David did seem to have a logical plan. Michael realized that he was tired of fighting. What he wanted was to sign back on and see this thing through. He looked at David. "What do you want from me?"

"We'd like you on board, Michael, but only if you share our vision. It's up to you. You don't have to come along. You can leave now, no questions asked. As long as you honor your confidentiality agreement, we will have absolutely no problems." He swirled his drink. "So, Michael: do you share our vision?"

Michael looked over at Dr. Tanaka, who was tapping his fingers on the armrest of his leather chair, staring right through him.

"If I stay?"

"If you stay, we'll bring you in as a full team member. No more secrets. And you will be part of one of the greatest acts of social responsibility in history. Aseso will do a lot of good." He grinned. "The pay isn't bad, either."

Dr. Tanaka smiled at this last statement. David poured himself a second glass of Scotch and turned back to Michael. "So what's it going to be? You want to do some good and get rich in the process, or you want to prove some moral point? Go back to shipping books and CDs, maybe?"

That last statement sealed the deal. Michael grabbed the glass of Scotch that was meant for him. For the first time, he felt part of the decision-making process at Aseso. He was in.

After drinking two more glasses of Scotch and discussing ways to move forward, Michael realized that he needed to go home to Caroline. And David needed to go celebrate with his employees. The three of them walked to the elevator. Michael still had many questions, but they would have to wait for another time.

"I just have one last question." After the elevator opened, Michael held the door for his two bosses." When you first knew you had discovered an anti-aging pill, didn't you feel like jumping up and down and telling the world?"

David leaned against the elevator wall. "When I was a kid, I was the youngest boy on the block. One day when I was running around with the other boys, I found a twenty-dollar bill on the sidewalk. I picked it up and turned around to tell the others what I had found. That was a mistake."

26

D r. Tanaka did what no one else wanted to do, to talk about, or to admit that they took part in, even indirectly. He took from the world what he wanted. Everyone who subscribed to Sinsen benefited from his doing so. Everyone else suffered. He never considered justifying his actions to himself or to anyone else. Sinsen had to be manufactured. Seeds had to be planted. Governments that helped him with this process were rewarded. Those that did not were replaced. His morality was uncomplicated. People were rich because the majority of others were not. Some people would get to live; others would die. It was that simple.

Dr. Tanaka began his life in Osaka. He was the only child of a banking executive and a nurse. Education was the only religion in his parents' house. He was sent off to boarding school in England at a young age. Although he was intellectually and athletically talented, the cultural differences were too great for him to excel socially. He studied medicine at Oxford and returned to Japan after graduation. There, he practiced internal medicine for two years before joining a pharmaceutical company as an executive. He married a woman seven years his senior. Their son, Clive, was born a year later. Dr. Tanaka moved quickly up the management ranks of his company. Everyone had high hopes for his success.

In the 1980s, he moved his family to Hong Kong when he was promoted to President of Southeast Asian Operations. The first year in Hong Kong was the most difficult of his life up to that point. He quickly learned that in many situations, hard work and talent were not enough. Many of the people he dealt with expected kickbacks for signing lucrative contracts on behalf of their governments. His early resistance to this practice resulted in fewer sales than expected.

His second year was even worse than the first. His wife was diagnosed with lung cancer. He spent half the time traveling on business in an attempt to meet the expectations of his employer. When he was not traveling, he was at the hospital. Any sense of fairness in life vanished.

After his wife died, he put all of his energy into his work. Now free of any moral convictions, he became the most successful executive in his company. When his superiors reprimanded him for questionable business practices, which included bribery and unauthorized political campaign contributions, he left the company to start his own firm. For many years he slaved away tirelessly to grow his business.

He sent Clive to boarding school, then to Oxford, as his father had done for him. After graduating from Oxford with a degree in biochemistry, Clive returned to Hong Kong to help with his father's business. By the mid-1990s, Dr. Tanaka's company was one of the most successful independent distributors of generic pharmaceuticals in the region.

Then, in 1998, one year after the Asian Financial Crisis crippled the region, President Suharto of Indonesia resigned amid political protests. Many Indonesians believed that corruption was a main cause of the financial crisis. Suharto's successor, in an effort to placate the restive masses, had scores arrested on corruption charges. Dr. Tanaka, who was in the country at the time, was arrested along with his contacts in the Ministry of Health. Dr. Tanaka, however, had the financial and logistic resources to leave the country. Bribery got him in, and bribery got him out. His contacts at the Ministry of Health were less fortunate.

In the eyes of Dr. Tanaka's clients, his arrest had left a permanent scar on the face of his company. Realizing that he would have a difficult time securing government contracts in other countries, he sold the company. Clive enrolled in a graduate program at Stanford University, working toward a Ph.D. in microbiology. Dr. Tanaka retired to Barbados, knowing he would be unwelcome in Japan.

A few years into his retirement, Dr. Tanaka became restless. He began looking for investment opportunities. He investigated replicating his former business in the Caribbean, but found that many similar companies already existed. He then turned to the United States, where there was promising new cancer research. He examined over twenty potential projects, but nothing inspired him.

Clive, meanwhile, grew interested in the fast-growing area of biology known as biomedical gerontology—the science of age prevention. Most of the work being performed at the time involved either pure science—determining the biochemical causes of aging—or the practical science of curing age-related diseases.

However, there were a few scientists who were looking directly at ways to prevent aging. One of the leading scientists in this area, Clive learned, was a former pupil of Clive's Stanford thesis advisor. The former pupil had gone on to work at NIH, and his name was Dr. David Oaks.

Clive decided to base his graduate thesis on some of David Oaks's pioneering work, which he had done at NIH. When Clive tried to contact David, he discovered that David had left NIH to return to California to start his own research-based company. David had left behind a team, headed by two other scientists, to continue the work he had started.

David's starting point was the theory that telomeres, the protective ends of chromosomes, became shorter during cellular replication, and that the shortening of telomeres led to the loss of genetic information and eventually to cellular senescence. The relative absence of telomerase in aging cells was the key. Telomerase could help prevent telomere shortening.

David discovered that a molecule found in the root of the Astragalus plant, used in traditional Chinese medicine, was a natural telomerase activator. He was convinced that he could easily secure financial backers to help him start his company, since his discovery would ensure unimaginable wealth for investors. To his surprise, however, there was very little interest.

David's business plan suggested that he would discover how to unlock the body's own telomerase-creating ability, thereby preventing the destruction of telomeres after cell replication. But this seemed too good to be true. The idea of preventing aging seemed too fantastical to contemplate as a legitimate business opportunity.

Unlike other potential investors, Clive Tanaka had enough scientific background to understand, a willingness to believe, and access to the funding that David needed. Dr. Tanaka, who had full faith in his son, agreed to meet with David. There were many additional meetings and countless telephone calls over the course of several months. Projections and timelines were drawn up. Each discussion brought the three of them closer together.

One aspect of the business proposition, however, bothered Dr. Tanaka. He was weary of bureaucracy and wary of intervention by the Food and Drug Administration in the important U.S. market. The government might slow down their drug trials if the results were inconclusive. In addition, if they applied for a U.S. patent, other companies, especially overseas, would not respect it, and that process, too, would take time and pose obstacles. Dr. Tanaka was not a patient man, and all of these possibilities made him nervous. But his biggest worry was that the government might decide that such a discovery was too great for any one company to control. That would be the worst outcome of all.

Dr. Tanaka finally approached David with a plan. They could perform human trials in Laos. Dr. Tanaka had many contacts in that country and could easily obtain volunteers. Relatively small amounts of capital would be necessary to conduct experiments that could prove the efficacy of David's drug, and there would be next to no government intervention.

But the key to Dr. Tanaka's plan was that their product would be sold not as a pharmaceutical product or drug but as an herbal supplement, which under U.S. law would require no regulatory approval. Rightly or wrongly, anything marketed as a nutritional supplement was classified as a food by the FDA. Unlike drugs, which had to go through multiple testing phases, nutritional supplements could be marketed and sold freely in the United

States. Only if consumers claimed that the supplement caused harm would the FDA get involved.

A happy coincidence was that several forms of Astragalus root extract were already being sold throughout Asia, the U.S., and Europe. The respective regulatory authorities would not concern themselves with a new brand in an established category. Dr. Tanaka's plan hinged on the assumption that by the time the world discovered that the new product was actually an effective anti-aging drug, the company would be too entrenched in society, and too politically powerful, to stop.

At first, David was opposed to this approach. He had been trained as a scientist in the United States and believed in the process that had been set up by his government. Dr. Tanaka, however, would not have it any other way. The potential for the project was great, but the risks of a traditional approach were greater. Finally, realizing that Dr. Tanaka's proposal was his only opportunity, David agreed.

That decision would change the course of history.

Working with Clive in a laboratory they set up in Laos, David discovered a fundamental flaw in one of the technical assumptions he and his NIH colleagues had made. His discovery was possible only through experiments on the Laotian "volunteers". It led to the genetic engineering of a new variety of subtropical Astragalus: the variety that would later produce Sinsen.

Most of the volunteers benefited from the clinical trials. A few paid with their lives as the drug and its dosage were perfected. The fact that they were all military prisoners helped to justify the activity in David's and Clive's minds. Dr. Tanaka reminded them of the old American saying: in order to make an omelet, someone has to break a few eggs.

PART THREE

THE FOURTH YEAR

27

Washington, D.C. The Fourth Year.

Alton, Gordon, Stevens, Harrison & Foley, commonly known as Alton Gordon, was established in 1934 as a Washington, D.C.-based law firm specializing in government agreements with New Deal contractors. Over the years the firm grew to over twenty offices worldwide, offering a full portfolio of legal services. Its marketing materials boasted that Alton Gordon was one of the world's largest and most prestigious law firms, citing its 1,000-plus attorneys and broad international presence. The brochures also listed the firm's thirty practice areas, which ranged from credit agreements, financial restructuring, and capital markets to white collar crime.

What the brochures did not mention was that Alton Gordon's most profitable business was executed by its lobbying group. This group did not formally advertise its services, and no business cards revealed its existence. Those in the know inside the Washington beltway used to say that if you had enough money, Alton Gordon could get you a meeting with God.

The K Street offices were furnished with traditional dark wood paneling and oversized leather furniture. Portraits of the founders and distinguished partners adorned the walls on all five floors that made up Alton Gordon's global headquarters. David and Michael had taken the forty-five-minute flight to D.C. that morning on David's private jet. As they waited alone in a conference room, Michael detailed his plan to set up a new processing facility in Lisbon, Portugal. He envisioned a direct shipment of raw extracts from the African plantations directly to the new facility, which would help meet the growing demand in Europe.

At that moment, the door opened, and three men entered the rom.

The first was Patrick Maloney, who had been Aseso's chief outside counsel for the past year. He was a tall, thin, completely bald man in a dark blue pinstriped suit. Patrick commuted to New York almost weekly to consult with David on a host of legal issues. The second man, shorter, with wire-rimmed glasses, was not familiar to Michael or David. The third was undoubtedly the former Speaker of the House. He had gained considerable weight since leaving office, and his face seemed as wide as it was long. Unlike the other men in the room, he did not wear a jacket, but rather his trademark suspenders over rolled-up shirtsleeves.

"David, I would like you to meet Representative O'Farrell." Patrick stepped aside to let the two most important people in the room greet each other.

"Pleasure to meet you, sir." David shook the former Speaker's hand. His gaze was direct and respectful, yet made it clear that as the client, he was the more important of the two that day. Since the Stanford press conference, David had spent most of his time traveling, meeting with the press and government officials throughout the world, but he had not spent much time in Washington.

"It's a pleasure, Dr. Oaks. I've been looking forward to this meeting for a long time."

"Please, call me David. Let me introduce you to my colleague, Michael Jeffs, who runs the operations at Aseso."

Michael felt a rush of pride at David's acknowledgement that he was in charge of running the company. "It's a real pleasure, Representative." Michael could not remember being so nervous. This was the first time David had brought him to such a high-level meeting.

"It's nice to meet you, son." O'Farrell introduced the man standing beside him as his right-hand man, Mark Joseph. Then he invited everyone to sit down.

Even before Michael had settled comfortably into his seat, Representative O'Farrell began to lecture his new client in a tone reminiscent of his days in office.

"I've got to tell you, David, I am very impressed with the number of people your company has managed to piss off in the last couple of years. Your partner Dr. Tanaka has everyone at the United Nations wondering if he's declared a personal war against democracy. And Michael, you've got everyone convinced that you're suffering from a God complex with that damn waiting list of yours. Everyone seems to get on but no one ever seems to get off!"

Michael froze. Being reprimanded by a powerful public figure, even in a private office, was humiliating.

"I had a lovely flight down here this morning; thanks for asking," David said.

"Now that we've gotten down to business," Patrick inserted himself into the conversation in an attempt to preserve Alton Gordon's relationship with his biggest client, "let me outline our thoughts on how to move forward."

"David," Representative O'Farrell went on, ignoring Patrick and continuing his oration, "I understand you want us to help you with government relations, but you have to help us. You gentlemen have been acting like the kid on the block that's got the ball. Everyone has to suck up to you, or there's no game."

"Look, Frank." David did not bother asking whether he could address the Representative on a first-name basis. "I can't control how the media portrays us. The bottom line is that we have what everyone wants, and there simply isn't enough to go around. Our original customers continue to be customers. Those who aren't already customers need to get on the waiting list. That's the only fair way to distribute Sinsen. What Dr. Tanaka is doing is making sure we have sufficient land to produce enough of what people want."

"What Dr. Tanaka is doing is creating a United Republics of Dr. Tanaka. He has every human rights organization protesting in front of Congress, opposing Aseso's practices and calling for its abolishment."

"There is not much I can do about that. The American people want civil liberties around the world as long as they don't have to pay for them. Well, now it's pay-up time. If Americans want more Sinsen at a reasonable price, they are going to have to turn a blind eye as to how exactly we provide it. Otherwise, they'll have to pay more for less."

"I'll agree with you there, David." The Representative's tone changed to one of deference. It was clear to everyone that David was not going to be intimidated by O'Farrell's stature in the Washington community. "This whole Dr. Tanaka thing will blow over. Your bigger problem is the countless baby boomers—a demographic that votes, I might add—who want to know why their government is standing by while Aseso decides who is worthy of buying its product."

"Some people around here want the FDA to get involved." Patrick, wanting to earn his fees, decided once again to try and jump into the conversation.

"What's the FDA going to do? Sinsen's not a drug. It's a nutritional supplement. Like children's chewable vitamins." Michael knew the last thing David wanted was interference by the U.S. government. Questions would be asked; limitations would be imposed. In public, David voiced a philosophical opposition to government intervention. He justified his actions by pointing to the ideas of contemporary conservative writers. In private, however, he disclosed to Michael his fear that if the government were to get involved the plan would be jeopardized.

Mark Joseph had been quiet, but now he spoke. "There is a movement among certain members of Congress to have the FDA classify Sinsen as a drug," he said ominously.

"To be classified as a drug, it has to prevent or cure a disease. Sinsen doesn't cure any diseases." David appeared unthreatened by this news.

"They want to have the FDA classify a new disease," O'Farrell said.

"What disease would that be?"

"Aging."

"Aging?" David and Michael said simultaneously.

"Yes. Senator Mathew Coves from Florida, who chairs the Senate Special Committee on Aging, has been over to the FDA several times now. His advisors are telling him that if he can get the FDA to classify aging as a disease, then Sinsen can be classified as a drug. If that happens, Aseso will no longer be free to sell Sinsen directly to its customers."

"Can you tell me whether the Senator's advisors graduated from high school?" David asked. "Why don't they just classify 'ugly' as a disease and get HMOs to pay for plastic surgery?"

"This is serious, David," Patrick said, his voice low.

"I am serious. The FDA doesn't just classify anything it wants as a disease. There would have to be some serious scientific backing to all of this, and there isn't any."

"Not yet," O'Farrell said. "One hundred and fifty thousand people die every day, globally. Of those, one hundred thousand die of illnesses that young people never die of. So, in effect, they die of aging—technically, of age-related diseases. If Slnsen can prevent aging, it can prevent age-related diseases...or at least that's the logic Senator Coves wants to use."

"There isn't enough evidence that Sinsen can prevent age-related diseases. It's only been on the market for a few years. My oldest customers are too young to prove anything."

"David." O'Farrell leaned forward. "In Washington, perception is reality. Senator Coves' constituents are older voters on fixed incomes. They are convinced that you have the fountain of youth and that it is their right as Americans to drink from it. Even if you took all of them off your waiting list and offered them Sinsen now, they probably couldn't afford it anyway. They believe the only way they're going to get their mittens on it is if Medicare pays for it. Since they are convinced, Senator Coves is convinced. And unless he does something about it, those older voters down there in Florida are going to vote him right out of office."

Listening to O'Farrell, Michael realized that there was a real possibility that the federal government could interfere with Aseso's operations. He had dedicated the last few years of his life to building up the company and was now recognized as the operating head. He had been worrying about meeting the growing demand for

Sinsen. Never had he entertained the possibility that Sinsen could be taken out of his hands.

"What can we do to prevent this?" Michael's mind was racing with alternative scenarios they could turn to in the event that Senator Coves' efforts proved successful.

"Start making some friends around here." O'Farrell stood up to pour himself some coffee.

David turned to Michael. "How soon did you say you could get that facility up and running in Lisbon?"

28

New York. March.

Caroline and Michael had moved into a 3,000-square-foot penthouse apartment on the 51st floor of One Lincoln Center Tower. Their apartment had the unobstructed view of Central Park that they had always dreamed of.

Over the past two years, however, their relationship had slowly deteriorated, in lockstep with Michael's success. They each took one side of the national debate that now comprised a large part of every American's daily dialogue: whether or not to take Sinsen. Michael had continually tried and failed to convince Caroline to participate in what so many people longed to secure: a subscription to Aseso's promise in a pill.

Tonight they ate in front of the television, as was becoming increasingly common. Dinner conversation had recently decreased to no more than a few sentences, and to cover up the uncomfortable silence, they would both watch the evening news shows while trying to maintain a semblance of domesticity.

"Joining us tonight is Dr. Joanna Hochberg, associate professor of sociology at the University of Wisconsin and a leading figure in the debate regarding Sinsen, Aseso Nutraceuticals' revolutionary health supplement. Dr. Hochberg, thank you for being on the show."

"Thank you for having me." Dr. Hochberg was an attractive woman in her mid-thirties, with long, wavy dark brown hair. She wore tortoiseshell glasses and a black turtleneck sweater.

"You were the first to publish evidence of the effects of Sinsen, which you documented in a study a few years ago. Tell us about that."

Dr. Hochberg seemed right at home in front of the camera. "I had been tracking the behavior of a group of elderly people over a five-year period, studying their attitudes toward their own mortality. I noticed that many of them turned to religion, while others decided to spend more time with family. Some tried to regain their youth through diet and exercise. A few of these people began taking anti-aging products such as Sinsen. At the time, I did not believe that they worked, but I found it interesting that people would put their faith in something that offered them hope of continued life."

"When was it that you discovered that Sinsen worked?"

"Well, to be clear, I didn't discover that it worked. I am a sociologist, not a gerontologist, and I'm not qualified to determine whether it did or did not stop aging. That said, it seemed to me that, at least on the surface, the people in my study who began taking Sinsen, all of whom were between the ages of eighty and eighty-five, did not seem to physically deteriorate as their peers did. None of the Sinsen takers got sick while many of the others contracted heart disease along with other age related diseases and died. I made that observation in my study as a side note, not as a conclusion. But that observation has received more attention than any of my other conclusions."

"So for all you know, their faith in the product could have kept their spirits up, which resulted in them not appearing to get older."

"Exactly. There are many possible explanations for the state of their health over the course of those years. However, now that a few more years have passed, I have gone back to conduct a follow-up study. And I am now convinced that these people—for whatever reason—are not aging. We have compared pictures of them now to pictures of them taken when the study began, and they look exactly the same. Their doctors have told me that there have not been any measurable differences in their physical health. In fact, objective measures of health in some of them have actually improved."

"So what do you believe, Dr. Hochberg?"

"I think that now, given the many other studies that support the original Stanford study, we have to believe that Sinsen does have some anti-aging properties. I am told by my biologist friends, however, that a lot more research has to be performed before we can conclude anything."

"Let's assume, for purposes of this discussion, that it does work. As a sociologist, what observations have you made about Sinsen's societal effects so far?"

"Well, I don't think the real changes have happened yet. Right now we have a divided world. Many people would not hesitate to take an anti-aging pill. But there are many others who would not take it if it were offered to them for free. A substantial number of people see a moral issue with this technology. Some moral conservatives believe that it amounts to playing God. Others believe that it's just the natural evolution of man's quest to stay healthy, as with anything else in medicine."

"But is this medicine?"

"That's an interesting question. Is vitamin C medicine? If you lack vitamin C, you could die of scurvy. During early maritime exploration, sailors on long trips would suffer from scurvy due to their poor diet. When it was discovered that ascorbic acid in things like oranges prevented or, in some instances, cured scurvy, the disease was no longer a problem. If Sinsen does work, it will keep the effects of aging at bay, just like orange juice keeps scurvy at bay."

"If you look at it like that, it sounds like a no-brainer. Let those who want it take it, and those who don't want it simply won't."

"It's not that simple. Right now there are people who claim they would not take it; but if all of this does turn out to be true, the game of life is going to change."

"What do you mean by 'the game of life'?"

"Life is a competition. You have to compete when you apply to college or for a job. You have to compete for that special someone everyone else seems to want. The world is becoming more competitive, not less. If life were a football game, the people taking anti-aging drugs—we'll call them subscribers— would be the team that had helmets and shoulder pads, while those who did not—the nonsubscribers—would be the team without protective padding. The game could be competitive in the first half if the nonsubscribers were a good team, but by the end of the game, the subscribers would have such an advantage over the beaten-up nonsubscribers that it would not be a fair game. All the subscribers would have to do is play the game, and eventually they'd wear the other team down, probably breaking some bones in the process.

"The same thing would happen in the anti-aging scenario. Society would expect ninety-years-olds to be productive members of society. Social security would disappear. There would no longer be old-age homes, since the demand for them would disappear. You certainly wouldn't want to be the only ninety-year-old looking ninety years old. If you were, you couldn't afford to live. I think everyone will see that this is what would happen, and people will eventually realize they don't want to be the only player on the field without a helmet."

"Then what you're saying is that everyone will want to take it."

"Well, I think there are many profound implications if it does turn out to work. And I think that, as a society, we have to think long and hard about whether we want this in our lives."

"I think everyone sees the benefits of something like this. What do you see as other potential problems?"

"As a society, we're used to seeing people go through a predictable life cycle. People come into the world, consume resources, have children, and die. Death allows human population growth to be manageable, and resource availability on earth can grow accordingly. There is a limit to how fast these resources can become available. If resource availability can't grow as quickly as the human population, then terrible things will happen, like hyperinflation and unbearable overcrowding. Back in the 1800s a famous economist, Thomas Malthus, predicted that if human population growth outpaced growth in available resources, a series of events would create devastation. This prediction is known as the Malthusian Catastrophe."

"And you think something like that is possible?"

"In 1800, there were 978 million people on Earth. In 1900 there were 1.7 billion. That increase, over one hundred years, was not quite double. Then, in 2000, there were 6 billion people. That was more than 3.5 times the population from a hundred years before. Today, there are almost seven billion people in the world. Our current rate of growth is unsustainable, let alone a sudden surge in population because no one dies. Whenever you have a sudden disruption in the natural course of events, there will always be unwanted consequences and human suffering."

Michael lifted the remote control and put the large-screen television on mute. He sat back in his chair and crossed his arms. "I'm not sure if that woman is helpful or hurtful to us."

"I don't think she's trying to be either. I doubt Aseso's well-being is on her mind at all. She just wants everyone to think about the possible consequences of all of this." Lately, Caroline had shown no qualms about picking apart Michael's comments.

"The last thing we need is for someone like her to use the word 'catastrophe' on national television. We already have enough problems with the government. We don't need to have public opinion turn against us."

"Don't worry, Michael. Everyone loves you guys." The insincere sweetness in her voice did nothing to mask her bitterness.

All of Aseso's top management, including Michael, had become wealthier than any of them could have hoped. At the same time, it was as though Michael had completely forgotten about Caroline. He never asked her about her photography any more, or about the shelter or the hundreds of unfortunate people who depended on its survival for their own.

Caroline had tried to get Michael involved in other activities to get his mind off his work. It was almost impossible to turn on the television or read a newspaper without seeing something about Aseso. She had suggested that they rent a cabin and go away for a few days, or take a trip to Alaska, as they had always discussed doing. Michael's answer was always the same: there would be plenty of time for trips when the media attention died down. She pointed out that the media attention would never die down as long as Aseso was the only provider of an effective anti-aging pill. Everyone would always want it, and the press would always want to discuss its ethics and consequences.

What Caroline hadn't suggested was marriage, and neither had Michael. Caroline feared that one day Sinsen would destroy their relationship. The stress had taken a toll on her. She was now noticeably gray. She was still beautiful; she was only thirty-two, and people still took notice whenever she entered a room. But for how long? Michael would continue to take Sinsen, and she was determined never to take it. Could their relationship survive if she looked fifty and he thirty?

Michael took the television off mute.

The interviewer was holding up a bottle of Sinsen. "So, Dr. Hochberg, do you take this?"

"Of course," she said, smiling. "Who doesn't want to stay young?"

Caroline grabbed the remote and turned off the TV. "Hypocrite! She just said it's evil, and now she says she's taking it? I'm so sick of hearing about this. There's more to life than deciding how long you want to live."

She went into the bedroom. Michael stayed seated, staring at the darkened screen.

Michael did not understand Caroline's resistance to Sinsen. Part of him thought she refused to take it just to spite him. He still loved her, but he was concerned about their future. He was now biologically younger than Caroline and was not yet ready to have children. He thought about how this would affect people's decisions toward potential partners. Among the various criteria, such as education, values, and good looks, Sinsen-taking was now on the list.

29

April.

Brad was finally going to consummate the deal he'd been pursuing for years. His firm had conducted a few business transactions for Aseso, but not the multi-billion-dollar deal he had pitched in London—until now. Everything had fallen into place, and Brad had arranged for Michael to meet with some of Bearing Brothers' senior management. He had promised his superiors that this meeting would be the last. Aseso, he assured them, was only one step away from going forward with the transaction.

For years, David had resisted outside investors and lenders, preferring to finance Aseso's operations from its profits. It had finally become clear, however, that the demand for Sinsen would soon be so large, and the public pressure to provide it so great, that he had to do something to show his willingness to meet everyone's needs. Senator Coves was using Aseso's inability to meet market demand as evidence that the national interest was being undermined by an unregulated industry. If David didn't do something soon, the government would.

The offices of Bearing Brothers & Co. were the nicest Michael had ever seen. The modern glass tower made a strong, not too subtle statement to everyone that passed by. Only the most successful of investment banks could afford to build such an opulent building in one of the most expensive real estate markets in the world: midtown Manhattan. Tourists took pictures of each other in front of the bronze plaque by the door. This was one of the money centers of the world. All asset classes—stocks, bonds, futures, options, currencies, gold, silver, oil, and other commodities—were bought and sold every day at Bearing Brothers. Now nutritional supplements would become a tradable asset class.

The executive dining room at Bearing Brothers, which seated sixty to eighty people during lunch, had been closed off to host the intimate meeting. Brad introduced Michael to the bank's CEO, Alistair Furman. Aseso's Chief Financial Officer, Brian King, rounded out the meeting. David, originally scheduled to attend, was once again traveling through Europe, securing assurances from heads of state that if he invested in Sinsen distribution for their countries, their governments would not interfere in Aseso's business.

Alistair Furman was a distinguished-looking sixty-something year old man who had spent his entire career on Wall Street, mostly at Bearing Brothers. He was known more for his ability to develop professional relationships than for his technical skills as a banker.

Brian had been excluded from the deal making process until now. Typically, the Chief Financial Officer would have led such a project, but David had preferred to have Michael arrange all the high-level discussions and lay the groundwork. It would be Brian's job to iron out the details.

Once the introductions were out of the way, the four sat down to lunch. After an appetizer of baby arugula and shaved Manchego cheese, they moved on to pan-roasted duck with parsnip puree. The conversation meandered. It turned out that Alistair kept a pied-a-terre in Michael's building, although he spent most of his time at his home in Greenwich. They had both spent time in Boston—Alistair at Harvard Business School and Michael at MIT. A year before, a meeting like this would have made Michael nervous, but his confidence had grown along with his authority. He belonged at this meeting, and the similarities between him and Bearing Brothers' CEO confirmed it.

During the previous year, Michael had become an important figure in the New York business community. He was invited to give lectures at universities and speak at industry conferences. Reporters called to request interviews. Headhunters called, wanting to steal him away from Aseso. He grew to love his position. He wanted more.

"I'm sorry David couldn't join us," he said, once they'd finished dessert. Michael had become as eager to start the process as Brad was. With the new money that Bearing Brothers could secure, Aseso would have the resources to become one of the most powerful companies in the world. "He asked me to convey his full support for this project," he added.

"You'll have to send him my regards." Alistair looked ready to launch into negotiations. He waved over the white-vested, black-bow-tied waiter to remove their plates. "Has Brad described our new ideas for Aseso?"

"He did outline them for me, but I'd like Brian to hear them directly." Michael wanted to include Brian as much as possible, now that the deal was basically done. Aseso's success had fostered jealousies among the top managers, all envious of Michael's heightened status. David was more interested in socializing than in office politics, while Dr. Tanaka could not possibly have cared less about the opinions of Aseso's employees. It had become one more issue for Michael to handle.

"I've spoken with many of our investors," Brad said, taking Michael's cue to begin outlining his proposal. "We believe that if you were to set up a slightly different subscription structure with your customers, investors would come in for seventy billion dollars."

"What kind of new structure?" Brian asked, taken off guard. He'd never conducted a financing of this magnitude; that kind of money would create one of the world's largest corporations.

"Investors want assurances that if Sinsen proves not to be effective and Aseso goes bankrupt, they will have the means to recoup their investment. Now, just to be clear, everyone here at Bearing Brothers has full faith in your company and your product. But if we are going to obtain this amount of capital, we need to offer some sort of security."

"What form of security are you talking about?"

"Allow me to be frank and to the point, Brian," said Alistair, taking over from Brad. There were good reasons he was always brought in to close the deal. His demeanor and experience instilled confidence in even the most skeptical of clients, and he could deliver difficult news without fumbling over his words, as Brad had started to do. Brian was sitting on the edge of his chair.

"The number of people on Aseso's waiting list is at least fifty times the number of current customers," Alistair continued. "At this rate, it will contain two hundred times the number of customers by year's end. Every day, more and more people are convinced that your product works, as more and more favorable scientific studies appear. We appreciate your loyalty to your original customers. But, Brian, the truth of the matter is that those customers are not as wealthy as many of the people on the waiting list. We estimate that there are at least one million people around the world that would be willing to give you twenty thousand dollars up front and sign a ten-year contract, backed by personal guarantees, to become an Aseso customer at ten thousand dollars per year."

It took Brian several moments to process all of this. "If we did that, we'd be forcing out many of the customers that have been with us since the beginning," he began. He paused, considering, and then went on, gaining momentum. "I've been with Aseso since the New York office opened," he said. "There was a time when David personally wrote to each new customer, thanking them for trusting Aseso. Now you want us to make Sinsen too expensive for those customers? They depend on us. We'd be giving them a death sentence."

"That is one way to look at this," Alistair said. "But another way to view it is that your wealthy new customers will pay for the expansion of Aseso over the next few years, so that you can grow quickly enough to accommodate everyone. You're growing now, but your current pricing scheme will not enable you to meet the growing demand. Within the next couple of years, you'll have millions and millions of people on the waiting list. With our plan, you will be able to accommodate many more people sooner. The reality is, Brian, that however you decide to move forward, there will be people who are left without. Our plan would maximize the number of people you could help." Alistair leaned forward earnestly, emphasizing the benevolence of Bearing Brothers.

Brian was visibly shaken. "My family and friends were some of Aseso's first customers," he said. "They've believed in what we were doing all along. What are we going to tell people like them?"

"Believe me," Brad said, "we understand the dilemma here. But I think everyone would agree that Aseso has a responsibility to humanity to try and maximize the number of people it can help, even if it has to be at the expense of a few early adopters."

"How will this all work with investors?" Michael asked, trying to move the discussion along. He didn't want Brian to spoil this for him. He no longer cared that he wasn't working on Wall Street; he was now involved in one of the largest Wall Street transactions in history. And he was running it.

"These contracts will come with three features," Brad said. Alistair remained quiet, watching contentedly as the deal went forward. "One, Aseso will make absolutely no claim as to the effectiveness of Sinsen. Two, the contracts will come with the explicit personal financial guarantee of every new subscriber. Three"—Brad paused for effect—"the contracts will be written as fully transferable financial instruments. Once we have gathered one million contracts, we will sell them as a pool to investors, and you will receive all the money at the front end. Seventy billion dollars."

"What if new research comes out showing that Sinsen doesn't work?" Brian asked. "In that case, Aseso would owe seventy billion dollars. Right now we have no debt whatsoever."

"No, Brian. As I said, the contract will be transferable financial securities. Once you've sold them to investors, they will bear all the risk. Regardless of what is later proven or unproven with respect to taking Sinsen, every subscriber will be obligated to make payments for the full term of the contract as long as you keep delivering the product, effective or not. If they don't pay, the loss will fall to the investors. You will have already received the money, and we will already have received our fee." Brad was now sitting back in his chair, confident in the soundness of his plan.

"And who are these investors?"

"Mostly commercial banks, insurance companies, and pension funds."

"And you are sure you can pull this off," Michael said, more for Brian's benefit than his own. He had been sold since shortly after the London meeting.

"We live in very interesting times." Alistair rejoined the conversation. "Today there are not many attractive investment opportunities, and people are willing to spend anything to remain healthy. This is a match made in heaven."

"So what do you need from us to move this forward?" Michael felt that he had given Brian enough input; it was time to begin finalizing the plan. David had finally given the go-ahead. They had waited long enough.

But Brian stared at Michael, dumbfounded. "Wait a minute," he said. "Is that it? Five minutes of discussion and then it's decided? What about our early customers?"

"Brian, Alistair is right. We need to help as many people as possible. I think it is an acceptable sacrifice to have a few of our customers age briefly while we secure enough funding from others to grow the company. In a couple of years we can come back to them with lower prices. By then we'll have enough land and infrastructure in place to meet everyone's needs." Michael had no way of knowing that would actually happen, but at this point, the argument seemed irrefutable.

"So okay, Brad. What is the game plan here?" Michael asked.

"What we need from Aseso is this: you'll announce to the world that two months from now, everyone, including new customers, will have to apply for a ten-year subscription to Sinsen."

"A ten-year subscription? Do you really believe people will commit to something for that long?" Brian interjected, still trying to keep the debate alive.

"One of our equity research analysts used to write extensively on Carotegen before they went bankrupt. He is very familiar with the industry and the market demand, and he tells us you'll have absolutely no problem securing these contracts," Brad said. He had brought together all the firm's resources to support this deal.

"How exactly would these contracts work?" Brian asked, his voice heavy with resignation.

"All applications will require an upfront application fee of one hundred dollars. Then, as Alistair said before, each accepted applicant will sign a binding contract with Aseso, entitling them to delivery of the standard daily dosage of Sinsen for ten years at ten thousand dollars per year. Their initial deposit will be twenty thousand dollars, and the balance will be covered by personal guarantees. We estimate that we will secure one million customers immediately."

"I just can't believe people will go for it." Brian was alarmed at the reckless financial contracts Aseso would be asking their customers to sign. He hadn't even been able to think through the many risks to the investors.

"I've been in banking for over thirty years. I can't tell you how many times I've heard that statement before the successful completion of a transaction." Alistair said as he leaned back in his chair. What he didn't mention was how many of those transactions eventually resulted in huge losses for those involved. Except for the bankers.

30

Brazil. June.

Two months after the meeting at Bearing Brothers, Brad and his team successfully placed seventy billion dollars worth of collateralized bonds with investors. There was a flood of applications from all over the world for the new ten-year Sinsen subscriptions. Two major accounting firms were hired to process the wave of applications and sort them according to credit score. Aseso's existing customers were furious. After a deluge of angry calls and e-mails, Brian convinced Michael and David to give preferential status to existing customers, and the vast majority converted to the new subscription program without having to pay the upfront fee.

Armed with fresh new funds, Dr. Tanaka began the process of locating and purchasing the largest tracts of land possible. The natural first choice was Brazil, the largest producer of sugar cane and, not coincidentally, the largest producer of sugar-based ethanol. Brazil had begun producing ethanol-powered cars in the 1920s, and the Brazilian government had invested in ethanol technology in an attempt to free the country from its dependence on oil. By the turn of the twenty-first century, the vast majority of cars in Brazil were fueled with an ethanol mix. Given the increasing global demand for ethanol, sugar cane had become a lucrative crop for Brazilian landowners.

Dr. Tanaka, with billions of dollars to spend, was prepared to buy those sugar cane fields. And the price he was offering was too attractive for even the most successful sugar-cane producer to turn down. The proposed land sales were opposed by consumer advocates and environmentalists. The price of food and fuel would surely rise as less land became available for traditional crops. Many argued that seeding for only one crop would disturb the natural equilibrium of the farmlands. But the government, influenced by politically powerful landowners, expedited the process, allowing Aseso to secure plantations throughout the southeast region of the country.

Michael recommended to Dr. Tanaka that he hire one of his business school friends as head of Aseso's Brazil operations. Marcus Silva, who was originally from the state of Minas Gerais, in the south of Brazil, was well connected and experienced in dealing with both farmers in the countryside and officials in Brasília.

After studying civil engineering at the University of São Paulo, Marcus had begun a banking career with a Brazilian bank which was the local subsidiary of a Dutch financial conglomerate. Specializing in Brazil's large agricultural sector, he had traveled throughout the country, offering export finance to farmers who needed capital to plant their crops. Although Marcus had very strong technical skills, it was his genuinely warm-hearted personality that gained him the trust of his clients. They, in turn, recommended him to others.

By age 28, he was the most profitable employee in his office of two hundred. Impressed by his drive and popularity among clients and colleagues, his Amsterdam-based superiors paid for him to attend business school in the United States. He met Michael at MIT, and they quickly became friends. After graduation, Marcus returned to São Paulo, and the two kept in touch.

Dr. Tanaka hired Marcus away from the Brazilian bank to lead a team that would identify and negotiate the purchase of land appropriate for growing Aseso's genetically engineered Astragalus plants. Marcus immediately began to assemble a team of horticulturists, plantation managers, and well-connected lawyers. In short order, Aseso purchased several vast sugar cane plantations.

Marcus met with Dr. Tanaka at Sushi Yassu in the Liberdade area of São Paulo the night before they traveled out to see the new plantations. Liberdade was home to the largest Japanese community in the world outside of Japan. It was known for its restaurants, shops, and museums, and, more notoriously, for its geisha services. Dr. Tanaka had not been back to Japan in more than ten years, but he took every opportunity to visit Liberdade and immerse himself in his native culture. This evening he was savoring every bite of his grilled white tuna. He was, in fact, giving more attention to the fish than to Marcus.

"Cut them all down," Dr. Tanaka said.

"Now, Dr. Tanaka? There are only two months left till harvest. If you wait, you can get millions of dollars for the sugar cane crops. If you cut them down now, it will all be lost."

"I don't care. Have your people arrange to cut them all down. I want to start seeding the fields as soon as the shipment from Nanning arrives."

Marcus wanted to impress his new boss. He had made all the arrangements for Dr. Tanaka's trip to Brazil and wanted the whole thing to run smoothly.

"You're the boss. When do you expect we will be receiving the seeds?"

"In two weeks."

"Two weeks?" Marcus stopped to collect himself. "Dr. Tanaka, as you know, Aseso just became the largest private landowner in the country. It is not possible to clear that much land in two weeks."

"You need to make it happen. Use whatever resources are necessary. I want those lands cleared."

"I'll coordinate the effort with the plantation managers," Marcus said, although he had no idea how. "Dr. Tanaka, there is another issue we need to address."

"And what is that?"

"The local affiliates of some environmental groups would like to have a meeting to discuss Aseso's long-term plans in Brazil."

"What is their interest in us?"

"Whenever foreign companies come to Brazil to purchase land for exploration or farming, environmentalists become concerned about the potential consequences for the environment."

"You can inform them that our long-term plan is the same as our short-term plan, which is to grow and export Astragalus plants."

"Yes," Marcus said, trying not to sound as though he were lecturing his employer. "But they would like to know if you have plans to purchase more farmland in the future."

"Why should they care if we purchase more land?"

"At some point, if Aseso continues to purchase arable land, the traditional crop supply will suffer. There is a fear that forests would then have to be cleared to make room for traditional crops."

"Is there a possibility that these people could impede our efforts here in Brazil?"

"Yes."

"What can be done?"

"There are certain groups here that have strong political influence. These groups sometimes gain popular support through their associations with certain charitable organizations." Marcus was determined to be as vague as possible while still getting his point across. He had been raised with a strict Catholic upbringing, and greed, bribery, and coercion were all things he struggled to mention out loud. It was culturally embarrassing for Marcus to suggest to his new boss that these actions were necessary. He was unaware that his new boss had not only embraced these methods as part of his standard business practice, but had personally perfected their technique.

"Then we need to make associations with similar organizations. Let's hire a PR firm to begin a campaign demonstrating how Aseso gives back to Brazil. Pick a few national charities. Make our contributions widely known. This has worked in all the other countries."

"I will begin that process tomorrow." Marcus was glad that at least one of Dr. Tanaka's requests was feasible.

"Good. Now, we need to discuss security. Have you hired a team?" This was a top consideration now that Aseso was a household name internationally. There were constant raids on Aseso's many plantations throughout the world. The increased demand for Sinsen and its limited supply had created a lucrative black market for the product. Many people wanted to acquire the plants, believing they could cure disease. Others wanted to destroy the plants, believing that growing them was an act against God. Regardless of the motivation, the constant threat of intrusion had led Dr. Tanaka to amass private security forces in each country where Aseso had a presence.

"Not yet," Marcus said. "I wanted to discuss it with you first. A friend from my tennis club knows many people in the state police forces. He can arrange meetings with officials who can assure the safety of the crops."

"Exactly what would we have to do to obtain those assurances?" This issue was one that Dr. Tanaka faced every time he began operations in a new country.

"Along with the cost of hiring ex-military or ex-police for the private force, we will need to make some donations to certain political associations."

"Why don't we just give your politically connected police friends the money, and then they can contribute it to whatever political campaigns they want?" To Dr. Tanaka, placating certain political figures was simply a matter of doing business. He had based his entire career on doing exactly that.

"Here in Brazil, corruption is very much frowned upon by the general population. If money is to be directed to certain political figures, it will have to appear as a legitimate campaign contribution." Marcus was an honest, hard-working man, but he was not naïve. From the beginning, he'd understood that, in order to work for Aseso, he had to embrace the realities of doing business when so much money was involved.

"Frowned upon?" Dr. Tanaka began to laugh. "Frowned upon? Well, let's not do anything that is frowned upon." He laughed even louder, putting down his chopsticks. "You can inform them that Aseso looks forward to participating in Brazil's democratic process."

"Of course. I will pass that along." Marcus had, up to this point in his career, avoided political entanglements. As a mid-level bank executive, he'd abided by rules that had been established by those before him. None of those managers had involved themselves in political matters. He had now graduated to a level at which it seemed that such activities were required to effectively execute his duties.

The next day, Marcus arranged for Dr. Tanaka and himself to fly from Campo de Marte Airport to one of the new plantations. From the helicopter, São Paulo's enormity was apparent. With over twenty-one million people in the greater metropolitan area, it was an ocean of humanity. Rows of high-rise buildings continued for miles. Tentacles of streets emanated from the center and terminated at a beltway encircling the city. As they flew further into the interior of São Paulo State, concrete blended into dirt and wood. An hour after taking off, they approached the first plantation.

Wide green rows stretched to meet the perfect blue sky at the horizon. Large steel silos lined one side of a reservoir. A few buildings were grouped together near the road. Men and tractors were scattered around the plantation house. When they landed, Dr. Tanaka was introduced to the plantation manager, who'd been kept on after the land was sold to Aseso.

After a short tour of the fields, Dr. Tanaka was taken to the main building, where the plantation manager outlined the timeline for converting the fields from sugar cane to Astragalus. He was shocked to discover that the schedule had been accelerated. Acting as interpreter, Marcus explained the plantation manager's concern that they did not have enough men or equipment to cut down all of the sugar cane stalks in so little time.

"Tell him that I understand," Dr. Tanaka said. His tone conveyed his experience with these situations. Marcus, relieved and surprised that his employer was being so reasonable, prepared to translate.

"I understand that there's not enough time to cut down the sugar cane," Dr. Tanaka continued. "Just have him burn it all."

31

New York. July.

"I can't believe this." Caroline walked into the room with the day's mail. She dropped the pile on the coffee table, except for a letter that she held in her hand.

"What is it?" Michael's back was to Caroline, his eyes focused on his computer screen. He was sitting in the apartment office, writing an e-mail to the Portuguese contractors Aseso had hired to convert an old factory into the new European facility. The process needed to be expedited. Dr. Tanaka had ordered that all possible resources be used to finish two months ahead of schedule.

"It's a petition. Look, Michael. They want to close down shelters in the neighborhood. It's being sent to Upper West Side residents."

"Who sent it?" Michael tried to pay attention while finishing the e-mail, but he'd never been very good at doing two things at once.

"Something called the Upper West Side Restoration Society. Have you heard of them?"

"Can't say that I have."

"What are we going to do about this?"

"One second, Caroline. I'll be right with you."

"Michael, could you please turn around?"

"Hold on. Almost done." Michael made a few last changes. He scanned the e-mail and pressed Send. He collected the printouts of the documents he was working on and put them into the electric shredder above the waste paper basket that sat next to his desk. Feeling that he had completed everything that needed to be done he spun around in his chair. "OK, I'm all yours. What's the problem?"

"The problem, as I already said once, is that there are people who want to close the shelters in our neighborhood. That includes the one I work at."

"Well, technically, you don't work there. Now, if they paid you..."

"Michael, you can be a real jerk sometimes." Caroline turned to leave the room.

"I'm just kidding. Just trying to make you feel better."

"This isn't funny, Michael. It's important to me. We're trying to help people, and now a bunch of rich New Yorkers are going to shut us down."

"Okay, okay. What exactly does the letter say?"

Caroline read the letter out loud, interjecting her own growls of indignation. The Upper West Side Restoration Society's stance was that the community's shelters attracted homeless people from surrounding areas, resulting in a reported increase in violent crime. As in all other neighborhoods, home values had been declining as part of the economic downturn. The above-average number of shelters in the neighborhood and the increased crime had put further downward pressure on real estate values. The Upper West Side Restoration Society felt that unless the shelters were closed down, the increased presence of homeless people would cause home values to fall even more, making the area an undesirable place for people to move to, perpetuating the vicious cycle.

"Well, they do have a point," Michael said.

"What point is that?" Caroline's icy stare dared him to go on.

"Caroline, I understand why you're upset. I know how much the shelter means to you. I'm just saying, people want to protect their neighborhood."

"As if people would ever really abandon the Upper West Side. But anyway, where are the homeless supposed to go? It's their neighborhood, too."

"Don't get upset, but it doesn't make much sense if you think about it," Michael said. "Why do homeless shelters have to exist in one of the most expensive areas in the U.S., on our tax dollars?"

"When did you become so cold?"

"I'm not cold. I'm realistic."

"Life has worked out well for you, Michael. This is a nice place you've got." Caroline spread her arms to indicate the wealth represented by their apartment and its trappings. A sprawling four-bedroom apartment with an outside terrace overlooking Central Park would be the envy of even the richest New Yorkers. "You could be more sympathetic to those whose lives haven't worked out so well."

"It's worked out for us, Caroline. It's our place. It's our life. And it's worked out well because I have worked for it."

"It feels a lot more like yours than ours."

"Fine," Michael said. "That's just great." He stood and started out of the room, but Caroline blocked his way.

"I'm not saying you haven't worked hard, but a lot of life is luck. You were lucky to have the parents you did and to have been born with the smarts you have. God, Michael, you were lucky that you failed to get a Wall Street job. Otherwise, you would have never taken the one you have now."

"I don't have time for this. I'm going to the gym. And for your information, Caroline, I didn't 'fail.' The economy was tough. And I beat it. Tell that to the people at your homeless shelter." He stared at Caroline until she moved aside. He strode into the bedroom, grabbed his gym bag, and headed for the front door.

"Please don't walk away from me," said Caroline, following him. "People are starving, Michael."

"Well, you have to die of something." Michael continued walking towards the door.

"Well, thanks to you, now that's only true for the poor."

Michael paused with his hand on the door knob. Caroline stood in the middle of the living room, holding the letter at her side. He turned to look at her then turned back and walked out the door.

32

Washington, D.C. September.

"Thank you, Dr. Oaks, for agreeing to come before us today."

"It's a pleasure to be here, Senator Coves," David lied. He was not pleased to be appearing before the Senate Special Committee on Aging. Although David had spent many weeks traveling to D.C. to attend meetings arranged by the team at Alton Gordon, Congress could no longer ignore the increasing public pressure for government intervention. He had aligned himself with the many members of Congress who resisted government intervention, but everyone still believed that a public discussion was necessary to placate the American people—to buy time, if nothing else.

Photographers snapped pictures of David sitting alone before the committee. Patrick Maloney sat just behind him, ready to offer legal advice if necessary.

"First of all, Dr. Oaks," said Senator Coves, "I want to congratulate you on your success. I understand that Aseso has become one of the most profitable corporations in the world in a matter of just a few years. It has also been brought to my attention that much of the public, as well as many within the scientific community, believe that your product, Sinsen, is in fact an anti-aging drug. I've called you here today because it appears that the ethical implications of Sinsen, not to mention the federal government's regulatory responsibilities, have been ignored.

"Before we begin our discussion today, I want to make it clear to members of the press and our public audience that this committee has not formed a view on the scientific merits of Sinsen as an anti-aging drug, or as any other type of drug. If Sinsen is indeed a drug, however, I will have questions for the people over at the FDA as to why they have not intervened to date. Before I begin, Dr. Oaks, do you have any opening remarks?"

"Thank you, Senator Coves." David felt comfortable in front of cameras. His demeanor was relaxed; he even spoke with a slight smile. "You mentioned the FDA in your opening remarks. The FDA categorizes Sinsen and other Astragalus products the same as all nutritional supplements, which is to say, as a food—not as a drug. We make no claim whatsoever about the ability of Sinsen to prevent or cure any disease. We never have. As we've said from the beginning, we believe that Sinsen should be taken to promote general good health. I am aware that many people believe Sinsen has anti-aging properties, but we certainly have not made that claim."

"I appreciate your position with respect to the FDA," Senator Coves said, "but you cannot ignore the scientific evidence that has been brought forward by researchers over the past few years."

"All the research to date has been performed by third parties, without our knowledge or consent. We do not comment on that type of research."

"Well, 'that type of research' certainly helps your sales. I can't imagine that you would object to it."

"Again, I can only speak to what we do as a company. If your interest lies in the research conducted on our product, then you should bring in the scientists who conducted it." David poured himself a glass of water from the pitcher placed on his table as cameras flashed in front of him.

"I have every intention of bringing in those scientists, Dr. Oaks. One thing at a time. Moving on: why have you not proactively been in contact with the FDA to submit Sinsen for review as a drug?"

"The FDA does not require us to do so. And, as I said, neither we nor they consider it a drug."

"But don't you think you should submit it? As the socially responsible company you purport to be?"

"I don't make the rules, Senator. I just follow them." David was becoming annoyed at Senator Coves' persistent line of questioning.

"You just follow them. I see." Senator Coves' tone revealed growing frustration as well. "Well, let me tell you what I follow. I follow the interests of my constituents. And they want to know why the government is standing by and letting a select few—the wealthy few—have exclusive access to your product, which could prevent many age-related diseases. Now what would you have me say to them?"

"I'd think you would give them the same rationale that you use to explain why the government doesn't provide universal health care. We live in a capitalist society, Senator. The markets provide for the formation of private health care services, which can be purchased by consumers."

"There's no point pretending the market has free reign as to private health care. Consider the extent to which the federal and state governments regulate insurance, doctors, hospitals, and pharmaceutical companies for the public good," returned Senator Coves. "We live in a democracy in which the government does have specific responsibilities that benefit its citizens as a group, and that's why we're here today. Dr. Oaks, what is the current cost of a subscription to Sinsen?"

"We require twenty thousand dollars up front and an annual subscription of ten thousand dollars, with a required subscription length of ten years."

"And how many customers do you have?"

"We are a private company and do not disclose that sort of information."

"Can you disclose where Sinsen is sold today?"

"We sell globally. We have customers in over fifty countries."

"I see. A back-of-the-envelope calculation brings me to the conclusion that you must make billions of dollars in profits."

"Again, Senator, we don't disclose financial information."

"So you believe the government should just stand idly by while potentially millions of people relinquish their hard-earned money to you, based on nothing but their own blind faith that your product will cause them to live longer?"

"Well, Senator, as an agnostic, I am dumbfounded that the government allows millions of people to pour their hard-earned money into religious institutions without requiring those institutions to provide evidence of the existence of God."

Senator Coves took a moment to regroup while the audience and some of the other members of the committee laughed. "I understand people here in the U.S. continue to be on a long waiting list to secure a subscription. What is causing the delay?"

"Astragalus plants take a couple of years to grow. We simply don't have enough product to meet the demand. We are constantly acquiring new land to grow more plants, but it is a slow process nonetheless."

"Why don't you simply license the technology to make it more available to everyone?"

"For the same reason we didn't file for a patent. We don't believe that our intellectual property rights would be respected."

"I'll tell you something, Dr. Oaks. They certainly won't be respected if someone reverse-engineers your product and brings their own version to the market."

"We are prepared to run that risk."

"So as I understand it," said Senator Coves, speaking slowly and deliberately, "you may in fact possess the secret to long life; but instead of saving lives, you would prefer to make yourself rich. Dr. Oaks, tell me why we should not just mandate that you license the technology."

"If the federal government were so interested in saving lives, it would outlaw smoking, which is a leading cause of cancer. It would work on eradicating hunger. If the government cared so much about social responsibility, it would at a minimum ensure health care for children, who can't make choices for themselves, rather than interfering in the health choices of adults. As I have said, it is not clear that Sinsen has the properties you suggest. I certainly don't make any claims with respect to its life-extending properties. What I do is provide a product that people want, that people are willing to pay for."

"What is very clear," David continued, "is that there is a lot of low-hanging fruit that the government could go after if it really wanted to save lives. My guess is that those in positions of influence in the government are only interested in saving the lives of those who vote for them."

"You're arguing that unless the government does everything, it can't do anything – it can never start anywhere. You seem to want to have everything both ways: you want to enjoy complete freedom in commanding top dollar for Sinsen, yet at the same time you want to remain so evasive as to your product claims that you can avoid any sort of responsibility to anyone. Heads, you win; tails, we lose." Coves paused for emphasis. "Don't you feel any responsibility to your fellow citizens?"

"Yes, as much as any other health care company. Sinsen is a resource that is available to those who can afford it, as are surgeries and pharmaceuticals, which also extend life. I would be very happy to participate in a universal health care program that included every aspect of medicine. But I will resist any effort by the government to discriminate against our company. If you go down this path, you will create a chain of events that will create enormous problems you have not anticipated. Believe me you do not want to open this can of worms."

The remaining time was taken up by questions from other members of the committee. Senator Coves had covered most of the ground already. Phrases such as "rights of the people" and "social responsibility" were brought up again and again. David played along, repeating his points and for the most part maintaining his poise. Patrick remained quiet behind him.

After the hearing, David and Patrick were escorted by guards through the halls of Congress to a limousine outside. The press, waiting eagerly on the sidewalk, bombarded them with questions, microphones, and cameras. A security officer opened the rear door of the limousine and ushered them in. As they drove back along Pennsylvania Avenue, the limousine passed the White House on its way to the offices of Alton Gordon. Representative O'Farrell was waiting in the conference room.

"God damn, David. You sure know how to start a public relations war." The former Speaker, sitting at the head of the table, didn't bother to stand. It was obvious that he was not happy with David's testimony. "Every major network has commentators on right now, stating that the government would be right to take Aseso away from you. Even Fox News is calling for government intervention."

"Nice to see you again, Frank. How are the wife and kids?" David wondered why he spent millions of dollars on legal fees only to be chastised by an old relic like O'Farrell.

"Do you want your company to survive?" O'Farrell continued. "Because I can tell you right now, you are doing a piss-poor job of being the nice guy."

"This is not a popularity contest. The only chance we have to win is to show the hypocrisy of politicians who win elections on free market campaigns but then turn around and support government intervention when it's in their own best interest."

"David, why don't you just license the technology?" Patrick chimed in. "You're already a billionaire many times over. Just save yourself this headache." It was the first thing he'd said all day, and it wasn't what David wanted to hear.

"I won't do it because it is not in the best interest of society," David said. "Sometimes the popular decision is not the right one. The problem with democracy is that everyone gets a vote."

Everyone paused, contemplating the implications of David's last statement, until Patrick asked, "By the way, David, aren't you a practicing Presbyterian?"

"That was last month." David smiled and winked at Michael, who remained quiet at the corner of the table.

New York. November.

Months had passed since David's testimony before Congress. The press had brought Senator Coves into the national spotlight to represent the American people's desire to have the government make Sinsen available to everyone. The cost of a subscription would be beyond the means of most people even if an adequate supply were available. This widely known fact suggested the need not only to have the government mandate Sinsen's availability to everyone and subsidize its purchase, but also to somehow resolve the supply issue.

The op-ed pages of various newspapers described diverse views within the international community. The sense of entitlement seemed to be a purely Western phenomenon. The Asian populace, or at least the papers' editorial boards, seemed to be very capitalistic in their philosophy. Naturally, the Chinese government had no appetite whatsoever for providing Sinsen to everyone. Although the European community exhibited a more egalitarian attitude, any coordinated effort to make Sinsen available throughout the region seemed logistically impractical.

Congress, led by Senator Coves, mandated a special commission to investigate the scientific merits and ethical implications of Sinsen. Aseso was allowed to continue normal operations during the investigation. David, having anticipated that this situation would arise, had two years earlier instructed his lawyers at Alton Gordon to re-establish Aseso's corporate structure advantageously. Aseso Nutraceuticals, Inc., which was entirely owned by David, was nothing more than an American distribution company. It bought extract from Aseso Sciences, a Hong Kong-based company that was owned by Dr. Tanaka, a Japanese national.

Using this structure and Alton Gordon's contacts in Washington, David circulated a rumor that if Congress decided to intervene, it would only be able to stop the distribution of Sinsen in the United States. Aseso Sciences could continue to do business in the profitable markets of Asia and Europe. Given the limited supply of product, closing down the American operations would do nothing to halt Aseso's growth. The product shipped from Dr. Tanaka's plantations would simply be redistributed elsewhere, and the U.S. would lose out. In effect, David was playing a game of chicken with Congress.

"Did you know that Hochberg was going to be on TV this morning?" David stood next to his desk with one hand on his hip while the other pointed to the flat-screen mounted on his office wall. He and Michael had agreed to meet at 7 a.m. to go over plans for the launch of the new Lisbon processing facility.

"I had no idea." Michael, sitting on David's couch, looked up to see a message indicating that Dr. Joanna Hochberg would be the special guest on the morning show.

"Who the hell made her the anti-Aseso national spokesperson?" David had become increasingly frustrated with Dr. Hochberg's celebrity in the national debate regarding aging. She appeared on numerous television and radio news shows. Her blog had millions of followers around the world. She had moved away from publishing academic articles and begun writing popular nonfiction books on the subject. What particularly galled David were her personal attacks on him. She, like many journalists, reporters, scientists, and politicians, had requested an interview with David and been refused. David preferred to meet only with those he knew would write or speak favorably about his company. His reluctance to meet with Hochberg had only solidified in her mind the evil intentions of Aseso.

"Thank you for joining us today, Dr. Hochberg." The well-known morning host sat across a small round coffee table from Joanna.

Michael stood up, ignoring for the moment the work he had woken up so early to address. He and David would watch Hochberg voice her opposition to Sinsen once again. There were few who openly supported Aseso and its activities, and naturally, they were part of the lucky few who were Sinsen subscribers.

During the previous year, public opinion had shifted towards embracing aging as a choice. Those who opposed taking anti-aging supplements were now in the minority. The vast majority of Americans now felt that Sinsen was something that should be available to everyone. They were not interested in hearing about the controversy over corruption charges, which involved Aseso's land-grab policies in developing countries. Although the potential harm to the environment or humanity itself from the widespread distribution of Sinsen was not completely lost on them, it seemed too esoteric a discussion and its consequences too far into the future to dampen their desire for an enhanced life span.

A very vocal minority believed that Sinsen should not be allowed to exist at all. Joanna had become the poster child for this group. Her books foretold dire consequences if the majority of humans were allowed to live indefinitely. She also predicted that society would adopt a very different view towards life if people could not easily estimate their time on Earth. She often argued that while she philosophically opposed Sinsen's existence, she would be foolish not to take it while others did. She admitted that she was conflicted.

"Dr. Hochberg, in your new book, you come out quite strongly against what everyone seems to want, which is to live forever."

"I'm not sure people know what they're getting themselves into. There are many situations where something might be beneficial for the individual but hazardous to society."

"Can you give us a couple of the scenarios you outline in your book?"

"Some of the things I predict in the book are happening now. The wealthy are becoming wealthier. People in their sixties who started taking Sinsen five years ago are putting off retirement for years. These people, who would normally start to live off their savings, are still contributing to their own wealth. These people are buying second and third homes, believing they will have many years to enjoy their new investments. By contrast, their contemporaries who are not Aseso subscribers are retiring and finding it hard to maintain their lifestyles as their income falls. Those people have to sell their homes and move into more affordable housing. Sinsen is driving a wedge between the haves and have-nots. Sinsen, I believe, will make the economy's imbalances worse, not better."

"What other societal changes are you noticing?"

"There seems to be a new type of discrimination. Employers want to hire people who will remain young and energetic while accumulating experience. It used be that gray hair and wrinkles had the benefit of being associated with wisdom. Soon young-looking people will have the experience of seventy-year-olds without the health problems. Also, we are seeing that young people only want to date others who are also Sinsen subscribers. They feel that otherwise, they might marry someone who will grow old as they stay young. Since today Sinsen is only obtained by wealthy people, a new class of dating discrimination will exist."

"So you believe Aseso is creating a dual-class society?"

"Yes, I do."

"Well, doesn't that support Senator Coves' call for universal availability of Sinsen?"

"Unfortunately, although limited availability of Sinsen is problematic, universal availability would be disastrous."

"Tell us what problems you foresee."

"I have been working with some agricultural economists who are trying to estimate the demands on our resources that would be necessary to create universal availability. We have come to the sobering conclusion that there is simply not enough arable land to produce both the required volume of Astragalus plants and enough crops to feed everyone on Earth. The problem is that the land requirements of the Astragalus plants used by Aseso are too great to make universal distribution a practical policy. It will be human nature for everyone to want Sinsen, but the reality is that everyone can't have it."

"So what are your recommendations?"

"Right now there is an opportunity to halt this process. Only Aseso has the technology, so a coordinated effort between it and the government could remove Sinsen from the market long enough for more research and planning to take place. I fear that if the technology is discovered by others or is licensed to others, there will be no stopping this. Once one person has it, everyone will want it, and I believe it is better if nobody does."

"Thank you for joining us today, Dr. Hochberg. You raise some interesting points." The host shook Joanna's hands and turned towards the camera. "Next, Chef Skyler Venice will join us to share his secrets on how to make a spectacular dinner for two in under thirty minutes."

David turned off the television as Michael sat back down on the sofa. These issues were not new to Michael. Caroline brought them up regularly at dinner. But David did not seem concerned about the potentially disastrous consequences that Hochberg predicted.

"That was not good. Millions of people watch that show." Michael was visibly upset.

"In a way, she's useful because she keeps the debate alive. Without her there would be no opposition to Senator Coves' universal coverage campaign." David walked passed Michael and stopped at the doorway. "Anne, can you bring me Dr. Hochberg's number?"

Joanna had called several times over the previous months, each time leaving her number with David's secretary. "Are you going to call her?" Michael asked as David walked back towards his desk.

"Sometimes you have to give your enemies a reason not to hate you. It keeps them guessing."

34

David arranged to have dinner with Dr. Joanna Hochberg that evening. They had never met, although they had often locked horns in the media. He frequently complained to Michael about her but had never revealed his attraction. She was not as universally beautiful as the other women he dated, but there was something about her that was magnetic. He had his favorite restaurant, Flatiron Tavern, reserve its best table.

"I have to tell you, I was surprised to hear from you," Joanna said as she studied the menu. "You finally decided to return one of my calls."

"My secretary must have misplaced your message the first time."

"I left more than twenty messages."

"In that case, I'll have to fire her tomorrow." David smiled and sipped his customary pre-dinner Scotch Manhattan. The restaurant was full and lively.

"Everyone here is looking at us. I'm sure they're wondering why you and I are having dinner together." Joanna set the menu on the table and leaned back in her chair. "In fact, I'm wondering why you and I are having dinner together."

"They're staring because everyone likes a good love-hate relationship."

"Yes, but in our case it's just hate." Joanna was determined to hide her admiration.

"You should thank me," David said. "I've made your career."

"You are quite sure of yourself, aren't you?"

"No, but you seem to be. You seem quite convinced that Sinsen should be made illegal, like some addictive psychedelic drug."

"Who decides, David? Who decides who gets to live or die? You? Senator Coves? I think God was doing a pretty good job of it before you showed up."

"I enjoyed reading your dissertation on society's changing attitude towards aging," David said. "You wrote it while you were at Princeton, right? Tell me, Joanna, who decides who gets to go to Princeton? Who decides who gets to come here and enjoy an extravagant dinner? There has never been and will never be enough to go around. Implicit in every new innovation is the idea that some more than others will get to enjoy the fruits of mankind's progress."

"You call what you're doing 'progress'? You are recreating the middle ages. Dividing the world into haves and have-nots. I don't see that as progress."

"Humans have been searching for the fountain of youth since time began. You can't construct a logical argument to convince them to stop looking for it. Even if you were successful in making Aseso go away, others would try to invent something similar. And believe me, those people wouldn't contribute as much as we do to charities, or limit product availability to avoid a human population explosion, or invite you to dinner to try and explain the rationale behind their actions. They would simply sell the technology to the highest bidder, walk away rich, and let humanity destroy itself."

"Some things shouldn't be invented at all, by anyone." Joanna sipped her dirty vodka martini, extra olives.

"That may or may not be true, but we don't have the luxury of getting to decide, do we? A lot of people were against the development of nuclear weapons during World War II. But think what would have happened if the Germans had invented it first. If they'd controlled that technology, the world would be a very different place today."

"You seem to have everything all figured out. Why did you invite me here?"

David signaled subtly to the waiter that they needed more time. "We share a common goal, Joanna. We both know that it's not in anyone's interest to have this technology available to everyone. The sad fact is that the only solution to twelve people in a ten-person lifeboat is two bullets. No one wants to get out, but tough choices have to be made."

"How uplifting. You still haven't explained why I'm here."

"Let's order. I'll share some of my ideas over dinner. You should try the lamb."

"I'm a vegetarian."

David thought to himself: *Yeah, so was the lamb.*

35

Lisbon, Portugal. December.

The private balcony outside David's suite overlooked Eduardo VII Park, St. George's Moorish castle, the Old Town, and, most notably, the Tagus River. The hotel topped one of the seven hills of Lisbon. The distant hills, peppered with small stone houses, made the ideal backdrop for a lunchtime celebration.

A bottle of Cristal chilled in a silver bucket, and a beautiful assortment of white lilies, peach roses, and gerberas bloomed in a crystal vase. A heat lamp provided warmth. It was a slightly cold but beautiful day. The Lisbon facility was now officially completed and operational. The finest equipment in the world had been installed and would be run by the best process engineers money could hire. Soon Aseso would have no need to depend on the U.S. facility to meet demand in Europe.

David and Michael had spent the morning at the new facility just outside the city, meeting with the Aseso-Europe management team. Marcus had flown up from São Paulo the day before to consult with his new colleagues. Half of his shipments would now be redirected to the Portuguese facility for processing, bottling, and distribution throughout Europe while the African plantations were being prepared for the next harvest.

David had hired away many exceptionally talented managers from the most prestigious European companies to run his operations in Portugal. Hans Schultz, a highly respected German chemical company executive, had been chosen for the position of president of Aseso-Europe over hundreds of other applicants. Hans had grown up in Berlin. Shorter than most boys and not particularly athletic he dedicated himself to academics as a youth. He studied physics at the University of Bonn before going on to earn his PhD in process engineering at the University of Munich. He was very personable and unlike many of his scientific colleagues he had an interest in the business side of the industry. David and Michael were impressed with his track record of efficiency and thought him perfect for the job. He reported directly to Michael who was in control of all matters relating to operations.

"Please, let's sit down for lunch," David instructed.

Marcus and Hans had been leaning over the railing, getting acquainted while admiring the view from the balcony. David and Michael enjoyed the view from their chairs. Now it was time to attend to business. Marcus had been working at Aseso for some time but had never met David in person. For Hans, who had just started, everything was new.

"Hans, when do you think the facility will reach full capacity?" Michael was eager to make the European operations completely self-contained. He would feel more at ease once the facility produced its first batch of bottled Sinsen. The pressure from D.C. was mounting, and Michael feared that the Boca Raton facility could be shut down any day. Caroline had pointed out to him that this was the same fear she had about her shelter.

"I believe the bottleneck will be the availability of root extract," Hans said. "The question should be how quickly we can get raw materials from Brazil." Hans had run several tests, using hundreds of tons of ginger root as a substitute for Astragalus.

"Marcus, where are we with the next shipment?" David asked. He spoke offhandedly, but Michael knew that he, too, must be feeling the pressure.

"We start the harvest in two days, but it will take time to fill the tankers and get the product shipped here." Marcus looked haggard. Over the past two years he'd had to fight countless legal and security battles regarding Aseso's use of land.

"Let's not wait for the tankers to fill," David said. "I've got a better idea. Arrange for cargo planes to carry the root extract here as it becomes available."

"That will be incredibly expensive," Hans said, looking unpleasantly surprised. He was the only one. Michael and Marcus were accustomed to David's lack of fiscal prudence and would once again comply with the wasteful demands of their superior.

"We need to start as soon as possible," David said. "I don't care what it costs."

Hans's cell phone rang. He answered and then quickly stood up. He appeared shocked as he listened. It took him a moment to respond to the caller. His expression made it clear to the rest of the table that something was desperately wrong. He finally uttered a few loud words in German and closed the phone with a snap.

"There has been an explosion at the plant."

Michael's heart missed a beat. He froze, imagining the worst. Marcus rose from his seat and looked to David for guidance.

"Let's go." David stood and walked decisively through the sliding glass door into the suite. He went directly to the phone and dialed the concierge. "This is David Oaks, in the penthouse. I need two cars now. I'm on my way down."

He hung up and reached for his sport coat. The others filed in and grabbed theirs, which they'd flung over chairs in anticipation of a long lunch. Within minutes they had made their way down and through the lobby. Two black cars were parked outside, a chauffeur standing in front of each.

"Hans, you and Marcus take that one." David pointed to the front car. Michael followed David to the second car, and they sped away. Michael could see Hans up ahead, holding his cell phone to his ear.

"Call the guys in Boca Raton and Nanning," David said. "Let them know there's been an incident here. I want extra security put in place until we find out what happened."

"Do you think it was a terrorist act?"

"Can't be sure, but I wouldn't be surprised," David answered.

There had been several threats against the company. The controversy surrounding Aseso had intensified over the past few months. There was a long list of vastly different groups that wanted it shut down. The wealthy had become obsessed with living longer, and they were prepared to do anything to ensure their own longevity. Many people saw Aseso as representing all that was wrong with the world. The top two percent of the world's population owned over ninety percent of the world's wealth and the situation was getting worse. To aid them in their quest, Aseso needed to acquire more land.

Most of the violent acts to date had taken place at Aseso's plantations in developing countries, where people and traditional crops were directly affected. Spillover effects, however, were felt in Europe and North America, where inflation was skyrocketing. The cause of the inflation was both the real scarcity of commodities that resulted from Aseso's activities, and the buying of commodities by financial speculators driven by their expectation that one day there would be too many people for the earth to support. The new facility in Europe, as the key to Aseso's global expansion, was an obvious target for Aseso's enemies who wished to make a statement.

The two cars sped along the winding roads of Lisbon, up and down its many hills. After half an hour, they were almost within sight of the facility.

The first thing they saw was smoke in the distance. As they got closer, they could see lights flash and hear sirens blare.

When his car drove through the gates of the complex, Michael could see the extent of the damage. Dark smoke billowed from a large hole in the facade of an otherwise pristine tan brick structure. Fire trucks and police cars were scattered throughout the parking lot. A helicopter hovered loudly overhead. A group of employees huddled at a distance, watching the events unfold.

Hans got out of the car in front of them and ran over to speak with his second-in-command. Marcus, not knowing what to do, walked slowly toward the building he had inspected only hours before.

As the second car came to a stop, Michael jumped out and ran to join Hans. Firemen ran past him toward the building. An ambulance raced in the opposite direction. David stepped out and paused to take in the scene. The message was loud and clear. Somebody did not want Aseso to exist.

Although there was clear damage to the structure, it was not as bad as everyone's worst fears. Within a few minutes, Hans had regained his composure. He beckoned Michael to follow him back toward the cars, where David stood waiting. Michael felt himself breathing hard as he walked. It was difficult to concentrate. The helicopter, the ambulance, the fire trucks, the yelling: the combined noise had risen to deafening levels.

"It was definitely a bomb," Hans said to David. "Thankfully no one was seriously hurt. The national police are on their way. The damage is mostly to the exterior of the building, but it will shut us down for a couple of weeks while it is being repaired."

David turned to Marcus, who'd rejoined them. "Well, Marcus, I guess you don't have to worry about getting those cargo planes."

Marcus managed a weak smile.

Michael didn't think it was funny at all.

New York. The Fifth Year. January.

The Lisbon facility was repaired and made operational again within weeks. The root extract arrived on schedule, without significant additional cost, which pleased Hans. Disaster had been averted. With the European operation in full swing, the threat of intervention by Senator Coves was now less ominous. Although the U.S. was a large market, the rest of the world was gaining in importance; within a couple of years, the U.S. would represent only ten percent of Aseso's total sales.

Yet no one was breathing easily. The bombing had sent a clear message against Aseso's acquisition of land. A radical political group in Morocco claimed responsibility, and it vowed to continue attacks against Aseso for as long as the company conducted business in Africa.

Dr. Tanaka decided to take a more aggressive approach to security issues. He once again contacted Black Falcon, his neighbor Dirk's employer, who had helped retrieve the stolen cargo from Bridgetown. After extensive discussions, he hired Black Falcon to coordinate a global security force to protect all of Aseso's properties around the world.

Meanwhile, Dr. Tanaka was undeterred in his intention to acquire as much land as possible. His original plan had been to diversify Aseso's land holdings geographically rather than concentrate them in any one country, thus diminishing the risk that intervention by any one government would thwart Aseso's efforts. But given the seemingly infinite demand for Sinsen, it was becoming increasingly difficult to find suitable plantations. He began returning to countries where Aseso already had plantations, purchasing land adjacent to the existing Astragalus farms, paying off government officials as necessary. Many locals felt that Aseso was encroaching. Traditional crops were being sacrificed in order to plant Astragalus. Food costs escalated, along with housing prices. In countries where Aseso had plantations, the chasm sociologists had predicted between rich and poor was forming at lightning speed.

Michael was constantly aware of the controversy surrounding Aseso. Of course, he wished that Sinsen could be provided without displacing people from their land, but these were the same issues that faced many oil companies and agricultural conglomerates. It was not his responsibility to interfere with activities in other parts of the world. As far as he knew, all of Aseso's actions were legal. However, Caroline suspected differently. Dinner conversations had become more contentious.

While local people in places like Paraguay, Zimbabwe, and Thailand fought to kick Aseso out, American consumers were fighting to become part of the Sinsen elite. The money kept pouring in. Meanwhile, Brad and his team at Bearing Brothers had conducted many successful CDO placements for Aseso with investors all over the world. Thanks largely to the fees generated from these transactions, Bearing Brothers was now the most profitable investment bank in the world—and Brad was one of the wealthiest bankers in New York. Aseso's CDO securities became the most highly traded corporate bonds in the market. Many banks were buying Aseso bonds instead of U.S. Treasury securities. Lenders began to secretly discriminate by giving preferential treatment to Aseso subscribers, reckoning that a borrower with more years to live would be more likely to pay off a loan.

Caroline frequently commented on the growing division between the haves and the have-nots, but since Aseso's contributions were the only means of keeping her homeless shelter open, she couldn't say too much. She was now the director; Christine Johnson had relinquished the position, disheartened by letter after letter threatening to close the shelter.

Now Caroline had to fight her battle with the community on a daily basis. Many politically influential groups with residential and business ties to the Upper West Side wanted the shelter shut down. As other shelters throughout the city closed their doors, more and more homeless people journeyed to the Upper West Side for their daily meals. Many had no place to go after the lunch service and stayed nearby to wait for dinner. Vagrancy and loitering soared. Fights broke out constantly. Residents continued to complain. Squad cars were a common sight. Arrests increased. The neighborhood Michael and Caroline had come to love was changing steadily for the worse.

Caroline tried to appease everyone, but letters from the city still poured in, reminding her that the shelter was violating the ordinance with respect to unlawful public gatherings. She tried to limit the number of persons visiting the shelter, but she quickly learned that when people lose everything, they hold on tighter to hope. And Caroline's shelter was their only hope.

"Caroline, what Aseso is doing has nothing to do with what's happening with the shelter." Michael was packing for another trip. He was now away as often as he was home.

"It absolutely does, even if indirectly. This new greed for life Aseso has created is translating into just plain greed. People are upset that Sinsen is only available to a select few, and it's causing free-floating resentment. People are out for themselves more than ever. The world is losing its compassion." Caroline watched from the bedroom doorway as Michael retrieved clothes from the closet.

"The world is losing its compassion because the economy sucks and crime is rising. We offer hope. We are the only thing right now that gives people something to strive for. People will work harder and be more productive, thinking that one day they can get a subscription."

"Hope and the willingness to work are not going to be enough to keep people from starving or help them get medical attention. We actually have to do something to help them. Not give them hope."

"That's exactly what we need to give them. People need to believe there is a better future out there, and we provide that belief." Michael did not know how much of this he actually believed, but it sounded pretty convincing when heard himself say it out loud.

"Will you provide more than a belief, Michael? Will you actually provide a better future? What is going to happen if one day you are shut down? What will you do then?"

Michael had secretly asked himself the same question, but he could not face this possibility. He simply didn't have an answer.

37

February.

I t was the coldest day of the year. Snow covered the ground in front of the shelter, crushed underfoot by the line of people waiting for lunch. The food line on this Monday morning was as long as Caroline had ever seen it. People were showing up earlier every day, worried that the shelter might run out of food before they had a chance to eat. They knew that after the crowd numbered 200, the remaining homeless would be turned away. Refusing food to hungry people was the hardest thing Caroline had ever had to do, but she knew that if she didn't, the shelter would risk being closed for a crowd violation.

Even after the volunteers had told them that they would not be able to receive a meal, many of the unfed lingered around the shelter for the rest of the afternoon. Any chance of getting something to eat, however slim, was better than no chance at all. And they had nowhere else to go.

The sound of sirens was nothing new to Caroline. Police came around often to investigate complaints of fights, public urination, and loitering. Today she heard the sirens as soon as she got off the phone with her lawyer. Aseso's contributions had allowed Caroline to hire a law firm to help address the city's complaints against the shelter.

A heavyset man in his early fifties, wearing a brown suit, entered her office, followed by two younger, uniformed police officers. The heavyset man's presence made it clear that this visit concerned more than the matter of loitering.

He introduced himself curtly as Lieutenant Martinez. "I have a court order to shut this place down, effective immediately."

Caroline shut her eyes briefly. Her heart sank at the news, but it was not a complete surprise. She'd been dreading this day for months. "On what grounds?"

"Please come with me and tell your staff to shut everything down."

"We're in the middle of lunch service! For many of these people, it will be their last meal of the day. Can't we wait until everyone in line has had a chance to get something to eat?" Caroline pleaded, but the lieutenant just shrugged. Not possible. She followed him into the main room. Several police officers were already escorting people out the door. She could hear a voice over a loudspeaker outside, directing the crowd to disperse. Red lights flashed just outside the window. As she trailed the lieutenant, her staff stared at her in bewilderment. She met their eyes, then held up the court order, as if they might find an explanation there.

She told everyone to comply with the police, then walked outside. What less than an hour before had been a long, orderly line was now a disorderly swarm of people in the street. The police gave no answers to their questions: Why was the shelter closing? When would it reopen?

And where were they supposed to go?

As she helplessly surveyed the scene, she noticed a familiar face. It was familiar but out of place: an older woman was asking one of the police officers if he knew of another shelter that provided free meals. "I don't know of any, ma'am," said the officer.

The woman paused, smiling hopefully, as though still waiting for the answer even though it had already come. Caroline knew that delay. The police officer gladly stepped aside as Caroline approached.

"Mrs. Klein." Caroline touched her on the arm. "It's me, Caroline."

Mrs. Klein stood there, motionless. She looked much older than she had when they'd last seen each other, two years before. Caroline had lost touch with Mrs. Klein after they'd moved to their new apartment. She'd tried to keep in contact at first, but her many responsibilities had pulled her away.

Standing there looking at her friend, Caroline wanted to say something; but she had no idea how to begin. Mrs. Klein grabbed Caroline's hand with both of hers. Tears swelled in her eyes.

38

Hong Kong.

Thailand, one of Asia's oldest producers of Astragalus root for Aseso, was now the largest. Shipments from semiannual harvests were flown from there to the Nanning facility for processing and bottling. During Aseso's early years, Nanning had acted as the laboratory and the plantation for creating the genetically engineered seeds, as well as the processing and bottling facility. Now, with root extracts coming from places like Thailand, the Nanning production facility needed to be expanded.

Aseso had hired several contractors to triple Nanning's processing and bottling capacity. The project, expected to take nine months, had turned into a year-old still-unfinished quagmire. Revisions to the architectural plans had caused multiple delays. Worse, there had been several security breaches.

First, employees of a Macau-based subcontractor hired by the architect had tried and failed to break into the laboratory, which was kept under tight security. Next, would-be burglars entered the complex disguised as food truck cooks. They, too, were discovered.

The most coordinated effort to steal Aseso's secrets had come from a group of men disguised as local policemen. They convinced the night security guards, who had been hired by regional Chinese officials, that they were responding to a phone call made from a woman in distress inside the laboratory. The faux policemen had made it as far as the lab's front door before they were apprehended.

The threat of attack on the Nanning facility was growing. More needed to be done. Black Falcon had arranged to keep a small force at the plant, made up of some of its own people and a number of former Chinese special-forces soldiers. Dr. Tanaka chose Dirk to direct these security operations.

Now Michael was on his way to Thailand to help supervise the largest Astragalus harvest in the company's history. He would first meet with Dirk in Hong Kong—for security purposes. Together, they would fly to Nanning to join Dr. Tanaka and Clive, who oversaw all Asian operations. Michael would inspect the progress of the new facility before continuing on to Bangkok with Dr. Tanaka and Dirk to observe the harvest.

The sixteen-hour direct flight from New York to Hong Kong promised to go by quickly. Michael had grown accustomed to first class, which had all the amenities of home. Equipped with a desk, a full bed, and a flat-screen television, his pod served as an office from which he could work on his plans for Asia.

But tonight he couldn't focus. Lately, these flights had become his only chance to relax completely. At the office, he worked feverishly. At home, he was too aware of Caroline's chilly silence to enjoy their time together. Now, alone in his pod, he watched three movies and played chess against the in-flight entertainment system. During the last hour of the flight, he managed to finalize some projections Dr. Tanaka would want to see. He really should have gotten more work done; when the Lisbon facility was being planned, he'd underestimated the European demand for Sinsen. Hoping to avoid embarrassment, he was looking for ways to compensate for his lack of foresight, and he hoped that the Nanning facility would provide a solution.

The hotel had sent a car to pick him up from the airport. Because it was a weekend, the drive to Hong Kong's Central District was relatively short. This was Michael's first trip to Hong Kong, and he was struck by the city's beauty. Traditional wooden fishing boats navigated Victoria Harbor alongside large shipping vessels. Modern skyscrapers lined the bottom of a mountain. Higher up, glass and steel gave way to a green landscape. Hong Kong's pristine streets were more characteristic of a high-end California suburb than a crowded Asian city.

Once he'd settled into his suite, Michael called Joon, his friend from MIT. Joon had moved to Hong Kong three months earlier to help his uncle run the family semiconductor business.

"Hey, Michael, are you in town?"

"Yeah, I just got to my room. I'll probably take a nap now, but I'm free tonight." Michael looked out the window onto the city streets below. People seemed very small.

"Great. It'll be good to see you! I'll pick you up at eight in the lobby. We'll have dinner with my uncle."

"See you then." Michael hung up the phone, laid down on the couch, and turned on the television to catch up on the international news. The sportscaster was reviewing the previous week's cricket scores. His eyes were too heavy to keep open. By the time he woke up, it was time to meet Joon.

It was a nice night, so Michael and Joon decided to walk from the hotel. Joon described their destination, Lan Kwai Fong, as a small area in the Central District that was packed with bars, restaurants, and clubs. As they meandered, they caught up on old friends and new gossip. Joon was impressed with what Aseso had achieved.

"Man, I can't believe what you guys have accomplished. Who would have thought you would be the most successful one in our class?" Joon said. They turned onto D'Aguilar Street. A few rowdy Australians brushed by them on their way to another bar. Throngs of expatriates and locals wandered the sidewalks. The area was bustling with pedestrian activity.

"I'm not sure if that's an insult or a compliment," Michael responded jokingly.

"C'mon. You know what I mean. You guys are Mount Everest big. And to think I warned you not to get involved with Dr. Tanaka. Good thing you didn't listen to me."

"I could tell from the start that this company was going to be huge." Michael was loath to admit that at the time, he'd had no choice but to ignore Joon's warning. There had been no other options.

They arrived at Joon's favorite Cantonese restaurant, where his uncle was waiting at the bar. "Michael, this is my uncle, Dan Kim," Joon said. Dan was in his sixties and completely gray. Michael thought he would be the kind of person who would be completely comfortable in the presence of Dr. Tanaka.

"Nice to meet you, Mr. Kim." Michael had heard a lot about Joon's uncle, and not only from Joon. Mr. Kim had received plenty of coverage in the Wall Street Journal. He was a very successful businessman, with operations throughout Asia.

"Please call me Dan. It's nice to meet you. I've heard a lot about you from Joon, even before you became famous."

Michael smiled, trying not to show how flattered he was. The three of them sat down to dinner, and Dan asked about Michael's visit to Asia and his intentions going forward. Joon remained relatively silent while Michael talked. When Michael boasted of Aseso's intention to grow by 300 percent in the region within the next year, Dan set down his chopsticks, his plate still half full.

"This can't end well, Michael."

"What can't?" Michael asked, confused by the sudden change in tone. The conversation had been going well. He'd felt more confident than ever.

"What you guys are doing. This is what Joon often refers to as a train wreck waiting to happen," Dan said, glancing at Joon.

"I think we have it pretty much under control," Michael said, in an attempt to turn the conversation back to the positive.

"The only reason it's under control is because aging is a slow death. People can afford to wait to see what happens. If you guys had found the cure for cancer, the world would have conspired against you by now. Everybody knows there will never be enough Sinsen to go around."

"Dr. Tanaka is getting new land every day. In fact, starting next week, we are going to have the largest harvest yet in Thailand."

"It will never be enough," Dan said.

"There is never enough of anything. Why is this any different?"

"This is different because it is completely changing the world. The middle class will disappear. My family's semiconductor business depends on a growing middle class that buys computers and stereos. Now people here are spending all of their money on Sinsen. I hear that a lot of families are forgoing college for their kids so the parents can afford to stay young."

"Those are the choices people are making. Having choices is good," Michael said, immediately aware of how much he sounded like David.

"It isn't a choice. These people are shackled to Sinsen. It would be more of a choice if you guys were offering cocaine. Surely you realize that to many people, you are offering life itself. They have to pay whatever you ask because it really is a matter of life and death. That's not a choice; it's a completely different thing."

"People should be happy that the choice is available at all, instead of complaining that it is not available to everyone."

"Don't get me wrong. I take Sinsen. Everyone who can afford it takes it, and don't believe them if they say they don't. Personally, I'm happy that it exists; but many of your customers, I would say the majority, spend most of their disposable income on Sinsen. That's a big problem for many reasons. One of them, which happens to be a problem for me, is that they are no longer spending money on stereos and computers. But that's the least of my worries."

"What would you have us do? We have a product that everyone wants, and it's in limited supply. You know how business works, Dan. We aren't forcing anyone to buy it."

"You know that if you drop a frog in boiling water, it will jump out. But if you put a frog in a pot of water at room temperature and turn on the stove, the frog will stay there as the water heats up. Eventually, the heat will kill it."

"Who is the frog here?" Michael asked with a forced laugh.

"The world is the frog. If you had announced early on that you had discovered the fountain of youth, the world's reaction against you would have been immediate. Instead, you have slowly allowed people to believe that you guys might have something that could possibly extend life, never really denying or confirming. But in the meantime, the number of people who want Sinsen will gradually but steadily keep growing. It's happening so gradually that people don't recognize the danger. In other words, people, like the frog, are unaware of the rising temperature."

Michael could see that Dan had made his fortune by understanding human nature as well as he understood technology. He wanted to say something that was dismissive of Dan's comments, but he couldn't think of a clever retort. This was the first time that someone had suggested to him that Aseso had known the truth about Sinsen all along. For the first time, he would have preferred not to be seen as the man behind Aseso. *Not me*, he thought to himself: *I wasn't the one who slowly raised the temperature.* But it was too late for disavowals. He was an integral part of Aseso now. When people talked about Aseso, they were talking about him.

39

Michael did not sleep well. There was something unsettling about what Joon's uncle had suggested. Aseso had attracted many critics for many different reasons. Religious fundamentalists, social liberals, politicians, academics, and talk radio hosts all had opinions about how Aseso should be controlled. But now, for the first time, someone had recognized David's plan, laid out the blueprints, and forced Michael to look.

Michael ordered room service and watched the international news network while he ate breakfast. There was an uprising in Thailand. Protestors were being shot. Scenes of rocks being thrown at a wall of heavily armed soldiers flashed on the wide-screen television. Michael was only half watching; the other half of his attention was on the local newspaper that had been delivered to his door. He poured the last of the coffee and looked at the clock. It was seven-thirty. He had plenty of time to get ready for his meeting with Dirk. He called Caroline, but she did not pick up. He always called her from his trips, always telling her that he wished she were there, always promising that next time she would come with him. The calls always ended with "I love you."

He left a message and got dressed for his day trip to Nanning.

Michael spotted Dirk as he left the elevator. It had to be Dirk: tall, short hair, rugged face, in his early fifties. This would be the first time Michael had been escorted by a Black Falcon agent. Michael had heard of similar organizations providing private security for oil companies in places like Iraq and Nigeria. He'd never thought he would be walking around an international city with a bodyguard.

"Mr. Jeffs." Dirk extended his hand.

"Yes. You can call me Michael."

"Very well, Michael. Everything has been arranged. Your transport is waiting outside."

The lobby was filled with businessmen and women on their way to and from meetings, and staff helping guests with luggage. Two tall, well-built men wearing dark suits and earpieces stood ten feet away. As Michael and Dirk made their way to the hotel entrance, one man walked ahead as the other fell behind. Michael couldn't help thinking that they must appear conspicuous to everyone; he'd probably be safer without the entourage. The welcoming receptions had changed dramatically since Michael's first trips to Barbados.

Two black Mercedes were parked outside. Michael and Dirk were ushered into the second car. The men with earpieces got into the first car, which quickly pulled away. Michael's car followed.

Michael felt a little awkward sitting in a car with someone he had never met—someone whose only job at the moment was to protect his life. There wasn't much to say. Dirk stared straight ahead for the duration of the ride. Within half an hour they had arrived at the airport, where a private chartered jet was waiting to fly them to Nanning.

Nanning was the capital of Guangxi province, a largely autonomous region in the southeast part of China. A subtropical, mountainous territory bordering Vietnam, Guangxi had long been China's largest sugar-producing territory. That had changed after the conversion of sugar plantations to Astragalus fields for Sinsen production. China, once a net exporter, had come to be the largest sugar importer in the world.

Two more black Mercedes were waiting at Nanning Wuxu International Airport, along with more tall, well-built men in dark suits. As Michael walked off the jet, he reflected that if nothing else, Black Falcon was consistent. The trip to the Aseso complex took another twenty-five minutes through a road carved into the jungle-covered mountains. Chinese soldiers patrolled the road leading directly to the gate of the complex. Men in black army-style jumpsuits stood guard inside.

Michael had never been to Nanning before, although he had seen numerous pictures. This, he thought, was the place it had all started. As they entered the complex, Michael was amazed by the progress that had been made. Although he had seen the architect's sketches of the proposed expansion, it was quite different to see it in person. The complex was now larger and more modern than any of their other facilities. The three original buildings had been transformed into white brick structures reinforced by an outer steel skeleton, while five new buildings had been built on newly-cleared land. Guards, some with dogs, were posted at every door.

Dirk and another Black Falcon agent escorted Michael into the main building. Dirk seemed to know exactly where they were going. The interior of the building was even more impressive than its exterior. A large marble reception desk, flanked by two stone and steel staircases, stood in the middle of a large lobby with a ceiling two stories high. Not a single security guard stopped them as they ascended one of the staircases. Michael noticed, as he walked along the long second-floor hallway, that everyone slowed down and drifted to one side to let him pass, as if they already knew who he was.

At the end of the hallway, they approached a glass-walled office where Dr. Tanaka sat behind a traditional dark wood desk, speaking to a younger man whose back was turned. He looked up as they entered.

"Welcome to Nanning, Michael." Dr. Tanaka stood as his colleague turned around. "This is my son, Clive." In response to a nod from Dr. Tanaka, Dirk left the room.

"It's nice to meet you, Clive," Michael said, extending his hand. "I've heard a lot about you." Although Michael had planned many trips to Asia over the previous years, the grueling requirements of the Aseso build-out in Africa, South America, and Europe had caused countless cancellations, and he had never had the opportunity to meet Clive.

"The pleasure is mine." Clive, like Dr. Tanaka, spoke with a British lilt. He was the same height as his father, but thinner. He was much more fashionably dressed than Michael would have expected of the technical head of the company. "It's hard to believe we are only now meeting. Father has told me a great many things about you. Not all of them bad."

Apparently, Clive's sense of humor was closer to David's than to his father's.

"Well, that's good. The facility looks great." Michael directed his compliment to both of them.

"Sit down, Michael. We'll get you up to speed and then give you a tour." Dr. Tanaka took his seat and pointed to the chair beside Clive's.

"The facility does look great, as you say, Michael. It is also now fully operational. With the help of the Chinese government, we will build a landing strip a couple of miles from here." Dr. Tanaka seemed very pleased.

"That's good news. The government here seems to be cooperating nicely."

"We are a very large contributor to their tax revenues. They have every desire to see us prosper," Clive said. "I've made quite a few trips to Beijing, and believe me, we have the full support of the government." He sat back in his seat. "How are things on your side of the world?"

"The Lisbon and Boca Raton facilities are at full capacity now. We will probably move forward with building the one we've been thinking about in Germany."

"I travel quite a bit to Hong Kong," Clive said. "I have friends there. Many of the Americans I meet praise you guys in New York. It's all they can talk about."

"Yes, we're very popular. We are getting a lot of pressure to ramp up production to increase Sinsen's availability." Seeing an opening, Michael added, "Will we be able to tap into this facility to meet some of the demand in Europe and the U.S.?"

Dr. Tanaka interjected. "We can do that for now, but the real problem is not going to be processing capacity. It's going to be land. It is becoming increasingly difficult to secure more land."

Michael was surprised to hear Dr. Tanaka admitting that there would be a limitation to Aseso's growth. At the same time, he was relieved that at least his miscalculations about the Lisbon facility would not be held against him.

"David has been making promises to all sorts of governments about our ability to make Sinsen more available to everyone. Have you spoken to him about this concern?" His relief evaporating, Michael suddenly worried that the company's plan and the projections he had laid out were not feasible. Many people believed that, one day, Sinsen would be available to everyone. Any suggestion to the contrary would be devastating.

"David has no choice but to make those promises. He is buying us time. We will need to figure out something. In the meantime, we will blame Sinsen's lack of availability on the limitations of our processing facilities."

"If people find out that there's an eventual limit to what we can produce, there is going to be chaos. We have half of humanity on a waiting list," Michael said, as the severity of the situation fully dawned on him. It wasn't just the lack of land that was the problem—it was the possibility of people finding out.

Michael had once been concerned that the public would panic if the Stanford study showed that none of the anti-aging products worked. That panic would have been nothing compared to what would happen if people found out the one thing that was supposed to preserve their lives would never become available to them. Now, he was starting to believe that he had been fooled, once again, to believe in the benevolent intentions of his superiors.

"The world has always been some variety of managed chaos. Now it will have to be managed differently."

Michael recalled the warnings Joon's uncle had given the night before. He was beginning to fear that even if there were enough land, things still might not turn out well. He saw now what a dangerous game David was playing. The situation suddenly seemed as volatile as a slow gas leak in the basement. All of the implications of not being able to deliver on David's promises raced through his head. The potential problems seemed biblical in size. Humanity would want to save itself on Aseso's life raft, but only a handful of people would be able to fit.

At that moment, Dirk rushed back into the room. His face was flushed from running. "Gentlemen, we have a problem in Thailand."

40

Nanning, China.

R iots had broken out across Thailand. Growing unrest over food shortages and local political corruption had driven people into the streets. Once the world's fourth-largest sugar cane exporter, Thailand had sold much of its arable land to Aseso. As in other countries where Aseso conducted business, inflation was skyrocketing. Many of the government's resources were directed towards maintaining the company's vast Astragalus plantations. Those who could take advantage of the new wealth-generating activities related to Aseso's operations prospered. The majority did not. Journalists began to refer to the cultivated Astragalus as "blood plants," analogous to the blood diamonds that had financed war throughout Africa in the 1990s.

The police tried to keep the peace through brute force. At first, most of the protests were regional in nature; each city had its own locally-organized riots. But the revolt quickly grew national in scope, and within a couple of days, protestors blocked roads leading into and out of towns. The situation drew international attention when groups of students blocked the highways leading to the international airport in Bangkok. Tourists were trapped, unable to catch their flights home. All incoming flights to Thailand were cancelled. The prime minister, watched closely by the international community, tried to relieve the situation through peaceful negotiation.

The airport blockade came one week before the largest harvest in Aseso's history. The company was already running dangerously low on inventory, and any delays in delivering extract from the plantations to the Nanning facility would cause shortages and bad press. David had placated his critics in the U.S. by promising availability to everyone within a couple of years. News that Aseso did not have enough product to meet demand would surely bring about public support for government intervention—something David wanted desperately to avoid.

The situation was made worse for Aseso by the fact that in two weeks, David was going to receive an international medal of recognition for Aseso's global charitable contributions. In order to improve Aseso's image, tarnished as it was by Dr. Tanaka's activities, David had given away hundreds of millions of dollars for education in developing countries. Aseso also sponsored youth sports programs in poor areas of the many countries in which Sinsen was sold.

Michael, Dr. Tanaka, and Clive monitored the evolving situation in Thailand from Nanning while David watched from New York. For three days the Thai government tried to negotiate with the students who were blocking the airport roads; the prime minister ordered the military to secure the area surrounding the airport but not to take aggressive action against any protestors. As a precaution, all other commercial airports in the country were closed until the situation could be resolved.

Meanwhile, Michael attempted to redirect to Nanning a shipment of extract from Brazil that was on its way to Florida, but he quickly realized that even if a rerouting were feasible, there still would not be enough to prevent an interruption in supply to customers. Until then, Michael had not fully appreciated the scarcity of the resources upon which Aseso depended to satisfy what was becoming an insatiable demand. It was essential that the harvest in Thailand go according to schedule. There was simply no other solution.

On the fourth day of the student protest, with the prime minister making little progress, Dr. Tanaka's patience ran out. He ordered Dirk to organize a meeting in Vientiane, the capital of Laos, Thailand's neighbor, with a few Thai officials he kept on a secret Aseso payroll. The Thai officials would be transported in Laotian military helicopters disguised as commercial helicopters, with the help of Black Falcon agents.

"The helicopters have left Thailand and are on their way to Laos now," Dirk announced early that afternoon.

"Good. How soon can we leave for Laos?" Dr. Tanaka was meeting with Michael and Clive in his glass-walled office in Nanning. They were planning a new, accelerated production schedule, to be implemented once the airports in Thailand reopened.

"We can leave in an hour." Black Falcon had resources in almost every country in the world. The coordinated effort was being handled with military precision.

"Clive, you stay here and continue with the preparations. Michael and I will take care of things in Laos."

Michael looked up from his laptop, stunned. He had come to Nanning from Hong Kong for a two-day business visit. Today was already his fifth day on the mainland. Convincing Caroline that Aseso had the best intentions was becoming increasingly difficult. He had not told her about his private security escort. He definitely did not like the idea of having to tell her he was traveling to Laos to involve himself in clandestine political operations.

"Are you sure you want me to go? I can stay here and help Clive with the preparations." Michael felt like a kid being dragged on a shopping trip. He had never directly participated in any of Dr. Tanaka's activities, and he preferred not to start now.

"If we don't change things in Thailand soon, there will be nothing to prepare. We are going to need you there once things start happening."

Happening? What was going to start happening? A week ago, he'd been having dinner with Caroline in his New York apartment. He had been doing his job as the operational head of one of the most successful companies in the world. Now he was about to become involved in a political imbroglio in a country he could not have pointed to on a map. Suddenly, the future of Aseso—as well as his own future—were in question. Dr. Tanaka's decisions were swift and free of doubt. Michael was exhausted from the stress.

The jet landed in Vientiane just over an hour after departing from Nanning. When it had come to a complete stop, Michael grabbed his briefcase from beneath his seat and followed Dr. Tanaka and Dirk down the steps to the tarmac. As he got into one of the signature black Mercedes, he felt as if he were in a dream he could not wake himself from. They were taken to a downtown resort. Once Michael had checked in, he got up the nerve to call Caroline.

"Caroline, it's me." Michael paced back and forth in the hotel gardens just outside the conference room where the meeting was to take place. His heart was racing and his hands shook.

"Michael, where are you? Is something wrong?"

"I'm in Laos."

"You're where?"

"Laos."

"What are you doing in Laos?"

"The situation in Thailand isn't getting any better, so Dr. Tanaka is coordinating a meeting here."

"You just hopped on a plane and flew to Laos while Thailand is falling apart? Who are you meeting with?"

"I don't know, but I'm about to find out. The meeting is scheduled to start in a few minutes."

"Why does he need you there? You don't know anything about politics."

"I think I'm about to have a crash course in politics. Caroline...." Michael said, but he was afraid to proceed.

Caroline must have heard the anxiety in his voice. She was silent.

"I'm not sure how long I'm going to be here," Michael said.

"You don't?"

"I don't think...Caroline, I might not be back for your birthday."

Caroline gave a sharp laugh. "Oh, well. I guess I should have taken Sinsen. Then I wouldn't have to worry about you missing a birthday. I'd have hundreds more."

A Black Falcon agent walked up to Michael. "They're ready for you, sir."

"Thanks. I'll be right there." Michael turned his attention back to Caroline. "Caroline, I love you and I'm so sorry. I've got to go. I'll call you tonight."

"Wait. Tell me you're not doing anything wrong."

"I don't even know what I'm doing."

"Michael, I fell in love with you because on top of all of your other amazing qualities, you have one of the biggest hearts of anyone I know." Caroline's voice began to weaken. "Please don't change."

"Don't worry. I'm still the same guy you met in Seattle. I'm not going to change."

"I love you, Michael."

"I love you, too."

When Michael walked into the conference room, Dr. Tanaka was inexplicably absent. Dirk introduced Michael to the Thai officials, two men in suits and two in uniform. Michael didn't take note of their long, complicated-sounding names, which he wouldn't have been able to remember anyway. They began to talk about the situation in Thailand, but Michael suggested that they wait until Dr. Tanaka arrived. He was feeling emotionally drained and socially inept, incapable even of small talk. He could not stop thinking that he was losing Caroline.

At last Dr. Tanaka arrived. In signature form, he dispensed with salutations, walked straight to the head of the conference table, and sat down.

"I am sorry, Dr. Tanaka, that we have to meet under such clandestine circumstances," said one of the men in suits.

"What is the current situation?"

"The student protestors have managed to attract popular support for their cause. The roads are now blocked by trees they have cut down with help from the locals. They have indicated that they will not leave the area until their demands are met."

"What are their demands?" Dr. Tanaka indicated a slight interest.

"Among many other things, they want land returned to the people."

"Returned to the people? Don't these students believe in property rights? This is outrageous. Why does the prime minister entertain the wishes of these radical students while the country remains frozen? Why doesn't he simply have the military remove them?"

"The prime minister does not have the political appetite to take military action in this situation. He is being watched carefully by the international community and wants to be seen as tolerant and friendly to democratic ideals. Therefore, this protest could last for months."

"In that case, I think Thailand needs a new prime minister." Dr. Tanaka sat back in his chair. Michael was aghast at his arrogance. One didn't just stroll into a country and replace the prime minister. Michael, embarrassed at how insulted the Thai officials must have been by the comment, did not want to make eye contact with them.

One of the officials stood up. He walked over to Dr. Tanaka and handed him a sealed envelope. Then he said, "We couldn't agree with you more."

41

Vientiane, Laos.

The coup d'état began two days later.
The two uniformed men in the meeting, Michael later learned, were generals in the Thai army who were sympathetic to a rival party leader's desire to become prime minister. A military overthrow of the existing prime minister's government had been in the works for over a year. Provincial governors and regional businessmen had met frequently with the political opposition. In addition, it was widely known that many leaders within the armed forces were dissatisfied with the size of the government's military budget. Once the conspirators had decided upon a new political leader, key generals were approached. A deal was struck.

The army was waiting for two things: a politically advantageous moment and the financial resources to execute the plan. The large popular uprising provided the first. Dr. Tanaka offered the second. The army moved quickly to oust the existing prime minister. Martial law was imposed. A bank holiday was declared and citywide curfews were enforced. Journalists were restricted to certain areas. Many student protestors fled to their home towns when they heard of the change in power. A few remained defiant to the end. The student casualties were few—but there were casualties.

Dirk and two Black Falcon operatives flew to Thailand to act as advisors to the military. Dr. Tanaka and Michael stayed at the resort hotel in Vientiane, watching the events unfold on television. A military representative visited them each day with updates from the front lines. His updates conflicted substantially with what they saw on the news.

The main subplot of the Crisis in Thailand, as it had been dubbed by the media, concerned the thousands of acres of Aseso's Astragalus plants that sat in the middle of the war zone. Journalists speculated as to what it would mean if the plants were destroyed. On fears of such an event, the Thai baht tumbled against the U.S. dollar and the euro. Stock markets around the world plunged when it was rumored that battles were taking place in the fields. A mild panic spread among the world's elite, who began to realize that this political event could impede their subscription to Sinsen. By the third day of fighting, the Crisis in Thailand was the most closely followed story around the world.

Senator Coves was having a field day—or, rather, a field week. He made the rounds on the talk show circuit, pointing out the problems that lay ahead for Aseso if the Thailand situation was not resolved quickly. Coves had recently declared his intention to run for president and was preparing to make Sinsen a matter of national debate. He was steadily attracting support for the idea of making Sinsen universally available—although it was not clear to anyone exactly how that would happen.

"When are you coming home, Michael?" Caroline asked. She called him regularly, wanting updates. "I can't sleep. I keep waking up and turning on the news."

"I'm so sorry to put you through this. I'm not sure when I'm coming home. It'll be as soon as possible, whenever this is all over. I'll make up for missing your birthday—I promise." Michael sat on the bed in his hotel room, watching the muted television. Images of soldiers fighting in the streets flashed across the screen.

"I don't care about my birthday. I care about you. I want you safe."

"I'll be safe. Don't worry. I'm staying at a luxury resort. There are guards everywhere. "

"Guards? Why do you need guards?"

Michael realized that he probably should have left out the part about the guards. Even he wasn't sure whether the Black Falcon operatives that escorted him everywhere made him feel better or worse. "We don't need guards. Dr. Tanaka just likes to have them around. Really, there's no danger here."

"Why can't you at least fly back to Hong Kong and wait there?" Through the phone, it sounded as though Caroline was watching the same footage in their living room in New York that Michael was watching in his room in Laos.

"Dr. Tanaka wants me here. As soon as the fighting stops, we're going into Thailand."

"What? Why do they need you there? That can't be safe."

"I'm sure it will be fine," Michael said. But of course he was not sure. He had never been involved in anything like this before. He did not know what was expected of him in Thailand. Would Dr. Tanaka want him to take part in some of the political activities that had become necessary for Aseso to function properly?

"Can I come and join you?"

"I don't think it will be safe."

"You just said it would be safe."

"I don't think it will be safe for you."

"Why would it be safe for you but not for me?"

Michael flopped back on the bed, exhausted. He did not understand why she so urgently needed to join him now. He reckoned Caroline would be safe at the resort in Laos, but he did not know what to expect in Thailand once the fighting stopped. He was both reassured and unsettled by Dr. Tanaka's confidence—not to mention the constant presence of the Black Falcon agents posted outside his room.

"Okay. Call my office and have them arrange for you to fly to Hong Kong tomorrow. You can wait for me there, and we'll decide where to meet. Joon can show you around. Once I'm finished here, we'll take a vacation."

"I'll call them right away. I can't wait to see you."

After Michael hung up the phone, he turned the volume back up. Even though he could hear everything that came from the TV, he wasn't really listening. He wished he could make Caroline stop worrying. He wanted Caroline to be there next to him, but he was too protective to have her see what he was involved in. Or too ashamed. What am I doing here? Michael thought. Then a familiar scene on the television stole his attention.

A reporter was standing in the middle of an Astragalus field. He and a cameraman had somehow managed to get past the soldiers protecting the plantation. The reporter, unshaven and slightly dirty, looked as if he had spent the night in the jungle. With the fields as a backdrop, he explained that the little plants he was standing in seemed to have caused all the suffering that was taking place in the country. The revolution was not the end, he said, but the means.

The image was reminiscent of one Michael had seen a few years before: a reporter covering the unrest in Nigeria, standing in the oil fields. He wondered if all wars were similar in origin. He wondered if all wars had their own Dr. Tanaka.

The phone rang, and Michael answered it, thinking it was Caroline calling back. Maybe she'd changed her mind. He knew that was not likely.

"Hello, Michael. It's David."

"David! It's great to hear your voice." Michael had always felt more comfortable working with David than Dr. Tanaka. In these troubling times, that sentiment was even stronger.

"Are you having fun over there?"

"I wouldn't say 'fun.' It's gotten a little crazy."

"Why don't you guys just take over China while you're at it?"

"You'd have to ask Dr. Tanaka about that."

"I'll do that. How are you?"

"Fine. I'm fine." Michael was miles from fine. He was slightly envious of David's cool demeanor. David never seemed to be unnerved by any of life's surprises. He was always sure of what to do and say, no matter what. Michael, by contrast, had never been more unsure.

"Hang in there," David said. "Listen. We're getting a lot of calls from nervous people who think if this thing in Thailand goes the wrong way, we won't be able to deliver on next month's orders. What is the situation, as you see it?"

"I can't lie, David: it will be tough. Our inventories are really low. We definitely won't be able to take on any new customers." Michael hated having to say that. He knew that customers would be disappointed in Aseso, and more importantly, he knew David would be disappointed in him.

"Well, thanks to your buddy Brad, we just took on twenty billion dollars' worth of new customers. They are going to be pissed."

"Dr. Tanaka seems very confident that this will be over soon."

"If it's not, I want you to coordinate the harvest from the Mozambique plantations."

"Those plants won't be ready for harvest for another six months," Michael said. Confident David always had a solution ready. The problem was, these solutions were never feasible. Just once, Michael would like to say no. To tell David that things weren't always possible just because he, David, wanted them to be.

"Our Bearing Brothers contracts don't say that we have to deliver effective Astragalus extract," David said. "All they state is that we must deliver Astragalus extract. People won't die if they age a few months. We should be back on schedule by the end of the year. If we start failing to deliver product now, the whole world is going to come down on us."

Michael tried to cover his shock. "I read you loud and clear," he said. The unspeakable truth was, he was relieved that there was a solution, even if it was an unscrupulous one.

"Good. I doubt it will come to that, but we need to be prepared."

"We'll be prepared," Michael assured him.

That night Michael barely slept. His mind raced. He began to wonder whether Aseso was becoming too big not to fail. The global demand for Sinsen would never be satisfied. Each new customer came at greater expense to the rest of the world. War had become a corporate necessity. How many lives should be sacrificed so that others could live longer? How many people should go hungry? How long would the world tolerate having a handful of people control so much power?

The moment he woke up, he turned on the television. Almost as quickly as it had begun, the coup had ended. Early that morning, the prime minister and his closest aides had fled the country. Michael watched the news all day, seeing the story through to its resolution. After the generals had declared victory, they quickly abdicated power to the new prime minister in a short public ceremony. The political transition was complete.

Over the next few days, soldiers remained in the cities to keep the peace. Roads were reopened. By the end of the week, the international community formally recognized the new government. Banks reopened and airport service returned to normal. The new government allowed Black Falcon to send private security forces to protect the Astragalus fields and major airports.

The Astragalus harvest went ahead as scheduled.

42

Washington, D.C.

A string quartet played as David, in a custom black tuxedo, walked into the grand ballroom of the landmark Waldorf Hotel. Crystal chandeliers hung from the eighteen-foot gold-leaf ceiling. Men in white formal jackets prepared tables for the 300 guests expected that evening. The 150-year-old hotel had hosted some of the most important galas in the nation's history. This particular event had been organized to raise money to combat hunger in the U.S. David was to receive a medal of recognition.

One of the event coordinators, Lisa, was notified through her earpiece that the guest of honor had arrived. But by the time she located David, he was already surrounded by people waiting for their opportunity to speak with one of the wealthiest, most influential men in the world. The event photographer took one picture after another of David with the many guests. Everybody there wanted to be associated with him. Every guest except one.

"David, I believe you know Senator Coves?" Lisa had pulled David away from the crowd to escort him around the room, introducing him to other VIPs individually.

"Yes, we've met before," David said, slightly surprised. "I wasn't aware you were a sponsor of this event, Senator."

"This is not official business for me. My wife is on the planning committee. Tonight I'm just a guest."

The photographer snapped away as the crowd looked on. David and Senator Coves had each been betting his career on the failure of the other's. Neither was feeling particularly friendly.

"Well. If you will excuse us, Senator, I need to introduce David to a few others before the ceremony begins," Lisa said, feeling the tension between the two men.

"Enjoy your evening, Senator," David said.

"Dr. Oaks. Perhaps we can have a drink in private after the ceremony," Senator Coves said. His tone indicated that it would not be a social meeting.

David smiled. "Have your people find me. I'll make myself available."

"I look forward to it."

David told Lisa to take a break and made his way to the bar alone. Waiters circulated with champagne, but he wanted something stronger.

"Dirty vodka martini, please." David began to reach into his pocket for his money clip. He was a notorious over-tipper.

"I'll have one of those as well."

David turned and found himself face to face with Dr. Joanna Hochberg. She wore a full-length strapless black dress, and her hair, uncharacteristically, was pulled up in a bun. She wore more makeup than usual. She looked beautiful.

"Nice to see you again, Joanna," David said.

The photographer had caught up with him and was going overboard with photos. The crowd clearly found David's interaction with Joanna even more interesting than his encounter with the Senator.

"I noticed your best friend is here tonight," Joanna said, referring to Senator Coves. She reached for her martini, thanking the bartender. Joanna had also made a career out of trying to destroy David's. Her intention, however, was the exact opposite of the Senator's. Like Coves, she had amassed a great deal of popular support for her cause. The country was gradually dividing its support among David, Joanna, and Senator Coves.

"Yes. It's ironic that his wife planned a gala to honor me." David dropped a large bill into the tip jar and reached for his drink.

"You two didn't seem to have much to talk about."

"No, we're more into awkward silences. But he wants to see me later." David smiled at Joanna and tasted his martini.

"Oh? What do you think he wants?"

"I don't think he's going to ask me for a campaign contribution."

"He might want to make peace with you."

"I hope not. What fun would I have then? I'd only have you to go to war with."

"Me and a few Southeast Asian countries."

David laughed briefly. "That's funny." Lisa was walking toward him; it was time for his speech. He handed Joanna his half-full martini. "Enjoy your evening."

"Knock 'em dead," Joanna said, raising both glasses in a toast.

David smiled. "That will happen by itself if you get your way."

David was escorted to the front of the ballroom, onto a small stage. The award was presented, and he made the requisite speech, thanking everyone for attending the gala and supporting organizations that sought to rid the world of hunger.

Then, fully aware of his audience, he moved on to the more interesting part of his speech. "I am not a complex man, but I live in a complex world," he began. "In such a world, actions might appear to be contrary to ideals. I live in a world in which we have figured out how to send a man to the moon and how to create identical clones of animals. Some people even believe that we will one day discover how to prevent people from getting older." David paused for the crowd's laughter. Senator Coves, standing near the front, did not smile.

"Despite all of these accomplishments, we have yet to figure out how to share. I am aware of the controversy that surrounds what I do for a living. But what I do is to offer a choice to adults who are capable of making decisions for themselves. Children cannot make their own choices; they must grow up before they can start to worry about getting old, and in the meantime they depend on us. We owe it to them to improve their lives before we concern ourselves with extending ours. Tonight, therefore, I challenge our government and the governments of all the countries on the earth to pool their resources to combat hunger among children—before spending any more time and energy on the selfish pursuits of adults."

His speech received a standing ovation. He spotted Joanna finishing the second martini as he took his seat. People rushed up to shake his hand; the press of his admirers abated only when dinner was served. David had been seated with, among others, the British ambassador to the U.S. and the most recent Nobel Prize winner in economics. His was at a table of people who could afford to share David's point of view. They were all subscribers to Sinsen.

The wait staff seemed less sympathetic.

After dinner, David joined some old friends on the balcony to catch up over a few glasses of Scotch. Private moments with friends were rare for him now. It was a constant battle to be able to enjoy personal time. Craig and Eric had flown down to support him. Their wives were busy socializing inside while they toasted David in private, away from the press and photographers.

"So when are you going to settle down?" Craig, once a notorious womanizer, was now married. He'd stopped dead in his tracks upon first sight of the woman who was now his wife. They'd eloped within six months of meeting and moved into a house in Connecticut, near the ocean. David hardly saw Craig any more.

"Not any time soon. I've got too much to take care of these days."

"Have you stopped dating because the press follows you everywhere? It must be tough to keep two girls a secret from each other." Eric seemed to enjoy playing out his own fantasies through David.

"There's no one serious right now, but I do have my eye on someone."

"Does that someone have their eye on you?" Craig asked.

"Look who you're talking to," David said, feigning confidence.

David had hardly started on his second glass of Scotch when he saw a young man walking toward him.

"Dr. Oaks. The senator is waiting for you in the presidential suite."

"The senator is in the presidential suite? That's very presumptuous of him." The aide didn't seem to get David's joke. Craig and Eric snickered. "All right, then. Let's go see what your boss wants."

43

"That was a heartwarming little speech you gave down there, Dr. Oaks." Senator Coves sat on the couch next to his chief of staff, Robert Dorsen, across the coffee table from David. Aides and security personnel waited in the hallway. The Washington Monument, lit up in the night, could be seen through the window.

"I was enjoying a nice glass of single malt with my friends. I hope you didn't interrupt just so you could congratulate me on my speech."

"They have Scotch here. You can pour yourself a drink." Coves pointed to the bar behind David.

David glanced at the bar. "They have blended whiskey here. Not the same thing."

"Dr. Oaks, let's cut the bullshit. Aseso's days as a free agent are numbered. You can play ball with us and make out like a king, or you can get crushed under the combined weight of my foot and your ego."

"Unfortunately for you, Senator, we live in a democracy. I don't have to play ball. I just have to wait long enough for you not to get elected."

"You'll have to wait a very long time for that to happen," Robert said, leaning forward with an arrogant sneer. "The senator is miles ahead in the polls."

"The only reason he's ahead is because he's promising something he can't deliver."

"Trust me," Coves said. "I can deliver a world of hurt to you."

"Imagine the world of hurt when I tell the American people that if you move against my company in any way, I will simply pull the whole goddamn thing out of the U.S."

"You won't do that. The U.S. has to be at least a third of your total sales," Robert rebutted. David wished he wouldn't speak. Coves was bad enough.

For a moment David stared at Robert before turning his attention back to Coves. "Listen, Senator. The U.S. is a third of my total sales because I don't sell what I sell here to the billion other people around the world who are already on the waiting list."

"You're bluffing." The senator's voice betrayed his nervousness.

"Am I?"

"You don't want to be seen as unpatriotic."

"Free market capitalism is patriotic. Even the Chinese aren't getting involved in my business. This meeting is over." David stood and walked toward the front door.

"You are fucking with the wrong man," the senator called after him.

David closed the door without looking back.

The Black Falcon agent acting as his security guard for the evening was waiting in the hallway. The two took the elevator down. In the lobby, two more Black Falcon agents were waiting to escort David to the large black SUV that was parked outside.

On the way to his hotel, riding in the back seat, David called Michael and asked him to look into moving the processing and bottling capabilities from Boca Raton to Canada. He then called Dr. Tanaka and suggested that he set up a meeting with their friends in Beijing.

By the time the SUV dropped David off at his hotel, it was past midnight. The lobby was empty except for a couple of bellhops and the night manager. In the elevator, David soaked in the silence. He pulled out the key card from his money clip as he approached his suite and opened the door. The television was on in the bedroom, and so were the lights. He walked toward the lit room while loosening his tie.

A woman reclined on his bed, a glass of wine in her hand. "So, what did he want?"

"He wanted me to help him secure the presidency." David took off his jacket and poured himself a glass of Scotch.

"Now that would be something," Joanna said as she put down her wine and waved David closer. "You two would make strange bedfellows."

44

Philippines. March.

The press had already abandoned the Crisis in Thailand in favor of more current events. The Astragalus harvest in that country went as planned. The new Thai government delivered on its promise to provide Dr. Tanaka with the logistical and administrative wherewithal to expedite shipments of his Astragalus roots. Meanwhile, the modernized Nanning facility was running with the efficiency that Dr. Tanaka had expected.

Michael was putting the events in Thailand behind him. He had known that big business and politics were often intimately involved; that was certainly no secret. But now that he had been an active participant, he understood that the victims were innocent people—real people. The Thai students that had died while demonstrating were not mere statistics. They were real people with families and friends. The problems behind the protests had not been solved. Instead, the protestors had been silenced.

Michael had decided to take a vacation with Caroline once he was satisfied that the harvest was successfully under way. He flew to Hong Kong, where Caroline had been waiting for him for the past week. She had tried to occupy herself with shopping and sightseeing, but all she really wanted to do was go straight to Bangkok to be with Michael. Despite the tensions between them she still loved him for the man she knew he could be.

On Joon's recommendation, they traveled to a small island called Boracay, located 200 miles south of Manila in the middle of the Philippines. Getting there from Hong Kong required two planes, a bus, and a boat. Caroline had asked Michael to find a place where there were no televisions to distract them or phones to interrupt their conversations. In Boracay, crystal-blue waters, powder-white sand, tropical palms, and flowering plants more than compensated for the lack of air conditioning and room service. For Michael, who had become accustomed to five-star resorts with all of the inconvenient modern conveniences, the cabana on the beach was a welcome return to an uncomplicated life—if only for a few days.

He sat at an ocean side bar, drinking a San Miguel beer as he waited for Caroline to return from a shopping trip down the beach. To call it a bar was generous. A local man had driven bamboo poles into the sand to support a thatched roof. Metal folding tables and chairs and a cooler of beer and bottled water completed the setup. A boy walking along the beach sold the only bar food available: grilled shrimp and fresh coconuts. All of the day's customers, with the exception of Michael, had left to get ready for dinner.

Caroline approached the folding table. She was wearing a new dress. "You look beautiful," Michael said. The sun was setting, and it was cooling down. Earlier, Caroline had had her hair braided by a woman on the beach. She looked like a traveling college student, no older than twenty-two.

Caroline smiled and sat down beside him, grabbing his hand. Together, they looked out at the ocean. The sun had turned to a darker orange as small boatloads of tourists made their way back to shore after a day of scuba diving and windsurfing.

"You want one of these?" Michael offered her one of his grilled shrimp.

"No, I'm going to wait till dinner. You should save your appetite, too."

"Are you kidding me? I could eat another plate of these and still have room for dinner."

For the first time in months, they were affectionate with one another. The previous two years suddenly seemed like ten. Aseso had grown, and they had grown apart. But now that they were alone on the beach, watching the setting sun, Michael was more relaxed than he'd been in years. The incident in Thailand shocked him into realizing what was important in his life. He was a changed man.

"Would you like a beer or some water, ma'am?" The bar owner was a short man in his fifties with a thin moustache and a friendly smile.

"Water, please."

The owner walked back to his ice chest.

"These local beers taste good. You should try one." Michael held up his bottle. Caroline hadn't had a drink since they had arrived, and he didn't like drinking alone.

"I'm sure they do," Caroline said. "Michael, you don't know why I'm not drinking, do you?"

"You're not giving up drinking as part of a new diet, are you?"

Caroline smiled. "I'm pregnant."

"Congratulations!" The bar owner had walked up with her bottled water, and he interjected before Michael could fully register Caroline's statement. Caroline laughed. The owner grinned, waiting for Michael's response.

"Really?" Michael looked back and forth between Caroline and the owner. "Are you serious?"

The owner nodded happily. Then he returned to the other end of the bar, realizing that he had interrupted their moment.

"You'd better say something before you make me nervous," Caroline said.

"This is great! Why didn't you tell me before? When did you know?" He pulled her into his arms. She pushed him away, just enough to look into his eyes.

"We are going to be parents, Michael."

"Wow—and I thought I had responsibility before."

"Do you think you can handle it?" Caroline asked with a smile.

"This makes everything worth it," Michael said. "I love you."

"I love you, too."

The breeze picked up as the sun sank lower. Aside from them, the beach was now deserted except for the bar owner emptying ice from the cooler. He was trying hard to be quiet, to keep from interrupting the new parents-to-be, but the tumbling ice made a distracting racket.

Later that night at dinner at a beachside restaurant they dined on whole fish roasted over a fire pit. Only their waiter, delivering and retrieving plates, interrupted their hand-holding throughout the evening. Caroline told Michael that she had known about the baby since the day after he'd left for Asia, but she had wanted to tell him in person—away from everything and everyone. After dinner, they went for a walk on the beach. The moon was reflected in the water just off the shore. There on the beach, he asked her to marry him.

"I want us to grow older together, Michael. I want us to have children and grandchildren and look the part. I want you to be a father that is always around, with a bald head and big heart. I want you to leave Aseso. Let's go back to Seattle."

Michael was torn. "I will be a great father, and I will be around. We can work out the age difference issue. We have plenty of time. But don't take me away from Aseso now."

"You don't have anything more to prove to anyone."

"I helped build that company. I'm not ready to leave it."

"That company will destroy you."

"Just let me stay for a couple more years. David and Dr. Tanaka need me now more than ever."

"Michael, they don't need you. They use you. Let them use someone else."

"Please. In a couple of years we'll have saved enough so that we can move wherever you want. We'll never have to worry about money again."

"We have enough now, Michael."

"I can't quit now just because we had a little hiccup."

"A hiccup? A civil war is not a hiccup."

"I have so many plans for the company. We're about to open processing facilities all over the world. I want to be there for that. Soon there won't be much left for me to do. Wait a couple of years, and you'll get everything you want."

"I have everything I want, and I don't want to lose it."

"A couple more years and I will have had everything I wanted, too. I will dedicate the rest of my life to you after that."

Caroline knew how much his job meant to him. She wanted desperately to convince him to quit immediately, but she knew that Michael would be crushed if he left right away. So she agreed. A couple of years of sacrifice in exchange for a storybook lifetime seemed more than fair.

A few days later, Michael and Caroline flew to Manila, where they had decided to spend a few nights before catching a connecting flight to Hong Kong. From there they would take the nonstop flight back to New York. Caroline had never been on a business trip with Michael, and he was eager to show her how he traveled: chauffeured town cars, nightly room service, and VIP treatment wherever he went.

They checked into the Shangri-La Hotel. Their room had all the conveniences of home but still felt a world away. They ordered room service for dinner and watched television; it seemed like quite a luxury after their time in Boracay. Caroline let Michael catch up on his e-mails while she treated herself to a massage.

The next day they did some sightseeing with a private tour guide. The tour included a visit to the old Intramuros section of Manila, an area filled with forts, fountains, and churches built by the Spaniards during the sixteenth century. There they bought a few Lumpiang Pritos, crunchy spring rolls filled with bean sprouts and pork, from a street vendor. In the afternoon, they came across the most imposing structure in the area, the Minor Basilica of the Immaculate Conception. The neo-Romanesque architecture seemed to represent a different time and place, and it stood out in sharp contrast to the tropical foliage surrounding the church.

They walked inside and found a small wedding taking place. Hand in hand, they watched from the back of the church. Neither spoke Tagalog, but they recognized every part of the mass. Both of them came from Catholic families, though neither practiced. The beauty of the ceremony was undeniable. Caroline only had to look at Michael once to make him understand what she wanted. They were married in that church the next day.

PART FOUR

THE SEVENTH YEAR

45

New York. The Seventh Year. March.

"David would fire Bearing Brothers if he knew we were meeting with you today," Alistair Furman said to President Coves. He took a seat beside Brad on the couch in the presidential suite at the Willard-Astor Hotel.

"Something has to be done before his damned intransigence causes this country to fall apart," said President Coves. He was in New York to give a speech before the United Nations, and he'd taken the opportunity to call up his old college friend.

Alistair was a year past retirement from Bearing Brothers. As one of the bank's few senior officers with strong ties to the new administration, he had stayed on at the request of the board. His friendship with the President had the potential to help many of Bearing's other clients, which included transportation companies and military contractors. He had been reluctant to meet with Coves, aware as he was of how David felt about the new president. But Brad had been in the room when Coves called, and he'd convinced Alistair that it would be in the bank's best interest to foster a better relationship between Aseso and the new administration.

Brad had attained senior status within Bearing Brothers, due in large part to his association with Aseso and the fees the relationship continued to generate. He now had ambitions beyond being a banker. Over the years, he had watched Alton Gordon's lawyers try without success to lobby for Aseso's interests. They did have Representative O'Farrell on their side, but he subscribed to an old school of thought, according to which all deals could—and should—be struck within the D.C. beltway. Brad had seen more and more Washington power brokers come to Wall Street to get things done. Washington still had the political capital to motivate legislation, but it had run out of the financial capital to implement it.

"David is stubborn. Everyone knows that. Everyone also knows he doesn't like you." Alistair grabbed a handful of nuts from the bowl in front of him and began to eat them one by one. He seemed much more comfortable in this setting than Brad was.

"Tell me, Brad," Coves asked, seated comfortably on the opposite couch, "how do you keep the Aseso account all to yourself? I hear everyone on Wall Street wants a piece of that business."

"I think Aseso's management appreciates the fact that Bearing Brothers is the best shop on the street."

"It doesn't have anything to do with the fact that you were swimming buddies with the chief operating officer back at Cal Berkeley, does it?"

Brad glanced at Alistair, hoping for a cue, but Alistair was going to let Brad handle this one on his own. "Well, Mr. President, I'm sure it didn't hurt when we were trying to land the account, but it's our continued—"

"Relax. I'm just busting your balls." The President leaned forward, resting his elbows on his knees. "Look Gentlemen, I don't have to tell you how bad it is out there. At first I thought that Hochberg lady was crazy when she said America was going to come crumbling down in some sort of Malthusian Catastrophe, but now I am not so sure. My Homeland Security Advisor tells me that the greatest threat to America right now is Americans. They're poor and they are pissed. We are on the verge of a French style revolution in this country if we don't turn this ship around."

"Mr. President, let us know what we can do to help." Brad saw Coves' agitated state as his opportunity to inset himself in the national scene.

"China is getting rich while we keep sliding. We need Aseso to get on board with America."

"As far as I know, Mr. President, the United States is the single largest national market for Aseso," Brad said defensively.

"The seeds come from China and get planted in Brazil. The only thing that goes on here is processing and distribution."

"Aseso is a Chinese corporation," Brad said. "Although David does own half of it, the other half is owned by—"

"That crazy ninja running around the world," Coves interrupted. "Yeah, I know about him. Listen, friends, we cannot have America become chemically dependent on something that can be pulled out from under us without any warning. What's more we could use some of those tax revenues Aseso is paying to Beijing."

"And how do you want us to help?" Alistair said, obviously trying to balance the desires of one of his oldest acquaintances, who happened to be the president of the United States, against the financial interests of Bearing Brothers.

"We need to lure Aseso here. I want seed production, plantations, processing, the whole thing done within the fifty states."

This was not what Brad had expected, but he was willing to help in any way he could. "David is stubborn, but he is not unreasonable," he said. "If there was a business opportunity that justified the move, he would do it." Brad was now playing with fire. He believed that if he could pull together an alliance between Aseso and the new administration, he would be seen not only as one of the most respected investment bankers on Wall Street, but also as one of the most savvy power brokers in Washington. On the other hand, he knew full well that his efforts could easily render him unemployed.

"What kind of business opportunity?" asked Coves.

"There would be some preconditions associated with something like that."

"I'm listening."

"You would have to give up on the idea of having the government regulate Sinsen," Brad began.

"That's not politically possible any more, anyway," Coves said wearily.

"You would also have to come up with a lot of money."

"We're America," Coves said, smiling. "We have a lot of money."

"I am talking about a lot, a lot, of money."

"To do what?"

Brad paused for effect.

"To declare a War On Aging."

"A War on Aging?"

"Yes. You would officially declare a War on Aging, and the U.S. would simply buy Sinsen from Aseso and distribute it to every American over the age of sixty-five."

"War on aging, huh? Isn't that a little over the top?"

"Why not? There has been a War on Poverty, a War on Drugs, and a War on Hunger."

"Fair enough. And you believe David would go for that?"

"He told you himself that he would."

Coves frowned. "When did he tell me that?"

"During the hearings before the Committee on Aging, back when you were in the Senate. He's not opposed to having the government buy Sinsen from him and distributing it to Americans. What he can't tolerate is for the government to tell him who he can and can't sell it to, and at what price."

Coves sat back, considering. "If we offered this to him, you think he would move production here?"

"I think he would have to."

"Tell me something, Brad. Is it really possible? Providing Sinsen for everyone?"

"Like I said, it would take a lot of money." Brad had no clue whether it was really possible; but if it were, he felt sure that a lot of money would be involved.

By now, the U.S. government had exhausted many of its funding sources. Domestic tax revenues had not kept up with government spending since the late 1990s. The situation forced the government to borrow more money from abroad by issuing U.S. Treasury bonds at progressively higher interest rates. Administration after administration had tried and failed to cut deficit spending. Taxes were lowered, then raised, then lowered again. But spending remained out of control. The government was running out of ways to finance even the most basic services.

As a result, the financial markets had no more appetite for U.S. government debt. America was still the wealthiest country in the world, but it did not have the financial resources it once did, and there was risk in buying U.S. government bonds. In contrast, the Aseso bonds that Bearing Brothers sold to investors were backed by the credit of wealthy Aseso customers all over the world. The markets had plenty of interest in taking on credit risk from wealthy individuals, and the Aseso bonds were in high demand.

"How do you propose we secure this money?" President Coves asked.

"We have an idea." Brad looked over to Alistair for confirmation. Alistair nodded.

46

Thirteen years after the first bottles of Sinsen were sold in Asia, and ten years after the supplement was introduced in the U.S., Aseso had become the most powerful company in the world. It had grown more than a hundredfold in the previous two years alone. Bearing Brothers continued to bring in plenty of new capital from its bond sales. Dr. Tanaka used the money to purchase greater and greater quantities of land, while David and Michael coordinated processing in various countries. Worldwide, over 200 Aseso facilities now operated twenty-four hours a day.

Governments the world over had threatened to regulate Sinsen. In response, David had threatened to pull distribution from those countries if they tried. His threats were real; Aseso had more demand for Sinsen than it could ever meet, and there would be plenty of eager new customers in other countries. Sinsen's removal from any given country would have meant political death for its leadership. Simply put, Aseso was now too powerful to regulate. As the threats of regulation gradually ceased, David's influence grew. He befriended influential political and business leaders around the world—all of whom were customers.

The price of a Sinsen subscription had fallen dramatically, giving more people the opportunity to maintain their youth. As

Alistair Furman had predicted, the wealthy original subscribers had made it possible for Aseso to grow enough to offer Sinsen once again to some portion of the masses. Now, more than two hundred million people around the globe were customers—albeit the wealthiest two hundred million.

Aseso's revenues now averaged over one billion dollars a day. The company had also become the largest private landowner in the world. It had Astragalus plantations in over forty countries, including Brazil, India, China, Thailand, Zimbabwe, and Pakistan. As many had predicted, Aseso's plantations had displaced traditional crops, causing food prices to rise as farmland became increasingly scarce. Governments used tax revenues from Astragalus exports and income taxes from local Aseso business activity to subsidize imported food. Local diets changed dramatically as imports replaced traditional diets.

To process all the Astragalus extract, Aseso had purchased pharmaceutical facilities throughout the world. The facilities' owners were happy to sell at the high prices Aseso was offering; over the past few years, pharmaceutical manufacturing had become less profitable as government programs and regulations drove drug prices down. Although the exit of many pharmaceutical manufacturers from the market did cause a slight rebound in prescription drug prices, it was expected that the business would remain tepid in the future due to lower demand from a growing population that did not age.

To protect all of its assets, Aseso had amassed the largest private security force in the world. Agreements with governments in countries where Aseso had plantations and facilities allowed Black Falcon to place and manage large groups of armed paramilitary personnel. Men in black uniforms carrying automatic weapons had become a common sight in many locales.

To win over the people in the countries where it conducted business, Aseso set up charitable programs. Most were dedicated to promoting education and ending hunger. David drew on his international prominence to convince local celebrities to act as "Aseso Ambassadors," aiming to create the image of a benevolent company with the local people's interests at heart.

To efficiently convert Sinsen from roots in the ground to capsules in a bottle, Aseso built up a large fleet of custom-designed aircraft to carry harvested roots from the plantations to the processing facilities. New local companies sprang up for the sole purpose of building and servicing the fleet. Aseso's global operations required thousands of personnel worldwide. The company had no problem securing new employees. The pay was above market, and the fringe benefit of free Sinsen was the biggest attraction of all.

Companies throughout the world found that they were able to secure lower group health insurance rates by providing free Sinsen to their employees. The logic was that the subscription price (two thousand U.S. dollars per year per employee) mitigated future healthcare costs by preventing age-related diseases. Norway became the first country to provide Sinsen to every citizen over the age of forty. Given its universal healthcare system, it projected that the reduction in healthcare costs for the elderly would more than offset the investment. Switzerland, Singapore, and Luxembourg soon followed what had become known as the Norway Model.

Aseso set up a sister company, Aseso Capital, to manage the massive amounts of cash coming in. Aseso Capital was quickly becoming the largest money manager in the world. It used Aseso's cash to purchase investment assets such as stocks, bonds, currencies, and commodities. The largest asset class that it purchased was government-issued debt. Aseso was now the single largest financier for countries all over the globe; in turn, many countries now relied on Aseso as their single largest source of financing.

The global economy had slipped even further during the last couple of years. Inflation caused by Aseso's activities, as well as lingering unemployment, drove more and more people into poverty. The average unemployment rate in the developed world reached over twenty percent. Inflation averaged thirty percent annually.

Although Aseso had managed to grow without any significant interference from governments, a public debate continued. But the issues had changed. At first, people had disagreed about whether Sinsen actually could prevent aging. But there was no longer much doubt that Sinsen worked. Over time, the scientific evidence supporting its efficacy had become all but irrefutable, and no one could deny that those taking Sinsen looked younger and healthier after years of daily use. David, now almost fifty, hardly looked forty.

The new public debate concerned practicalities surrounding the idea that Sinsen should be available to everyone. David knew that this, as a practical matter, was impossible. There was simply not enough land in the world. One in thirty people had become Aseso subscribers. The resources needed just to supply them had dramatically changed the earth's economic and environmental landscape. David worked hard to keep public attention away from that issue. He had to keep fostering the belief that one day Sinsen could be available to everyone.

Keep 'em guessing.

—

David was having coffee with Joanna on a beautiful spring morning at their favorite East Village coffeehouse. She had moved to the city after accepting a position as full professor at New York University. In half an hour, David would head off to a meeting at Bearing Brothers. Brad had arranged for a group of officials from the Department of Health and Human Services to fly up from Washington, D.C. He had an idea, although he wouldn't reveal what it was.

No one was more surprised by David's falling for Joanna than David himself. His initial courtship of her had been based on ulterior motives. She did not fit the profile of the women he had been known to date. Although attractive, she was not exceptionally beautiful. She was opinionated and slightly older than the others. But their senses of humor were perfectly matched. She thought that every dry comment he made was hilarious. And he found her intellectual curiosity refreshing.

More surprising to David than falling for Joanna was that she did not fall for him. She thought he was handsome, charismatic, and brilliant. But he was not her soul mate. They would never share the same philosophical approach to life. They had the same intellectual curiosities and a strong physical attraction to each other. But that was it. They agreed to continue as friends. She had become one of his closest confidantes. He remained hopeful.

"Don't let them convince you to try and please everyone."

Joanna, now forty-one, looked extremely young for her age.

"Don't worry, I won't. But he is President now, so I should at least talk to his people." David thought, as he watched Joanna stir her cappuccino, that she looked as confident as she did happy.

"I think you've painted yourself into a corner."

"Why do you say that?" David loved to hear Joanna speak. She made the esoteric sound beautifully simple.

"David, more than forty percent of the people on earth are under the age of twenty-five. Within a couple of decades, those people will all want Sinsen, and they'll want to eat, too. The way things are going, the world will not be able to provide them the opportunity for either."

"I guess I'll have to work on a pill that keeps you from getting hungry."

She smiled and reached over to touch his hand. "I'm afraid you're not going to charm your way out of this one."

47

Silvia Gutierrez, a fifty-six-year-old with short salt-and-pepper hair, was not unknown to David. As Secretary of the Department of Health and Human Services, she oversaw the activities of the FDA as well as the National Institutes of Health, where David had begun his professional career. Although not a doctor herself, she was respected within the medical community. She had entered politics shortly after her second son graduated from high school, representing California's 19th Senate District, which encompassed her hometown of Santa Barbara. As an advocate for healthcare reform, she was successful in passing employee-friendly legislation that extended mandatory employer-subsidized coverage to every full-time worker in the state. She and her husband, a retired appellate judge, moved to Sacramento when she was elected Commissioner of the California Department of Insurance.

Shortly after Coves won the presidential election, Silvia was appointed to his cabinet as HHS Secretary. Her predecessor had acted in accordance with the former president's hands-off attitude toward healthcare coverage. Silvia, with the explicit blessing of the newly-elected president, intended to be quite hands-on.

Alistair had arranged a lunch in the executive dining room he reserved for his most important clients. "Secretary Gutierrez, I'd like you to meet Dr. David Oaks."

"It's a pleasure to meet you, Dr. Oaks."

"The pleasure is mine," David said with a perfunctory smile. He had been suspicious of her from the onset. After all, she was working for Coves. David, who had been surprised when Coves had been re-elected senator, had been even more surprised when he'd won the race for President.

"Let me introduce my chief operating officer, Michael Jeffs."

Introductions continued around the table: Alistair, Brad, and then Dr. Sanjay Bhatia, the Assistant Secretary for Health. As lunch was served, they proceeded with the customary innocuous pre-entrée conversation. Michael enjoyed his appetizer; being at the offices of Bearing Brothers gave Aseso the home court advantage, and he could relax.

"I have to say, Dr. Oaks, I am quite impressed with what you've accomplished in Norway and the other countries where Sinsen is universally distributed." Silvia seemed nervous. It was one thing to serve as State Insurance Commissioner, even for a large state like California; it was quite another to hold a cabinet post through which the President intended to make his mark on history.

"Thank you. We've worked very hard with each country to establish the programs." In fact, establishing the programs had not been hard at all. All of the countries had relatively small populations, above-average GDPs per capita, and well-established universal healthcare programs. David had merely agreed to what was, in essence, a group discount.

"I understand there are a few other countries you are working with now on similar programs." Sanjay spoke up for the first time. He looked very young to hold such an important position.

"We are. We expect to make an announcement soon." David smiled. "Dr. Bhatia, if you don't mind my saying so, either you have incredibly good genes, or you are a long-time Sinsen subscriber," he said.

Michael was thinking the same thing. By now, the two of them had encountered many customers who appeared to be in their early thirties, even though they were actually over forty.

"Yes. Both, I guess." Sanjay blushed. "I was an early adopter. I began taking Sinsen as a med student. All my classmates thought I was crazy. But now I still have all my hair, and they're as bald as bowling balls." He laughed briefly.

It had become culturally impolite to ask if someone was taking Sinsen; but in Sanjay's case, the answer was obvious. Michael couldn't tell whether Silvia was a customer.

"Dr. Oaks, I believe you have met my new boss," Silvia said, alluding to Coves.

"Yes, we've met on several occasions."

"He has an interest in working with Aseso." Silvia spoke carefully. It was clear that she was prepared for confrontation but was trying to be diplomatic.

"I can't say I'm surprised. In what capacity, exactly?"

"The President would like to open up a conversation with Aseso to discuss the possibility of a public-private partnership." This Silvia said quickly. She seemed anxious to get the statement over with.

"A partnership to do what?"

"A partnership to produce Sinsen here in the U.S. as part of an entitlement program."

"Entitlement for whom?"

Sanjay stepped in. "For the sake of argument, let's say everyone over the age of sixty-five."

"Over sixty-five? That's over forty million people," Michael said, unable to hide his concern. Aseso's growth had slowed dramatically during the previous year. It was becoming increasingly difficult to secure new plantations. Civil unrest in the countries where they already grew Astragalus was making it difficult to harvest the plants and ship them to the processing facilities.

"Assuming that eight million of those people are already subscribers, and that half of the remainder will opt not to take Sinsen, that leaves us with a much more manageable number," Sanjay said. He'd obviously done his research.

"I think your first assumption is right, but your second is way off," David said. "The experience in Norway, Switzerland, and Luxembourg suggests an almost universal acceptance. Sinsen is like cell phones in those countries. Plenty of people did not immediately adopt the technology, but now everyone feels naked without it."

"OK, then. Let's assume forty million. Is that possible?" Silvia asked, tension apparent in her voice.

"Not any time soon," Michael broke in.

"When, then?" Sanjay asked.

"When they colonize Mars," David said.

"Dr. Oaks, we know that you're in talks with Australia. We want Aseso to do something similar in America. We want you to do it here first."

David paused. "Australia is contributing large amounts of land to support its own domestic consumption."

"We could do that, too," Silvia said.

"Australia has more land than the U.S., and its population is only seven percent of ours. They can afford to do it."

"We can afford to do it," Silvia said urgently.

"I don't think you can." David spoke slowly, as though talking to a grade-school student. "The only land we could use is in Hawaii, Florida, and Texas. And that's not exactly cheap real estate."

"We can afford to do it if we prioritize the use of our natural resources," Silvia persisted.

"I'm not sure you appreciate the amount of money we're talking about."

"David," Brad interjected. He'd been silent the whole time, picking at his food, listening closely. Now he set down his fork and leaned forward. "We have a willing partner."

48

"China?" David and Michael glanced at each other, sure they couldn't have heard correctly.

"Yes, David." Alistair spoke up. "As you know better than anyone, China generates a lot of taxes from sales of Sinsen around the world. Aseso is, after all, a Chinese corporation. China also generates export revenues from sales to the U.S. They have a real interest in seeing Sinsen widely distributed here in America. They are looking for new sources of oil, which we have. This is how it will work: the U.S. government will sell oil exploration and drilling rights directly to China, and then it will use the proceeds to buy suitable private land. That land will then be leased to Aseso. You can figure out the rest."

"I'm not sure the administration will get away with selling off America's oil exploration and drilling rights to a foreign government," Michael said, genuinely unsettled by the proposition.

"We think it will," Brad said. "People will gladly swap their environmental conscience for more time on earth."

Michael could not make the math add up, especially when faced with Brad's smug grin. Every time he turned around, another country was part of the Aseso equation. And what about America's own energy needs? He couldn't decide which of his many objections to raise first. He took a breath. "Well, even if the American people did agree to it, why would China agree?"

"Let me break it down for you," Brad said. "All of the world's available sugar plantations are slowly being converted to Astragalus to service Aseso. Soon, sugar-based ethanol will disappear as a viable energy source. Without sugar, corn-based sweeteners will become the most widely used around the world, which will push out corn-based ethanol, which never made sense to begin with. We calculate that China, along with India and Brazil, will have to start importing larger and larger amounts of oil to satisfy the demand for consumer goods as the global population increases."

"And you believe that China will pay a high enough price for these reserves to make this plan happen," David said, his tone skeptical.

"It's going to be a race to the top for oil. The population will grow, and there will be more people demanding Chinese-made products, which in turn will require more oil, which in turn will drive up its price. China sees this coming. They want to own the reserves now, at a cheaper price, rather than watch their production costs skyrocket over the next few years."

David held up a hand to stop Brad. "I'm not sure your scenario is going to play out like you say it will, but let's assume, for the moment, that the Chinese believe it will, and they agree to this deal. Countries like Norway and Singapore have so few people that they can implement universal coverage. In the U.S., forty million people will become eighty million in the not too distant future. This will not be a viable long-term solution. The U.S. simply does not have enough subtropical farmland for the volume of Astragalus that will be required."

"With a healthier, more productive society, we will leap ahead of the rest of the world, regaining our former standing. The U.S. once produced over thirty percent of the global GDP. We are down to less than twenty percent now. This could help us get some of that back. After we rebuild our economy, we'll just have to buy land overseas. I hear your firm is very good at doing that."

"Yes, we're good at buying land, Silvia. The problem is finding it. Most of the world's usable land is already committed to servicing our current customers."

"We could convert more traditional crop lands to Astragalus plantations."

"We've already looked into that. Food is becoming scarce and will become even scarcer as the population grows. Widespread starvation will be a real threat. The only solution would be more deforestation, and I would highly recommend against going that route."

"The President has made up his mind," Silvia insisted.

David looked over at Brad, who looked back nervously.

After lunch, David and Michael took the elevator down by themselves. The tension between them was palpable.

"Brad must have traded in brains for balls right before he came up with that stupid idea," David said.

"He can get a little ahead of himself," Michael allowed. He didn't know what else to say.

"At least with O'Farrell," David added, "you know what side he's on."

n the eight years since Caroline and Michael had moved to New York, Caroline had not realized her goal of becoming a professional urban landscape photographer. She had never invested enough time. There had always been distractions and excuses: the shelter became a full-time job; Michael's job exhausted her as much as it did him; the apartment always seemed to need attention. When Gregor came along, she threw herself into motherhood. The pregnancy, the birth, the doctor's appointments, the mommy groups, the play dates—they all took up much more time than she could have imagined.

Above all, there was the daily struggle over whether or not to take Sinsen. She and Michael fought about it constantly. He could not understand her reluctance, and at times, neither could she. Originally, she'd claimed that she did not want to stay young while her family and friends aged. Michael countered by getting them all on the subscriber list. Her real fear was that Sinsen was an ill-advised attempt to mess with Mother Nature.

It had been much easier to stick to her decision as a twenty-nine-year-old. But she was turning thirty-six tomorrow, and her worries were mounting. She'd stopped looking forward to birthdays. Michael was approaching forty, and she wasn't far behind. But Michael still looked like he had when he was thirty. His haircut was different—styles had changed—but he had not aged at all. Caroline had. Not that she was old; she was still an attractive woman. But things were changing quickly. The media had been obsessed with youth since long before Sinsen was invented. Now it seemed that aging at all was a sin. The vast majority of Americans still aged, but not by choice. If Sinsen were cheap, everyone, it seemed, would take it.

On the eve of her birthday, she went to a salon and had her hair colored for the first time. As she sat with her head under the dryer, she worried: could she and Michael last forever? Would he be happy, married to an old woman? Would he eventually leave her?

"Hey, babe, how was your day?" Michael came in as Caroline was giving Gregor his dinner.

"Pretty quiet. How was your meeting with Brad?"

"Not just Brad. The Secretary of Health and Human Services. You are not going to believe what they want us to do. And by 'they,' I mean the administration and Bearing Brothers." Michael set his briefcase down on the kitchen island and got a beer from the fridge.

"What?"

"They want us to provide Sinsen to retirees."

"But that's what Coves has wanted all along." Caroline was trying to listen and at the same time keep Gregor's food from running down his face.

"Yes, but now the plan is simply to buy it and hand it out to everyone over sixty-five."

"Have they totally given up on having the FDA regulate it, then?"

"I think so. If the FDA got involved, they'd take Sinsen off the market for years while they did clinical trials. There would be no popular support for that. Also, Coves would look foolish if he pushed that change through and caused Aseso to stop distributing in the U.S." Michael sat down at the table, watching his son and his wife. They made a beautiful picture. He didn't say anything about her hair.

"So in that case, will it be available only to people over sixty-five?" Caroline asked hopefully.

"No. They're not planning to regulate its sale. We'll still be able to sell it to anyone who can afford it. The government will hand it out to seniors in parallel."

At that moment, Caroline understood that Sinsen was a problem that would never be solved. It would never be regulated or abolished. Although she hadn't realized it until now, she had secretly hoped that the government would force Aseso to sell Sinsen only to the elderly. That way, she would no longer have to decide whether or not to take it.

Caroline had always hoped for a less complicated life, a natural life, in which people worked, raised families, and grew old together. She wanted to get older with Michael and to see Gregor grow up and go through life as she had. She didn't want to have to decide how long she would live. That, she believed, shouldn't be anyone's decision to make.

50

Harare, Zimbabwe. June.

The world was changing rapidly. India had become a divided country: the majority of people in the poorer South had become almost entirely dependent on the government's Aseso-backed food distribution programs, while the wealthy northern Indian nationals continued to prosper under modernization. India had a relatively young population, and many investors saw it as the future of global consumerism. China, which guarded Aseso's secret facilities, continued to benefit from Sinsen-related revenues. Brazil suddenly found itself in a particularly good position compared to the developing world powers, since it had a relatively small population to feed.

There was mounting pressure for Aseso to expand its distribution footprint. Leaders of wealthy small countries reached out to David, anxious to implement the Norway Model. Until then, David had been very secretive about Aseso's distribution capabilities. Soon he would have to start telling the world that they were quickly approaching the limit.

The situation in the less-developed countries was even more sobering. Even the most corrupt governments were now resisting Dr. Tanaka's requests for more land. Civil unrest was becoming commonplace as the authorities seized arable land to satisfy Aseso's voracious appetite. Black Falcon's footprints across the globe were becoming more widespread as well. Fear and anxiety often escalated to panic in the streets. A fundamental change in humanity was now almost unavoidable. The wealthy had tasted immortality, and they were not prepared to give it up.

"Dr. Tanaka. We have to leave now!" Dirk stood in the doorway of Dr. Tanaka's Harare hotel room, visibly concerned. Two Black Falcon agents stood behind him. Gunfire and yelling could be heard in the streets below.

Dr. Tanaka was on the phone. "The situation here in Zimbabwe is bad, Michael. I am leaving now for the airport. We'll fly to Johannesburg and stay there for a couple of days. I will call you when I arrive. We can't count on an upcoming harvest from here. It might take some time for the government to regain control."

He hung up the phone and waved in Dirk and the agents. They helped gather Dr. Tanaka's belongings and escorted him downstairs, where a car was waiting. Dirk ushered Dr. Tanaka into the back seat, then climbed in himself. The police escort that Dr. Tanaka had been promised, by the mayor he'd helped get elected, was disappointingly absent. A Black Falcon SUV, leading the way out of town, was the only other vehicle in their group.

Since the successful overthrow of the previous regime in Thailand, Dirk had secretly been promoted to the role of Head of Special Operations of Aseso. Although he was still employed by Black Falcon, his only role was to aid Aseso in the execution of paramilitary actions. Ten such actions had been executed flawlessly since Thailand. Zimbabwe was different.

Zimbabwe's history was inundated with political turmoil. It had been the last African nation to achieve independence from a European power. Since it had achieved autonomy in 1980, political uprisings had been a common occurrence. Accordingly, political suppression had become a frequently-used tool for keeping order. The most controversial example of this took place in 2000, when the government forcibly redistributed land from the white population to the black population. Until then, the white population had owned seventy percent of the arable land while making up only one percent of the population. Decades later, backed by considerable government resources and assistance, Dr. Tanaka re-concentrated the land away from the people, making Zimbabwe one of Aseso's largest plantation countries.

Although most of the strategic planning and high-level operations were conducted by Dirk and his Black Falcon colleagues, local militaries had always been essential to Dr. Tanaka's special operations. Without military support, no regime could hope to hold power. In most cases, the military were unified around a group of coordinated generals that could be persuaded to act in their, and Aseso's, financial interests.

But Zimbabwe had proved too fragmented to control. A portion of the military remained loyal to officials who allowed it to profit by forcing local villagers to mine diamonds. Another portion was vehemently opposed to supporting foreign interests, given the embedded anti-colonial sentiment of the people. The part of the military that Aseso did control was the best equipped, but it was small. Capable of suppressing small uprisings, it was no longer able to hold back the popular revolt that was gaining momentum.

All along, Dr. Tanaka's basic assumption had been that he could always buy someone's cooperation—and if not, then the cooperation of that person's enemy. Ironically, Aseso's presence in Zimbabwe had improved the average citizen's standard of living by every possible metric. Aseso's food distribution and education programs had raised conditions to levels never before seen. But the new, overwhelming sense of nationalism was something that Dr. Tanaka could not bribe away. The people of Zimbabwe had come together to expel Aseso, as they had expelled the British decades earlier. They were prepared to be free and hungry rather than fed and shackled.

"How long will this take us?" Dr. Tanaka had stayed too long in Harare, he thought, looking out the window of the Mercedes. People filled the streets. They were in the midst of an anti-government demonstration. Parked cars, their windows shattered, had been lit on fire from within. Young men holding signs high above their heads were restrained by the few soldiers who had not yet deserted. Those few soldiers were all that kept the city from exploding into utter chaos. Dr. Tanaka had thought that if the country descended into civil war, he could at least count on the capital remaining loyal to the politicians he controlled. Now everyone was fleeing. The politicians were nowhere to be found.

"I don't know. It will depend on the roads to the airport. If they aren't blocked, we could make good time." This situation was not new to Dirk. In the course of his career, he had taken part in many activities that had led to similar demonstrations. It was, however, new to Dr. Tanaka. This incident would undoubtedly be the worst in Aseso's history. The government Dr. Tanaka had helped organize had stayed in power for less than a year, and no viable governing groups remained with which he could coordinate another coup. The revolt was overwhelmingly popular and immediate. The nationalist movement had raced through the country like wildfire through a dry field, taking everyone by surprise. All the plantations in Zimbabwe would be lost. His efforts there would be seen as a failure.

Not since his 1998 arrest in Indonesia had Dr. Tanaka felt so ashamed.

"Here, take this." Dirk released the safety on a 9-millimeter semiautomatic pistol and handed it to Dr. Tanaka. "If the car is stopped on the way to the airport, we'll get out and make our way to the woods. There's a safe house nearby where we can stay until we figure out what to do next."

"If that becomes necessary, I will walk back to town and use this on the mayor who deserted us," Dr. Tanaka said, still furious at the mayor's betrayal.

"That coward is probably out of the country by now." Dirk watched the road ahead, on the lookout for road blocks.

"That coward has my money!"

People wanting to avoid the conflict were streaming out of the city. Others, wanting to participate in the revolution, were streaming in. No one was standing in place. Everyone was in a hurry to get somewhere. It seemed, as the Mercedes and the SUV drove out of the city, that everything that could catch on fire already had.

People threw rocks at every car heading out and cheered the cars heading in. The dust stirred by the SUV up ahead blocked Dr. Tanaka's view of the road. The constant sound of rocks hitting the Mercedes made everyone inside flinch at the thought that the next sound could be that of bullets streaming in. Dirk looked unusually nervous. He kept both hands on his machine gun and his knee against the door, ready to burst out of the car if necessary.

Surprisingly, the group made it to the airport without much incident, although the forty-minute drive seemed like an eternity to Dr. Tanaka. News crews had been reporting on the events from Harare International Airport for the past two days. Cameramen filmed as businessmen, diplomats, and other foreign nationals tried to flee the country. Long lines wrapped around the main terminal. Luggage was abandoned as some passengers bribed their way onto cargo planes with no extra room. The sun was setting. People were growing desperate, terrified of staying another night in the country.

Dr. Tanaka's car pulled up to the private jet Dirk had chartered. The driver jumped out to open the rear door. Dirk, glancing constantly behind him, followed Dr. Tanaka up the jet's stairs. Two Black Falcon agents entered the aircraft with more suitcases; once the Aseso country manager had boarded, the jet door was secured.

The pilot wasted no time in taxiing to the runway. Dr. Tanaka could hear the copilot requesting clearance to take off, but a commercial aircraft stood in their way, and confusion in the tower delayed taxiing. The jet was instructed to wait 100 feet from the runway while takeoff instructions could be organized.

As they waited on the tarmac, safely aboard the aircraft, everyone relaxed. Relief set in. Dr. Tanaka asked the stewardess to pour him a gin and tonic. The country manager tried to reach his employees by cell phone to get an update on the situation.

Dirk turned away from his window to face Dr. Tanaka. "To be honest, Dr. Tanaka, I'm surprised that we weren't stopped on the way here. My intelligence team informed me this afternoon that there was a plot to assassinate you. I didn't tell you earlier because I didn't want you to panic."

"Now, who would want to kill me?" Dr. Tanaka said, smiling. The stewardess arrived with his gin and tonic, and he quickly took a sip.

The shoulder-launched missile hit the aircraft a second later.

51

Washington, D.C. July.

David took Dr. Tanaka's death particularly hard. He had been a mentor, an enabler, and a friend. Although they had not always agreed, they had always respected each other's opinions. A decade before, David had grudgingly accepted Dr. Tanaka as his financial backer, unable to secure financing from prestigious Silicon Valley venture capitalists. Now, sitting in his private jet on his way to meet with the President of the United States, he understood that meeting Dr. Tanaka had been the best thing that could ever have happened to him.

Throughout the early years, Dr. Tanaka had never hesitated to do whatever was necessary to assure David the success he was seeking. Dr. Tanaka had made him feel bulletproof. Now more than ever before, David felt vulnerable. He struggled to maintain his confidence. He never really knew whether his success was due to Aseso being loved or feared. Perhaps it was both.

As the jet approached D.C., the monuments appeared beneath the sunset. Memories of countless flights from New York to D.C. swam through his mind. Dr. Tanaka had never joined him on any of those trips. He had left the glory to David, content to perform the necessary work no one else wanted to do. David gripped his armrests, imagining Dr. Tanaka strapped into his seat on that fatal flight, only minutes away from escape.

The in-flight phone rang. David recognized the number. "Clive, how are you doing?"

"I'm doing better, David. Thanks. How are you?"

"I miss your dad."

"I miss him, too."

"Nothing is going to be the same now."

"Father loved working with you. He was never good at showing his feelings, but I could tell."

"Thanks. I appreciate your saying that."

"He would want us to push forward, David."

"I know he would. On that note, did you speak with your contacts?"

"I did. I just got off the phone with them."

"Is it good news?"

"Very good news." Since his father's death, Clive had hardly spoken a complete sentence. Now, for the first time in a month, he sounded energized. "It didn't take much persuading. In fact, they approached me with the same idea before I had a chance to ask them."

David sat up straighter. "Great. When do we get our Zimbabwean plantations back?"

"Soon. Very soon."

52

New York.

Michael had never felt so uncertain about his future. Aseso had thousands of employees, offices in over a hundred countries, and numerous business partners ranging from suppliers to consulting firms. Nevertheless, Michael felt overwhelmed. Dr. Tanaka had been Aseso's operational visionary. Although the company had a manager in every country, Dr. Tanaka had always been the one to ensure the safety and efficiency of the harvests. Dr. Tanaka's death, in the midst of the situation in Zimbabwe, had shaken Michael's confidence—and right now, he needed confidence more than ever. Everyone throughout the Aseso organization looked to Michael for direction. Above all else, the new responsibility of directing Black Falcon's operations weighed heavily on him.

"Did they finally figure out who did it?" Caroline sat on the bed as Michael prepared for his morning flight to D.C.

"The people at Black Falcon believe that the same group responsible for the bombing in Lisbon helped the rebels in Zimbabwe kill him."

"Why would they do that?"

"They want Aseso out of Africa."

"What are you guys going to do now?"

"We have to keep doing exactly what we have been doing. Millions of people depend on us."

"David can't expect you to take over Dr. Tanaka's duties, can he?"

"There's no one else. I always thought that if Dr. Tanaka decided to retire, we would have Dirk take on that role. But he's gone, too." Michael's sense of order had vanished. The world seemed a chaotic, dangerous place.

"Isn't there anyone else at Black Falcon?"

"Sure. But I don't know them very well, and neither does David. Dr. Tanaka dealt with them almost exclusively."

"What about Clive?"

"As far as I know, the only thing he has ever done is work in laboratories. Besides, he's actually the most important person in the company. He runs the Nanning facility. He and David are the only people who really know the secret of Sinsen."

"Michael," Caroline said tentatively, "maybe you should think about leaving now."

Michael paused in the middle of choosing a tie. He turned to face Caroline. "Why would I leave now? David needs me more than ever."

"Stop thinking about David! I doubt that he thinks about you the same way. You have a family now. Your priority is us. Dr. Tanaka was assassinated because of his association with Aseso. How do you know they won't come after you?"

"Let's keep this in perspective." Michael sat down beside Caroline and took her hand. "He was killed in Zimbabwe by revolutionaries. I'm going to D.C., not Zimbabwe. I'll talk to David when I see him this afternoon. We'll figure things out."

"I really feel like things have gotten out of control. You don't have to stay. You've made enough money. We could stay here or move back to Seattle."

"Caroline, I can't leave David now. I owe him."

"What do you owe him? He's the richest man in the world. He could leave if he wanted to. Maybe he will. Why do you have to be a hero? There are plenty of people at Aseso who would love to jump into your position. Let them do it."

"You know how much this job means to me."

"How much does this family mean to you? If I think for one second that staying here will put us in danger, I will take Gregor and leave."

That was all Michael needed to hear. Over the years, Michael's position at Aseso had been in question several times. This, however, was the first time he had felt as though his relationship with Caroline was in jeopardy. He had promised her on their vacation in the Philippines that it would only be a couple more years; it was already going on three. "I know you're worried. I'll discuss everything with David. I promise, Caroline, I am not going to get assassinated. When David and I get back to New York, I will let him know I'm leaving."

This seemed to satisfy Caroline. "Is David flying down with you?" she said.

"No, he's flying in from Chicago on his jet. He's been visiting his folks. We'll meet at Alton Gordon, then we'll meet with Coves."

"What is David going to tell him?"

"That he can't have what he wants."

"Coves promised to make Sinsen available to everyone," Caroline said bitterly. "I think that now, everyone feels entitled."

"I think you're right. Everyone is making promises they can't keep."

"What's worse is that people are starting to die."

Michael sat there for a moment, contemplating his situation. The hairs on the back of his neck rose at the thought that he was responsible for everything that was going on. "I'm not sure which is worse—telling people you don't have the fountain of youth when you do, or telling them you do when you don't." Michael looked at Caroline, thoroughly disgusted with himself.

"What do you mean? Doesn't Sinsen work after all?" Caroline was surprised to hear Michael's change in tone.

"It works for those who can get it. People will not be happy watching others live while they die. It would have been better if we could have invented Sinsen either for everyone or for no one at all."

"Then they should just make it illegal."

"It's too late. Millions of people depend on it who will surely die within a few years if they stop taking it. My grandmother is ninety-five, and she takes it. I just don't see a solution."

Michael took a chartered jet down to Washington from Teterboro, the airport in New Jersey used by corporate aircraft. Aseso had recently contracted a new private jet service company to fly its top managers. David flew his own private jet, making Michael the highest-ranking corporate officer who used the service. The brand-new aircraft, decked out with all the newest amenities, would, on an ordinary day, have occupied Michael's attention for the entire forty-five minute ride. But that day his mind was elsewhere. He never would have thought he'd react so emotionally to Dr. Tanaka's death, or that it would be so hard to stop thinking about it.

During his first few years at Aseso, Michael had preferred to spend as little time as possible working with Dr. Tanaka, preferring to share the limelight with David. Dr. Tanaka had been a series of contradictions: polite but unfriendly, impatient but hard-working, ethically questionable but unquestionably fair. It had never become clear to him whether Dr. Tanaka really enjoyed playing the bad guy, or whether he did so because somebody had to. Regardless, Dr. Tanaka had done what was necessary for Aseso's success, and everyone else had benefited. Everyone knew that David was responsible for creating Sinsen. Few knew that Dr. Tanaka had made the phenomenon possible.

Once the jet had reached cruising altitude, Michael attempted to read the brief prepared by counsel at Alton Gordon. As usual, the brief was anything but. It contained the lawyers' assessment of the government's desire to have Aseso produce and help distribute Sinsen to beneficiaries in the United States. Michael thumbed through the hundred-page memo before putting it down in the empty seat next to his. He had meant to tell them to make it shorter than a textbook. An eventual consequence of paying people by the hour, he reflected, was a loss of brevity.

The sun was high off the horizon. There were few clouds, affording a view of the Atlantic Ocean off the Jersey Shore. Below, the East Coast was moving toward lunchtime. For the first time, Michael seriously considered leaving Aseso. He had never seen such worry and desperation in Caroline's eyes. He had never felt so worried himself. With every new day, the world would want more from Aseso; and with Dr. Tanaka gone, that meant they would want more from him. David had allowed everyone to develop unrealistic expectations. Michael realized, sitting in his chair looking out the window, that the world that had come to love Aseso would surely end up disappointed.

"Can I get you anything to drink, Mr. Jeffs?" The flight attendant was a pretty brunette in her late thirties.

"No, I'm fine, thank you."

"We have an assortment of newspapers as well."

"Thank you. I'm fine."

She disappeared toward the rear of the aircraft, but then returned. "Do you mind if I ask you something?" She stood with her hands clasped. There was a childlike innocence about her.

"Go ahead," Michael said. He welcomed the distraction.

"I was a regular customer of yours before you guys made everyone sign up for long-term contracts. I couldn't afford the new subscription, so I stopped taking Sinsen. Women like myself who haven't had children yet...well, we could really use it."

"I'm sorry to hear that we lost you as a customer." Truth be told, Aseso had not lost her. Aseso had kicked her out. "But now it's more affordable. The price has come down a lot since we established the long-term contracts."

"That's true, but it's not available. When I decided to start buying it again, I tried to sign up, but I was just put on a waiting list."

Michael heard this complaint often. When would more be available? How much more? How many more desperate customers could be accommodated? The questions kept Michael up at night. He did not have any answers. Now, with Dr. Tanaka gone, he was even less sure. Each day brought greater and greater expectations that could not possibly be met.

"Give me your name and contact information, and I'll see what I can do." Michael knew that he couldn't do much. Every new bottle had been promised three times over to friends, families, business contacts, politicians, and celebrities. Everyone was reaching out to someone at Aseso to try and secure more. There would always be too many people wanting more.

- 257 -

"Really?" She looked stunned. "That's great! I really appreciate it. I don't mean to seem ungrateful...but my family also needs it."

"How many are there in your family?"

"Seven, if you count my sisters' husbands."

"I'll see what I can do." It was all that Michael could think of saying.

"Thank you so much!" Her face glowed like a child's on Christmas day. "Mr. Jeffs, I've been following the news, and I've been wondering. Do you think one day it will be available for everyone?"

First you, then your family, then the world. Sure, why not? Michael thought, suddenly tired. He felt sick to his stomach. He had just made a promise that he knew he would not be able to keep. As the plane touched down at Reagan National, he knew that he had just shown a piece of candy to a child. He would soon take it away.

53

Washington D.C.

David and Michael arrived at the offices of Alton Gordon within minutes of each other. Patrick Maloney and Representative O'Farrell were already in the conference room. Brad was on the speakerphone, piped in from his office at Bearing Brothers in New York. They worked through lunch, strategizing their response to President Coves' request. Brad, Patrick, and O'Farrell disagreed with David's position.

"You have to be seen as cooperative here," O'Farrell said. "You can't give Coves a reason to take aggressive action against you. It was okay to fight him when he was a senator, but the presidency is a whole different story."

"They don't have any idea what they're asking for." David stood at the window, looking down at the people below. Dr. Tanaka's death had drained him of the energy he needed to vigorously oppose President Coves.

"You have to be very careful," Patrick said. "And I'm not talking about legal liabilities. I'm talking about personal safety, David. They are asking nicely now. But that can change."

"We've already informed Secretary Gutierrez and her team that their plan is not going to work. They don't seem to want to listen." David's mind was not on the impending meeting. He recalled the first day Sinsen was sold in Hong Kong. He recalled the opening of the New York office and the launch of Aseso's European operations. Each time they had expanded their operations, they'd faced greater challenges and opposition, but David had always been ready to meet those challenges. Ironically, this would be the biggest expansion in the company's history, but David had no enthusiasm about pursuing it.

"I've got to agree with Patrick here." Brad's voice came over the speakerphone. "Even if you guys end up doing nothing with this administration, you should at least pretend to be cooperative. It would be in everyone's best interest."

It was this comment that set Michael off. "No. I think what would be in everyone's best interest is if all of us stopped pretending. Coves needs to stop pretending that he can deliver on his promises. We need to stop pretending that there will someday be enough Sinsen. Between ourselves and Coves, we have set up such unrealistic expectations that we're all doomed to fail."

"What do you suggest we do?" O'Farrell was taken aback by Michael's angry tone.

"We need to manage the situation. Coves got elected because of promises he won't be able to deliver on, and we've been left alone for similar reasons. The game is over. The harvest from Zimbabwe was intended for Norway. We will not be able to deliver that shipment. When that happens, everyone will know we don't have a backup plan. We don't have any extra inventory. Unless we get back those fields in Zimbabwe, there are going to be some very disappointed old Norwegians that might die in the next couple of years."

"Just ship them some extract from somewhere else." Brad did not seem to grasp the severity of the situation.

"There is nowhere else!" Michael was exasperated. "We have run out."

There was silence in the room.

Everyone had understood the scarcity of Sinsen, but no one had understood how close to the edge Michael ran the company. No one had believed Joanna's predictions. No one had wanted to.

"Michael's right." David continued to stare out the window. "We should begin to lower expectations. But most importantly, we need to get back those fields in Zimbabwe as soon as possible."

"David," O'Farrell said, "This meeting today might still be of use to you. If you appear cooperative, you could probably convince Coves to arrange for the U.S. military to help you get back those plantations."

Patrick spoke up, "The U.S. has no strategic interest there. How could Coves possibly justify sending troops?".

"He'll make something up. What's the big deal?"

"Just make something up? Are you serious?"

O'Farrell shrugged. "Sure. Why not?"

"Well, for one thing...."

"A U.S. intervention is not going to be necessary, gentlemen," David interjected, turning away from the window. "I spoke with Clive on my way down here. The Chinese government is arranging to send troops to Zimbabwe tomorrow. Those rebels down there are dead men."

54

After being received at the White House, David and Michael were given a courtesy tour. A pleasant African-American woman guided them through the first floor, where they peered into the Vermeil Room and the library. The tour continued with a walk upstairs to the State Floor. They received lengthy descriptions of the East, Green, Blue, and Red rooms as well as the State Dining Rooms before finally being escorted to the West Wing. There, they were shown into the Roosevelt Room, where Secretary Silvia Gutierrez and Sanjay Bhatia were waiting.

"Nice to see you again, Dr. Oaks." Silvia seemed extremely uncomfortable.

"Dr. Oaks, I am sorry to hear of your loss," Sanjay said. He seemed sincere.

"Thank you," David replied. "I appreciate the sentiment. You remember my colleague, Michael Jeffs."

"Of course. How are you, Mr. Jeffs?"

"I'm fine." In fact, Michael was far less than fine. His facial expression showed it. A year before, he would have been beside himself with excitement about a high-level meeting at the White House. Now it looked as though every meeting from that point on would involve disappointments.

Silvia invited them to sit, but David waved his hand. He wanted to make this meeting as brief as possible. "You will see the President in a few moments," Silvia said. "But first, it's my duty to inform you that we have to hold off on the discussion scheduled for today. The President is inside with the Secretary of State and the National Security Advisor."

"Why are they involved?" David asked. He seemed taken aback.

"I will let them explain the situation to you. I apologize for not informing you of the change in advance, but my understanding is that this is due to events that have unfolded as recently as this morning."

The distance from the Roosevelt Room to the Oval Office was a mere few feet, but to Michael it seemed as vast as a continent. Meeting the Secretary of Health and Human Services was one thing, but the President, Secretary of State, and National Security Advisor was altogether different. As they entered the Oval Office, Michael felt his stomach fall a couple of feet below his navel.

President Coves looked newly confident. The last couple of years had been a stalemate between him and David. Coves had won the election but had failed to have the government intervene in the activities of David, the richest man in the world. But now a shift had occurred. David felt powerless without Dr. Tanaka, and Coves sensed that he had new leverage.

After the obligatory salutations and introductions were made, Coves invited everyone to make themselves comfortable. Large couches faced each other in the middle of the room. Aides stood at attention against the walls.

"I have to say, I am surprised to see you here," Coves said.

"That's funny; I was just thinking the same about you," David replied. One of the aides laughed. Other than Michael, no one else found it funny.

Coves frowned. "Let's get down to business. There seems to be a bit of confusion regarding what to do about Zimbabwe. The government there has nationalized all lands, including your plantations."

"Yes, I am painfully aware of the situation. The confusion you mentioned is among whom?" David asked.

"The plants that were to be harvested in Zimbabwe were to be sent to Norway; is that correct?"

"Not exactly," Michael broke in, anxious to avoid any misunderstandings. "They were going to be sent to one of our processing facilities in Portugal. But yes, the end product was to be warehoused in Norway for distribution there."

"We have already informed our contacts at the Ministry of Health in Norway that there will be delays in delivering the shipment. We are working with them to figure out a solution," David said. "We have it under control."

"Yes, well, the Minister of Health contacted the Prime Minister, who was surprised to find out that Aseso does not have enough reserve inventory for a situation like this."

"We never said we did," David said.

"You also never said you didn't. And I can tell you that the Prime Minister is not very happy."

"Not very happy with whom?"

"Let's just say he is not very happy with the situation."

"What does that have to do with you?" David asked, his voice rising.

"He gave me a courtesy call this morning, as a fellow NATO head of state, to inform me that he intends to send troops to Zimbabwe to get the plants that were meant for his country."

"If that is the case," David said, "I guess we're in a bit of a pickle."

"A Chinese pickle, I'd say." Cove said, making it clear that he knew about the Chinese troops that were preparing to invade Zimbabwe. Michael wondered what else about the company the President knew. Paranoia set in.

"You can inform the Prime Minister that we should have the plantations back soon enough," David said, clearly implying that the situation was none of the President's business.

"Dr. Oaks," the Secretary of State broke in. "The situation is complicated. We would prefer to have a NATO force in Zimbabwe, as opposed to the Chinese army."

"Aseso, as you know, is a Chinese corporation. The company that distributes Sinsen here in the States is merely a distribution subsidiary, as is the company that distributes it in Europe. What's more, those roots were to be delivered initially to our processing facility in Portugal. In view of all that, I think the Chinese have more justification than the Norwegians."

"Fine. We'll get the Portuguese to go down there and kick some ass." The National Security Advisor was not as soft-spoken as the Secretary of State. "Dr. Oaks, it is not in the best interest of the United States to have China post troops in Africa. We suggest you tell your friends in Beijing that NATO will take care of this."

"Don't you guys have a red phone around here that you can just pick up and call them directly? Why do you need me to do it?"

"We would like to avoid any unnecessary political entanglements," the Secretary of State responded, attempting to lower the tension in the room.

"First of all, I don't know the people in Beijing. Dr. Tanaka dealt with them. His son, who lives in China, is in contact with them now. I doubt they are going to listen to me," David said. "Second, what business is it of the U.S.?"

"David, let me make this very clear." Coves stood up. "The Chinese want arable land more than they want oil. If they get into Zimbabwe, they are not going to leave. The next time an African country decides to have a little coup and Aseso's lands are threatened, they will be right there to take over. We can't let that happen."

"You guys were about to sell them America's oil reserves to buy Sinsen. Now you want to stop them from helping us get our plants back?"

"Like the Secretary said, the situation is complicated," Coves said.

It suddenly became clear to Michael that while President Coves' legacy would go down in history as a success if he could deliver universal coverage, it would go down as a humiliating failure if the Chinese took over the world on his watch.

55

After the meeting at the White House, David and Michael rode back to Alton Gordon. As they drove north on Connecticut Avenue, Michael noticed pedestrians staring, wondering who was riding in the back of the police-escorted limousine. Dr. Tanaka had also received armored escorts, Michael reflected. And that's what had attracted the attention of his enemies.

O'Farrell and Patrick Maloney greeted David and Michael in the conference room. Clive dialed in from Nanning; David had called him from the limo, waking him up. It was the middle of the night in Asia. The mood in the conference room was tense.

"Clive, here is the situation. We need to tell the Chinese that we don't need their help any more. NATO will take care of it." David sat with his elbows on the conference table, leaning forward to speak into the phone.

"Why doesn't NATO tell China that NATO will take care of it?" Clive asked, sounding tired.

"Everyone is trying to avoid a confrontation."

"Well, there is definitely going to be confrontation if NATO shows up in Zimbabwe. The Chinese will be there in a couple of days."

"The Chinese are ambitious, not stupid. I don't think they'll risk war over this."

"I'm not so sure, David. They've had big plans for Africa for some time now. This is a perfect opportunity for them."

"Patrick, from a legal point of view, who do you think has the most rights to the fields in Zimbabwe?" David asked, looking for any angle that could help shed light on the situation.

"We set up Aseso Zimbabwe as a local subsidiary. It owns the fields, and it is subject to the laws of Zimbabwe. But now that the new government has nationalized all of the lands, it owns those fields...according to its own law, anyway." Patrick threw up his hands. He wasn't being much help.

David looked to Michael. "Is there any way we could get some inventory from our other facilities to satisfy the Norwegians?"

"We are completely out of product. Completely. We would have to take away from another country's quota, and that would probably make things worse." Michael was getting more and more nervous. "Why do we have to get in the middle? We asked the Chinese for help. They agreed. The Norwegians will just have to wait."

"It's not that easy, Michael." O'Farrell spoke as if he had been in similar situations before. "NATO has been very critical of China's military involvement in Africa. China has sent advisors in the past, but they have never invaded a country. This will be viewed as an act of aggression."

"Gentlemen, I don't have to remind you that the reason we originally secured so much land in Zimbabwe was because the Chinese introduced my father to their friends in the previous Zimbabwean government." Clive's voice cracked. "The current leaders killed my father. I hope the Chinese kill every one of them when they get there."

"Clive, I loved your father, too, but we need to stay calm and focused." David's voice betrayed a nervousness that no one had ever heard in it before.

"David, while everyone at Aseso, including me, worked comfortably behind a desk, my father went out there, never avoiding confrontation, to make sure the rest of us lived the good life. He tried to prolong life in Zimbabwe, and they took his life away. You can tell President Coves that if he wants to stop the Chinese government from sending troops to Zimbabwe, he can call them himself!"

There was a loud click as Clive hung up the phone. The conference room was silent.

"The kid's emotional. He'll get over it," O'Farrell said.

"No, Clive is right," David said. "We don't need to be Coves' messengers."

The Washington Mall was alive with tourists and joggers. Street carts selling everything from hot dogs to t-shirts lined the streets in front of the Washington Monument. Tour buses let people off before new crowds hopped on. The sun was setting below the ring of flags around the monument as David and Michael walked along the Mall, followed closely by Black Falcon agents.

"What are you going tell Coves?" Michael asked.

"I'm going to tell him the truth. We are not going to intervene on his behalf. He's going to be pissed, but Clive is right. The Zimbabwe situation has nothing to do with the United States."

"What are you going to do about the Norwegians?"

"I'm going to call the Minister of Health and tell him that we intend to get the plantations back with the aid of the Chinese government. I'm sure he will tell the Prime Minister. If the Prime Minister has a problem with that, he can call the Chinese."

They strolled alongside the reflecting pool, making their way toward the Lincoln Memorial. "That whole 'we will do a lot of social good' idea didn't quite work out did it?" Michael asked, thinking again he had been a fool to believe something good could have come from their actions.

"We're not to blame, Michael. We played by all the rules."

"Countries might go to war,"

"Countries always go to war. If it's not over Sinsen, it will be over something else."

"What will happen if someone else figures out how Sinsen works?"

"Someone will. In fact, I'm surprised no one has yet. Once the technology is leaked, the only thing that matters will be the land. I suppose people have figured that out."

"If you had to do it all over again, wouldn't you do things differently from the beginning?"

"Not really. Well...the Laotian prisoner thing was a bit questionable." David chuckled.

Michael and David picked up their pace as they came upon the Lincoln Memorial. They both knew that Aseso as a company, and their lives as they had known them, were about to change forever.

"Do you remember, David, when you asked me, the first day we met, what I would do if I learned I had one thousand years to live?"

"I remember. Do you have a better answer for me now?"

"Yeah," Michael said. He looked at David. "I wouldn't take the first job offer."

56

Two days after the meeting with Coves, Chinese troops landed in Mozambique, Zimbabwe's ocean side neighbor to the southeast. A longtime recipient of Chinese developmental aid, Mozambique welcomed the troops to its shores. News crews filmed as thousands of men in tan uniforms with red accents marched toward Zimbabwe from Maputo, the capital, while JF- and FC-class fighter jets practiced maneuvers overhead. Aircraft carriers were visible just offshore, some Russian-made, others manufactured more recently in China. Now and then the media diverted their attention from Zimbabwe to pay lip service to a new strain of influenza in Asia. All other news seemed to be on hold.

"Pissed does not even begin to describe Coves' mood right now." O'Farrell paced the length of the conference room. Patrick sat quietly, letting O'Farrell do the talking.

"Look, this thing has nothing to do with the Unites States," said David, calmer than anyone else in the room, more comfortable in the offices of Alton Gordon than in the Oval office. At the request of the President, he and Michael had remained in D.C. after their meeting at the White House. "If Coves wants to act the hero, that's his decision. He doesn't have to involve us."

"You are involved!" O'Farrell was more animated than he had been in any of the previous meetings. "Jesus, David, will you just face facts? The Chinese are trying to take over Africa in your name."

"First of all, the official statement from the Chinese is that they are there to help the legitimate government recover from the illegal coup that displaced it. The fact that their actions will result in us getting our fields back is great, but incidental. Second of all, they won't listen to me anyway." He leaned back in his chair, hands behind his head.

"Everyone knows they're down there to protect the Astragalus fields. You know it, I know it, and NATO knows it!"

Before David could respond, a woman walked in, sober and purposeful. She handed Patrick a note and whispered in his ear. Patrick thanked her, and she walked out of the room. He unfolded the note and read it. "Gentlemen, your presence is requested at the White House immediately."

"Again? You'd think they'd let me stay in the Lincoln bedroom," said David, making no move to stand.

Michael thought he heard O'Farrell mutter "Smug bastard," but he couldn't be sure.

Patrick had grabbed the remote control and turned on the TV. "This thing just got more serious," he said. "Look."

An anchor was describing the latest developments from CNN's studios in Atlanta. BREAKING NEWS flashed under the anchor's image. "Sources tell CNN that both Russia and Belarus have joined a coalition with China to oust the dictatorship in Zimbabwe, which achieved power through a recent military coup. Both countries are expected to send troops immediately to aid in the effort. China has given the military leaders of Zimbabwe forty-eight hours to abdicate power or face a coalition invasion."

"Forty-eight hours?" Michael said. "It takes the postal service a week to process a letter in that country."

"It's over." O'Farrell took his seat. "The Chinese own that country now. David, do yourself a favor and try not to piss off those boys over at the White House any more than you already have."

David and Michael arrived at 1600 Pennsylvania Avenue in what they agreed must have been the fastest time conceivable, thanks to a convoy provided by the Secret Service. This time, they did not receive a tour. No friendly African-American woman greeted them at the main entrance. Instead, a stoic man in a dark suit with an American flag pin escorted them through the West Wing to the

Oval Office. Secret service agents followed. As before, the President waited with the Secretary of State and the National Security Advisor. Secretary Gutierrez was nowhere in sight.

"Nice job with the Chinese, Dr. Oaks. Can we count on your support with Al-Qaeda, too?" President Coves stood behind his desk. David and Michael took seats opposite the Secretary of State and the National Security Advisor.

"Mr. President, the Chinese are not going to listen to me. Aseso is half owned by Dr. Tanaka's son, who lives in Nanning. I couldn't convince him to speak with them." David was notably less confident than he had been during his last visit to the Oval Office.

"I tell you to call off the Chinese, and instead you call off the Norwegians. Whose side are you on?"

"If I can add something here," Michael interjected. "I've been traveling to Africa for a while now. Everyone down there knows the Chinese have been looking for an excuse to develop a stranglehold on the region. They were going in regardless of what we told them."

"The kid's right, Mr. President," said the National Security Advisor, his tone suggesting that this was not the first time the President had been apprised of the fact. Michael was surprised to hear himself referred to as a "kid." He still looked thirty, but he felt much wiser. "Even though Aseso is the largest Chinese corporation in Zimbabwe, there are a few Chinese mining companies that could make just as good an excuse."

"Fine. Mr. Jeffs, since you seem to be our resident expert in the region, tell me: Why are the Russians there? What's in it for Moscow?" Eyes narrowed, Coves stared at Michael.

"I think by now it's clear to everyone that one day we're going to run out of land. The Russians have no way to grow Astragalus plants domestically, so my guess is that they want to secure some fields for themselves. That's probably the same reason the Norwegians wanted to go down there."

"I see. And exactly how soon do you boys expect to run out of land?"

There was a pause while David and Michael exchanged glances. They both knew the answer, but neither wanted to disclose it.

"You must have some idea."

"Well, Mr. President...." Michael hesitated. Coves raised his eyebrows, impatient for an answer. "If we don't move forward with your plan for universal coverage here in the States, we have about four more years before we would have to make a serious dent in the world's forests or food supply. Take your pick."

"And if you do go forward with my plan?" Coves was noticeably nervous. His legacy was threatening to fall apart around him.

"Then we have already run out of land."

Silence fell over the room. Coves looked as if someone had just informed him of a domestic invasion. Michael felt helpless. David, on the other hand, almost looked relieved that the truth had finally been revealed.

"Excuse my ignorance in all of this, but isn't there a lot of land out there? The world is a very big place." The Secretary of State was visibly confused.

"The problem," David said, "is that we are dealing with a very highly concentrated extract. It takes a large quantity of Astragalus root to make one Sinsen pill. And on top of that, only very specialized subtropical land can support Astragalus cultivation."

"Tell me, Dr. Oaks." Coves had recovered from his shock enough to continue his questioning. "How long have you known this?"

"Sinsen was never supposed to be for everyone. It is a luxury good, like a Mercedes-Benz or a heart transplant. Not everyone can afford it."

"Well, whatever the problem may be with making those little pills," the National Security Advisor said impatiently, "we cannot have the Chinese and the goddamn Russians joining forces to take over Africa. So what I would suggest you do, Dr. Oaks, is go down there after they've taken over Zimbabwe, thank them for their help, and tell them to get the hell out."

"You know, that's a good idea," David said. "And while I'm down there, I'll tell the Chinese to stop picking on poor little Tibet."

"Let's save the pissing contest for another day," said Coves, attempting to behave presidentially. "This situation presents a clear and present danger to the national security of this country."

"Mr. President, I would argue that the clear and present danger exists more for the Europeans," Michael said. He'd been playing these scenarios over and over in his head for the past few days.

"Why do you say that?"

"There is not one European country that can grow Astragalus plants. In the U.S., it would be unimaginably expensive to clear enough land, but it would be possible. It would require deforesting much of Hawaii. Australia has plenty of usable land, as do China, India, and most of South America. The Europeans are completely dependent on overseas fields."

"As are the Russians," the Secretary of State said slowly, painting a picture in his own mind.

"As are the Russians," Michael concurred.

"That's all I need to hear," Coves said. "This is going to be a land grab if we don't stop it. NATO needs to send a message. The Chinese and Russians can stay, but they can't stay for long."

Coves pressed a button on his phone and told his secretary to put a call through to the Prime Minister of the United Kingdom. David, Michael, the National Security Advisor, and the Secretary of State fell silent, waiting for the call to connect. Everyone could feel the awkwardness of the moment. Coves looked at them expectantly. When no one moved, he announced, "That will be all, gentlemen."

57

New York.

Ordinarily, the deaths being caused by the new strain of influenza in Asia would have caused panic in the United States. The World Health Organization had now classified the epidemic as pandemic in nature. Unlike previous pandemics, this strain seemed to be potentially lethal in anyone, regardless of age or social status. "Like death used to be," Caroline commented as Michael changed the channel. He, like the rest of the country, only wanted updates about the standoff between NATO and China.

Michael flipped the channel to BBC just as the latest news in the story broke. The African Union, led by South Africa, had declared the actions of the coalition of China, Russia, and Belarus to be an act of aggression against the Union. It warned that if the troops were to move into Zimbabwe from Mozambique, the Union would retaliate with force. It also stated that African countries would freeze the assets of Chinese entities domiciled within their borders. Those assets included the financial and physical property of Chinese corporations doing business in Africa. Because Aseso was based in Nanning, the African Union viewed it as a Chinese corporation, despite the fact that most of the management resided in New York.

A collective decision had been made by the majority of the African member states, with the notable exception of Mozambique, to prevent the harvest of Aseso's fields in their countries until the Chinese-led coalition withdrew from the continent. This would mean that most of the NATO countries would not have access to Sinsen in the coming months.

Aseso's fields had been taken hostage.

"This is insane." Michael leaned against the kitchen counter, drinking a beer. He had finally come back from Washington to spend the weekend with Caroline and little Gregor.

"How did all this happen?" Caroline asked. She hadn't turned off the television in days, but the television news, as usual, was woefully short on analysis.

"You know, a professor at MIT once told me that situations like these always last much longer than you would think probable, and end much more quickly than you would think possible."

"Situations like what? I don't even really understand what the situation is."

"The land situation," Michael said. "We were taking over land all over the globe on a daily basis. It wasn't sustainable. David knew that one day something had to give. Well, now something is giving."

"But why now?"

"We couldn't make the shipment to Norway. We've had a few close calls before, but this was the first time we failed. The Norwegians have figured out that there's no backup inventory because there's no backup land. Everything we make now is already spoken for."

"What can you do?"

"Nothing. There is nothing to do except try to get our plantations back and make good on our promises to our existing customers."

"And if you don't get them back?"

"I don't even want to think about that."

The public understood very little about the situation. All they knew was that Sinsen would soon be unavailable. Within days, panic spread. The people of NATO's member countries called upon their leaders to take action against either China or the African Union, or both—no one was quite sure who to blame. A request from the United Nations to the Security Council member countries to convene an emergency session went unanswered. There was no time to talk.

58

Two Days Later.

Over the weekend, the situation in Africa worsened. The Chinese were in full control of Zimbabwe. Russian and Belarusian troops arrived in Mozambique in large numbers—much larger than would be required to regain control of Zimbabwe. NATO issued an official warning to China to cease any further aggressive actions in Africa. It simultaneously warned the African Union's member nations that it recognized the expropriation of the Aseso fields as a hostile act. It was now a three-way conflict.

The situation was escalating from alarming to desperate. One African nation after another announced the annexation of Aseso's lands. On Monday, NATO sent a unilateral message to the government of Zambia, the largest producer of Aseso's Astragalus plants, that if it continued to prevent the harvesting of the plantations, troops would be sent to assure the safety of Aseso's European employees and contractors. On the evening news, political commentators predicted that Zambia would not comply and, instead, would look to the African Union for military support.

In Asia, another potential catastrophe was forming. A second strain of influenza had been reported. More deadly than the first, it was also spreading. The media had nicknamed this second strain "Dragon Flu" because of its mysterious tumor-creating potential. While mortality from the first strain resulted from pneumonia, the second, more mysterious strain caused an unusually rapid onset of tumors throughout the internal organs, followed by death within weeks or even days. The media, while continuing to report on events in Africa, now turned their attention to the unprecedented looming disaster in Asia.

Clive, in Hong Kong on business, was prevented from returning home to mainland China due to travel restrictions. He called Michael on Monday night to let him know that he could not be reached in his office. "People are dying here every day," Clive said. "Have there been any cases on your side of the world?"

"More and more are dying each day here in the States." Michael put Clive on the speaker phone and leaned back in his chair. It was late, and he was alone in the office. "But as far as I know, there have only been a few in Europe. Hey, Clive, I hate to be all business, but the guys in Brazil are bugging me. They want to know when they can expect the next shipment of seeds."

"It's difficult to say. The travel restrictions are making things impossible around here. This side of the world is shutting down. There won't be any seeds coming out of here for a while."

"While your part of the world is shutting down, the western hemisphere is heating up. The situation in Africa is out of control. Is there any way we can get some product to Europe from the warehouses in Asia?" David had instructed Michael to try to ease the tension in Europe by shipping Sinsen from any part of the world where it was available, regardless of the consequences.

"We have some inventory in Japan, but I doubt it will be enough."

"We'll take what we can get. I'll tell Jason to make arrangements with our guys in Japan."

"The Japanese will be upset," Clive cautioned.

"Everyone has to share the pain."

"I doubt they'll see it that way. But I'll do my best. By the way, Michael, it looks like I'll be in New York for Christmas. I've been dating a lawyer at the Alton Gordon office in Hong Kong. We've gotten to know each other while I've been stuck here. Call it a perk of the Dragon Flu." Clive laughed. "She's an American expat from New Jersey. I'm spending Christmas with her and her family."

"That's great," Michael said. It was the first time in over a month that he'd heard Clive bring up anything besides Astragalus and his father's death. "It'll be good to see you. Maybe we can plan something for New Year's Eve."

"We'd like that. I can't wait for you guys to meet her." Clive sounded like a schoolboy in love.

"I'll talk to Caroline, and you and I can speak again on Friday. Take care of yourself over there."

"I'm fine. Just waiting it out at Alton Gordon. If you want to worry about anything, worry about the Japanese."

59

One Week Later.

Caroline stood in front of the bathroom mirror with her hands on her stomach. She noticed a few more wrinkles around her eyes. Her face was still prettier than most, but it had aged. She was now in her late thirties. There were long-time Aseso customers who looked similar to her, but they were in their late forties. For the first time in her life, she felt like she was getting old.

She was pregnant. The blue test strip on the counter confirmed it. She was going to have another child. It had been much easier to refuse Sinsen before. She had looked young and felt energized. Things were different now. She really was getting older. Running the household, keeping up with little Gregor, and sharing in Michael's stress had taken their toll. She would be well into her forties by the time the new one entered preschool.

When the news had broken out, years before, that Sinsen really did prevent aging, she had not been alone in abstaining. Many people shared her view that it wasn't natural. Life had to take its course. It was unfair that it would be available only to the rich. Unwanted consequences were almost certain. Now those people had disappeared. The country was obsessed with youth. The new president was going to make it possible. Everyone desperately wanted what was so readily available to her. Had she been a fool? Why was she holding out? Didn't she owe it to her family to stay young? Was it too late?

She and Michael had had many arguments over the years about her not taking Sinsen. The arguments were mostly intellectual in nature, never threatening. Michael always supported her decision, even if he didn't agree. Would he do so in the future? She turned to the top of the linen cabinet and picked up a small framed photo of them from Michael's graduation. She looked at it often. Michael's appearance still hadn't changed; he now looked years younger than she did. It would only get worse. Should she just give in? Was it worth risking Michael in order to stick to her beliefs, beliefs that, now, very few people shared?

That night she prepared one of Michael's favorite meals, miso-glazed hanger steak with wasabi mashed potatoes. It was something Michael always ordered back at their favorite restaurant in Seattle. Whenever they flew back to visit their friends, Michael insisted on returning to the same restaurant, and he ordered the same meal without fail. She wanted to make it a special dinner. They were leaving the next day for Dallas, to spend Christmas with his family. Tonight she would let him know that she was pregnant, and they could surprise his parents with the news at Christmas.

After picking up Gregor from his preschool, she walked over to the gourmet food market at Columbus Circle. She always preferred to do her own shopping, even though they had plenty of hired help who could do it for her. The store was a madhouse. During the holiday season, food shopping meant fighting crowds and waiting in long lines. Gregor was tired and troublesome.

Most of the conversations she overheard in line for the register related to the high price of food that had become the norm. Even successful professionals were feeling the effects of the inflation caused by Aseso's activities. Tropical fruits had become a luxury. Few could afford to drink coffee every day. Chocolate was for special occasions. Food was becoming scarce.

After she checked out, she ordered the groceries to be delivered to her apartment. Next was the local wine shop. Michael was fond of Oregon Pinot Noir, which would go very well with the steak. At least they do not grow Astragalus in Oregon, she thought, otherwise wine would become unavailable. Some beer for the appetizer and Scotch for after dinner rounded out her list. Orchid Bakery, Caroline's favorite dessert shop, was her last stop before returning home.

She put Gregor down for a nap and began to pack before getting the apartment ready for dinner. In the time it had taken her to go shopping and come back, she had convinced herself that she would begin taking Sinsen after the baby was born, then changed her mind several times. She began to get excited about the future again. Soon Michael would have nothing to do with Aseso. They would have enough money to live anywhere they wanted. They would have a full family, perhaps one more baby in a couple of years. It was the prospect of one more that finally made her decide to take Sinsen. As she set out candles, occasionally looking at her reflection in the dining room mirror, she reassured herself that she was still fairly young; with Sinsen, she would stay that way forever.

Mrs. Klein, whom Caroline willingly overpaid as Gregor's nanny, arrived to help. After the shelter shut down, Caroline had made sure that she would never lose touch with her again. Together they packed Gregor's clothes and toys. Caroline's suitcase was next; then came Michael's. Michael's was easy. All of the money in the world would not change his fashion sense. It was always the same: jeans, button-down shirts, his favorite t-shirts, and slacks that went into the suitcase but were never worn. Once the packing was completed, Caroline went to the room that she and Michael used as an office, and Mrs. Klein prepared to give Gregor a bath.

"Congratulations, Caroline!" Mrs. Klein exclaimed from the office doorway, taking Caroline by surprise.

She stood there with the biggest smile Caroline had ever seen her wear.

Caroline instantly realized that she had left the blue strip indicator on the bathroom counter. She stood up as Mrs. Klein came to hug her. "Thank you. This is one of the best days of my life."

"Did you find out today?"

"Yes, this morning."

"Does Michael know?"

"I'm going to tell him tonight over dinner."

"He is going to be very happy. You have a beautiful family, and now it is going to be bigger."

"Thank you, Mrs. Klein." Emotions flooded Caroline, and she began to cry.

By seven p.m., everything was set. All the suitcases were in one of the guest rooms, ready for the next day's travels. Mrs. Klein had left for the day. Caroline eagerly waited for Michael to come home. He was going to be so happy at her news. She thought back to their time in the Philippines, when she'd told Michael she was pregnant with Gregor. She laughed, remembering how the waiter had congratulated her before Michael could say anything.

As soon as she heard the door open, she rushed into the foyer to welcome him. She slowed down when she saw the expression on his face.

"What's wrong, Michael?"

"Clive passed away a couple hours ago in a hospital in Hong Kong."

60

December.

W hen the first research supporting Aseso had come out, the World Health Organization in Geneva cautioned its member nations to perform further studies before allowing distribution within their respective jurisdictions. But the desire by people in those countries to believe in and obtain an anti-aging drug had been too great for their political leaders to ignore. Now almost every country in the world was involved in either producing or consuming Sinsen. The WHO watched helplessly. Countless policy papers recommending regulation and investigation went unheeded.

When David's phone rang on Wednesday morning, the caller ID showed a number in western Switzerland. David had conducted enough business with the WHO over the years to recognize the country and area codes. He hesitated before answering, prepared to field a question about the global availability of Sinsen.

"Hello, David. It's Alex."

"Alex! What are you doing calling from Geneva? I saw the number and thought you were the World Health Organization." David laughed. Dr. Alexander Block had been both David's and Clive's thesis advisor at Stanford. David hadn't heard from him in years.

"Actually, David, I am calling from the WHO. I'm a guest scientist here."

"That's great! I've been meaning to call you." David had been intending to call for a long time, but it seemed as though the world tugged at him every second of the day to solve a problem. He hadn't had time to reach out, and the two had grown apart. Alex was a scientist and felt uncomfortable in David's world. But now David felt a need to reconnect with old friends, and he was surprised at how happy he was to hear Alex's voice.

"I heard about Clive. It's a horrible thing. He was one of my best students."

"He was a dear friend. So was his father."

"I never met his father. I wish I could have stayed in touch."

"You know, when I first met him he couldn't stop talking about you, Alex. Dr. Block this and Dr. Block that."

"Me? No. He was your biggest fan. He thought you were a genius."

"I'm not a genius. I learned everything from you," David said. He meant it.

There was a pause on the other end of the phone. Then Alex cleared his throat. "Is there going to be a funeral?"

"No. Given the flu situation, Hong Kong is quarantined. I can't even fly there with a private jet."

"Actually, David, the flu situation is why I'm calling. I'd like you to come to Geneva. There's something we need to discuss."

David laughed. "Alex, in case you haven't noticed, I'm in the middle of trying to prevent World War Three."

"I'm aware of your situation, David, but we have a situation here, too. You need to come now." Alex's tone was serious.

"What is this all about?"

"I can't say over the phone. No one can know before you arrive. I'll tell you when you get here on Friday."

"Friday? That's two days from now."

"This is serious, David. Very serious. Listen to me. We need to have a good understanding of where Sinsen is sold and where the next shipments are going. How many people are taking it, how long have they been taking it, and a demographic description of those people."

"My chief operating officer, Michael Jeffs, has that information."

"Then bring him."

"Alex, I'm not exactly an expert on infectious disease. I can't imagine that the flu is being spread through Sinsen shipments, but I'll leave that to you to figure out. Why don't I give you Michael's number, and then you can do your job and I can do mine?"

David did not need a new distraction from all the issues that competed for his attention.

"David, only you can help. And let me be clear: you do want to know about this. Come to the entrance on Avenue Appia in Geneva at nine a.m. Friday. I'll be waiting for you."

Michael was scrambling to move inventories around the world. He had spent the week in South America, coordinating a harvest to be sent to a processing facility in Germany for European distribution. The harvest had been intended to supply Argentina. Argentina would be upset. It was a logistical nightmare. He flew into New York on Wednesday night, only to return to the airport early Thursday morning to fly to Geneva.

He boarded David's private Jet at seven a.m. David was already in his favorite seat. The pilot immediately asked the tower for takeoff clearance. They were running late.

"Good morning, Michael. Glad you could make it."

"Sorry I'm late. Caroline was feeling pretty miserable this morning, so I had to stick around for a bit."

"Morning sickness?"

"I'm not sure what is wrong with her these days."

"I'm sure she'll be fine."

"Yeah, I'm sure she will," Michael said.

"What time did you make it into New York last night?"

"Late. Because of weather they had us in a flight pattern for hours." Michael slid into the seat across the aisle from David's. He leaned his head back and closed his eyes. "So, why are we going to Geneva?"

Michael was exhausted. The stress was taking a physical toll. There was tremendous pressure on him to solve the shortage problem facing the world—an impossible problem to solve because, in fact, there was no solution.

"Alex will tell us when we get there."

Michael opened his eyes. "You mean we're flying halfway around the world, hoping this guy has a good reason for why we are flying halfway around the world?"

"It's just a quarter of the way around the world, and anyway, I have to go. I owe him everything, Michael. He's the one who discovered the anti-aging properties of telomerase. I was just a graduate student who rode on his coattails."

"You mean he discovered how anti-aging works?" This was the first time Michael had heard David allude to anyone other than himself and Clive as responsible for the discovery.

"No, but he came close. With the help of Clive, I got lucky and solved the last part of the puzzle. But without Alex there would be no Sinsen."

"Do you think he ever begrudged you your getting rich off his initial research?"

"I don't think so. He always was and always will be a scientist. He doesn't care about money. I offered him a position at Aseso many times, but he never took it."

The trip to Geneva seemed odd to Michael. Over the years, David had been known to make very unusual requests, but flying off to visit an old college professor in the middle of an international crisis was the strangest yet. What was the urgency? Who would take care of the matters that needed immediate attention? But Michael was too tired to argue.

Seconds later, the aircraft raced down the runway. Michael was asleep before the wheels left the ground.

61

Geneva.

David and Michael arrived in Geneva late that night. A car was waiting to take them to a hotel. They would have a few hours to sleep before their meeting. In any other situation, Michael would have been glad to travel to Geneva, a city he had never seen before. This time, though, the trip was a distraction. The pressure was mounting. His subordinates were upset that he was traveling around the world while the crisis unfolded around them. He had been playing referee between the country managers and facilities operators, all of whom were being pressured by their clients. Every distribution head had called, wanting to know when they would receive their shipments. Jason had been left to coordinate with them. There was no solution. Michael's absence only added to everyone's frustration.

Lawsuits were being filed. Shipments were being stopped at ports on orders from local judges. Michael worried that Aseso itself would crumble internally before the world fell apart. But he had to address the problems in person. And now he was flying off with David to meet with a scientist at the World Health Organization about a flu outbreak in Asia, something he knew nothing about. The mystery added to his anxiety.

Caroline had not been herself lately. At first he'd thought it was the pregnancy, but now he wasn't sure. She looked exhausted. He should have listened to her before; now it was too late. There was no quitting now. He had a social responsibility. Without him, Aseso would surely fall apart, and the millions of people that depended on him would suffer.

When he met David in the hotel lobby after a brief, restless nap, he saw that David looked as exhausted as he did. They could hardly summon the breath to speak as they got into the car that would take them to the WHO. They were surprised to find that the car had a police escort, not unlike those they had become accustomed to in Washington. The convoy sped past stoplights as traffic was directed away from them. The urgency of Aseso's situation would have monopolized their conversation if it were not for the constant phone calls they had to answer, receiving updates and giving instructions. Frantic voices wanted answers. Everyone, including President Coves, wanted to know why the two of them were in Geneva.

As they turned onto Avenue Appia, they noticed a small group of people waiting by the entrance. They were expected—and not just by Alex. A few guards stood by, waiting to escort them in. Alex stood by the door, accompanied by men that looked more like administrators than scientists. David began to fear the worst.

When the car finally stopped, one of the guards opened the rear door. David got out, and Michael followed. Alex greeted David and then quickly introduced everyone as they walked into the building. Michael's anxiety rose to unprecedented levels. At the end of the long gray hallway, another guard stood at attention in front of an open door. Alex guided everyone inside and motioned for them to sit down. Michael had no idea why they were there; David had his suspicions.

The small group huddled at the end of a massive table in a large room meant for seminars and presentations. The two administrators seemed to be there as witnesses, not as participants.

"This is all my fault, David. I didn't sleep again last night, trying to reconcile everything that has happened with what I intended." Alex looked as if he had not slept in days.

"What has happened?" David asked.

Alex took a deep breath. "I have been here for a year now, working on policy issues with regard to telomerase activators...."

David interrupted rudely. "That's great, Alex. We can catch up on your career later. But why are we here?" His characteristically cool demeanor had evaporated under the stress.

"That *is* why you're here. Telomerase activators. Sinsen."

"You told me this had to do with the flu strains in Asia. One of them, the Dragon Flu, killed Clive."

"Clive died of a strain of influenza known as avian flu."

"Clive didn't die of the avian flu. He died of the Dragon Flu," Michael said.

"No, he died of avian flu," Alex repeated.

"No, he died of the Dragon Flu." Michael was getting upset. He'd been dragged to Geneva in the midst of a crisis for nothing. "I spoke with him a week before he died."

"There is no Dragon Flu!" Alex pounded the table.

"OK," David said. "OK, there's no Dragon Flu. What are you telling me, that Clive died of an imaginary strain of flu?"

Alex tried to calm himself enough to deliver his point. He had never been good at taking charge of a conversation when he was upset. He poured himself a glass of water from the pitcher, his hands shaking. "There is only one flu. Avian flu. And it is spreading around the world."

"Fine. There's an avian flu pandemic. We know that. But there also seems to be a more deadly strain."

"There isn't, David. We thought that at first, too. There were markedly different causes of death among those infected."

"Then what is causing the cancerous deaths?" David asked.

"Avian flu combined with Sinsen, David. There are not two types of flu. There are two types of people. Those who take Sinsen and those who don't." Alex paused for a second, letting David digest the news. "I'm sorry, David."

Within seconds David's face had lost all its color. He sat there, expressionless. Michael looked between Alex and David, hoping one of them would say something. No one did. The temperature in the room seemed to fall with each passing second. Michael felt as if he had lost the ability to breathe.

"How?" David asked softly.

"It's the tumor suppressor TP53 gene. After a person takes Sinsen for many years, it can't code an efficient enough protein."

"What is a TP53 gene?" Michael's frustration overpowered his fear. He needed an explanation fast, before he grabbed Alex and shook it out of him.

Alex, back on familiar ground, turned to Michael to explain. "All animals grow and age because of cellular replication and division. At inception, one fertilized egg becomes two cells, which become four cells, and so on. This happens continuously until death. Every once in a while, a tumor will grow because of a mutation or viral infection. The p53 protein, which is coded from the TP53 gene, acts as a tumor suppressor. It can activate programmed cellular death, known as apoptosis, of the tumor cells if the body can't repair them."

"So what does Sinsen have to do with that?" Michael was drowning in his own ignorance. He desperately needed an explanation. Maybe there had been a mistake. Maybe it could be fixed.

"Sinsen is an incredibly good telomerase activator. It protects not only the genetic integrity of good cells, but also the genetic integrity of tumor cells. With the protective shield afforded by Sinsen, a tumor cell will replicate indefinitely, completely unchecked by the body."

"And this is what is causing all these deaths?"

"Yes, Michael. Anyone who has been taking Sinsen for years no longer had the ability to naturally combat tumor growths in the body. Once a strong viral infection genetically affects cells a wide spread tumorous growth is almost inevitable."

"And nobody knew this before?" Michael looked to David, who remained speechless, his elbows on the table, hands supporting his face.

"The full effect of Sinsen is realized only after it's been taken for years," Alex said. "At first, it only looks like people stop aging completely. What really happens is that aging slows down considerably. During that time, the p35 protein—the tumor suppressor—remains somewhat effective. But after a few years with Sinsen, aging really does stop completely. By the time cellular senescence—aging—has completely stopped, the tumor suppressor is completely ineffective. Then a tumor resulting from a strong viral infection, like the avian flu, is almost unstoppable. Some Asians were exposed to Sinsen for years before it was introduced to either the U.S. or the European markets. In Asia, we are just now noticing the consequences of attempting to stop aging."

"Do you think the same thing will happen in the rest of the world?" Michael felt as though he were watching himself ask the question from some place outside his own body.

"There is no doubt," Alex said, not meeting Michael's gaze. "This is my fault, David. I neglected my scientific duty to consider all the potential consequences. I encouraged you to continue the research. I desperately wanted you and Clive to succeed."

There was a long pause. "I didn't exactly avoid shortcuts myself," David said finally. He sat up in his chair and cleared his throat. "There is no doubt about this?"

"None, David. The data are unquestionably conclusive."

"What do we do now?"

"We have assembled a team. We need to know where Sinsen is distributed so that we can work with local authorities to disseminate the information. We must not cause a panic."

"There will be a panic. I can guarantee you that," Michael said. "Our customers panicked when their supply was threatened. They are sure to panic now that their lives are threatened. Two hundred million people take it!" Michael thought about his family, about Caroline. What if she had secretly begun to take Sinsen? He had asked her to so many times. And what about him? He'd been taking it for years.

"We need to save the lives of those most at risk and worry about the reaction of everyone else later." Alex stood. "There is a team waiting in the next room. These men have been assigned to you."

David looked at the men sitting beside them. They had not said a word during the meeting. He turned back to Alex. "These men aren't from the WHO, are they?"

"No, David. They are from Interpol. I'm very sorry."

Michael stood up. David stayed seated. He couldn't move.

62

"Please tell me you have not been taking Sinsen," Michael said, unable to hide the panic in his voice. He was calling Caroline from a phone at the WHO, where he had spent six straight hours with a crisis management team. Only after they were satisfied that he had given them sufficient information had they let him make a phone call.

"Michael, what is going on?"

"I'll tell you everything. Just tell me if you've been taking Sinsen."

"I've told you a million times, I haven't. I thought about it, but no...and I've decided that I never will."

Michael let out all of the breath in his lungs, relieved that he had not brought her harm. "Thank God. It kills, Caroline. There is no Dragon Flu. People who take Sinsen and contract a strong viral infection like the avian flu are dying of cancer."

"What?" Caroline started to fire off questions, near hysteria. The emotion in her voice and the speed of her words made it impossible for Michael to understand exactly what she was asking, but he had a good guess.

"Caroline. Listen to me. Listen. Right now I don't have any answers. I can only do the right thing and hope for the best."

"What about your family and mine? Beth? Our friends? What about you?"

"I don't know. An announcement will be made soon. Go get food and whatever else you might need for a couple of days, and stay put."

"Michael, what are you saying?"

"I'm not sure how the world is going to take this. I think there might be a panic. Get supplies and stay inside."

"Why, Michael?

"People are going to see this as the end of the world. Most people are already on edge. This will make them insane. Sinsen subscribers might come after me if they know where I live."

"Oh, my God." A flood of fear washed over Caroline.

"I'm going to call the office and have Black Falcon send people over. They'll protect you. I'm sure there's nothing to worry about. I'm just trying to be safe."

"When are you coming home?" It was as much a plea as it was a question.

"I'll try and catch a flight tomorrow."

"Catch a flight? Isn't David coming back with you?"

Michael took a deep breath. "David's been arrested."

Michael was right. There was a panic. A statement transmitted by the WHO to all of its member countries warned of the harmful effects of Sinsen. The statement was immediately transmitted to local authorities, who, in turn, instructed the media to release it. Once the message had been received by the masses, it ignited hysteria. The WHO wanted to be cautious, so the statement warned of potential death from a viral infection of any sort. As a result, people who had taken Sinsen locked themselves in their homes for fear of contracting anything at all. People who did not take Sinsen smelled the blood in the water.

The WHO's crisis management team had contemplated the reaction of the two hundred million people who took Sinsen. What they had not contemplated, what no one had contemplated, was the reaction of the billions who did not. It was those billions—the billions who had suffered rising costs, unemployment, hunger, illness, political unrest, threats of war, and aging discrimination—who reacted most violently. For years, those billions had watched world leaders waste valuable resources to keep the wealthy young. The sacrifice and pain they'd had to endure was mitigated only by a promise that, one day, the future would be better. Now it was clear that the future would be worse. The threat of World War Three had created a powder keg out of society. This announcement ignited it.

"My God! They are going to destroy everything." Caroline stood in the living room, with both hands covering her mouth, watching the events unfold on television. Mrs. Klein sat on the couch with little Gregor by her side. Just a few feet away, two well-armed guards in dark suits peered out of the floor-to-ceiling window of the fifty-first-floor apartment. They could see the chaos in the distance. The riots had begun earlier in the day. Now night was approaching.

"Don't worry, Gregor, we'll be fine here." Mrs. Klein held his tiny hand. Gregor was young, but he could sense the fear in the room.

That morning, one day after the announcement was made, the natural order of the city collapsed. Many people were too afraid to leave their homes to go to work. Several countries declared a bank holiday until further notice. The stock markets opened briefly, only to be closed by the authorities after panic trading commenced. By noon, it was reported that businesses were no longer taking credit for transactions. A run on ATMs ensued. By 2 p.m., all of the cash had been withdrawn from the machines. No one knew when they would be replenished. By 3 p.m., the stores that had remained open were sold out of inventory. Opportunists brought out what they could from their homes and sold it on the streets for ten times what it would have cost the day before. By 4 p.m., almost everyone with a car had left the city. No one was picking up the hitchhikers desperate to get out. By 5 p.m., the Governor had declared martial law. Everyone had to remain indoors after sunset.

The looting started around 6 p.m. The National Guard was called in to maintain order, but they were hours away. By 7 p.m., all ground transportation came to a standstill. All stores were closed. Every channel on television was broadcasting the news. Much of the information coming through was contradictory. There were more rumors than facts. One fact was indisputable: a catastrophe was unfolding.

"Why are they doing this?" Mrs. Klein stared at the television. Throngs of looters lit ablaze any car that remained parked on the street. Almost every large window within throwing distance of a sidewalk was broken. The rioters were now only a few blocks away.

"Let them eat cake" was all that Caroline could say.

"What's that, my dear?" Mrs. Klein asked.

"That's what they told them. 'Let them eat cake.' Everyone should have seen this coming. It's ironic that the one thing that couldn't possibly hurt them would cause this."

63

I t was ironic. The majority of the physical damage was caused by those that did not take Sinsen but had suffered indirectly, nonetheless. They were the masses holding on to a fragile string of hope that had just snapped. Realizing that their future had turned from bad to desperate, they flooded the streets exacting revenge on anything that they felt represented the Sinsen Elite.

The world continued to spiral into chaos in the days after the announcement. Every Sinsen subscriber thought they would die within weeks, despite the WHO's vigorous attempts to convince them of the contrary. Information was disseminated inconsistently by governments. All the major countries put out reports on their understanding of the situation, often in sharp contradiction to each other. Rumors swirled furiously throughout the world, aided by financial speculators hoping to cash in on the madness. Each time the stock markets opened, a flood of sell orders poured in, forcing trading to a halt. A few religious fanatics preached the end of man. People purchased guns in large numbers. All airlines were grounded to prevent further contagion of the flu. The military became the de-facto police in many major cities. Looting was prevented only by the threat of force. Society, it seemed, had utterly broken down.

Aseso's plantations, once worth trillions of dollars, lost almost all of their value, as did the bonds that Bearing Brothers had sold to investors around the world. The company's assets were frozen. Its headquarters in New York and Nanning were taken over by the WHO crisis management team. All documents were confiscated. Incalculable numbers of lawsuits were filed in empty courthouses. In less than a week, the most powerful company in the world collapsed.

Deaths continued to mount in Asia, but not at the same accelerating rate as before. Relatively few deaths were reported in the Americas and in Europe. The grounding of the airlines and self-imposed isolation within the masses had helped to prevent further spreading. Still, hospitals were overwhelmed with people claiming to be infected, which only prevented the system from helping people who actually were.

The potential world war had been averted. China withdrew from Africa and disbanded its coalition with Russia and Belarus. NATO rescinded all declarations against the African Union and its members. President Coves called on all countries to unite in an effort to restore world order. The same countries that had threatened to go to war only days before now came together to find a solution.

No one knew how long the chaos would last. No one knew how long Sinsen's harmful effects would remain in the body. The best scientists from each country were sent to Geneva to form a task force to study the problem. Time seemed to stand still while everyone waited to find out what would happen to them. Throughout those weeks, David stayed at the WHO under Interpol surveillance, helping as best he could.

"Deep down, I knew this would not end well. I just never expected it to end this way," David told Alex over dinner at the hotel in Geneva.

"There is a bit of irony in all this," Alex said.

"What is that?"

"I think we'll find that cellular senescence will restart very quickly without Sinsen. Without telomerase activation in the body, the threat of death due to viral infection should dissipate within a month, at the most."

"That's good news, but I don't see the irony."

"I've asked some of the statisticians to predict the total number of deaths that will occur if my theory about a month-long recovery to normalcy is correct."

"What have they come up with?"

"One percent of those that would have occurred if all those countries had gone to war."

"That's ironic, but it's not comforting."

"I then asked them to predict the number of deaths due to starvation if Aseso had been allowed to continue."

"And?"

"That was the largest number of the three scenarios. One hundred times those of war."

"Is that supposed to make me feel better?"

"This 'Dragon Flu' was the best thing that could have happened. It prevented many more deaths than there would have been otherwise."

"The world is in chaos," David said. "In case you haven't noticed."

"The world needed this chaos. Better to get past this quickly than to have the world slowly decay into extinction."

Logically, David knew that this was true, but he could not see past his depression. Nothing would ever be the same. There was no going back to New York. Everything for him there was gone. The only thing that helped him retain his sanity was his efforts to help the team at the WHO. Once that was over, he would have nowhere to go.

Each night at his hotel, David would watch television and witness how the world that he thought he had changed for the better had suddenly changed for the worse. What was most surprising was not the reaction of his customers, who feared death, but the reaction of the many who were not his customers, who feared their new lives. They were angry. They were angry at David. He had created this mess. His worst crime was that he had given the world false hope.

Death threats arrived constantly. Several countries threatened to charge David for crimes against humanity. Aseso's former activities would no longer be ignored. Somebody had to pay. David had to pay. He would be allowed to move around freely in Geneva long enough to help the WHO, and then there would be a trial. There could be many trials. If there were no existing laws under which to charge him, then governments would create them. The catastrophe could not go unanswered.

The nonsubscribers' reaction was immediate and violent, motivated by anger. The subscribers' reaction was no less immediate, but in their case, the motivation was fear. No one who had been a subscriber wanted to come into contact with the general population for fear of contracting the flu. The highest economic level of society was paralyzed. Expectations had been crushed.

For almost a decade, they had prayed at the altar of Aseso, only to find out that their god did not exist. They were mortal once again.

64

Washington, D.C. Two Weeks Later.

The impact on Manhattan was not trivial. Many buildings throughout the city were damaged. The looting was finally suppressed when the National Guard arrived, two days after the announcement had been made.

The harm to Michael and Caroline's apartment building was mostly superficial. The two Black Falcon agents who had been sent to protect Caroline had called for support when they saw that the mob posed a real threat to the building's residents. Within minutes additional agents had arrived, this time more heavily armed. They surrounded the building, brandishing semiautomatic rifles. Some of the rioters came dangerously close to losing their lives. The mob taunted the agents, but kept its distance when it became clear that the agents were prepared to use force.

No one at One Lincoln Tower Plaza was hurt that night. No shots were fired. The mob moved on to less protected buildings. There were assaults and muggings along with the looting. The police were overwhelmed. The angry mob fed on its own energy. Greater numbers came out to join them. The common people had been ignored for too long, and it was their night to be heard.

A similar scene unfolded in Washington, D.C. The army was quickly brought in to prevent the city from exploding into chaos. President Coves was flown to Camp David, where he remained for the next week. Silvia Gutierrez's department coordinated with the Federal Emergency Management Agency (FEMA) to provide support for cities where most of the rioting was taking place. For ten days, it seemed that the world was looking into the abyss. With one more step, civilization could be turned back five hundred years.

Then another announcement brought society back from the brink. The WHO announced that the detrimental effects of taking Sinsen, and specifically the risk of cancer from contracting a strong viral infection, should disappear within a month of ceasing its use. This announcement was based on a theory put forward by Alex and David and supported by the international scientific community. The world only needed to wait three more weeks, and then everyone would return to normal.

Aseso, through its regional offices, sent every customer an email, drafted by the WHO, detailing what to expect. A dedicated website explaining the situation was set up. Michael had agreed to cooperate fully with Coves and his administration to minimize the damage created by the crisis. A month after the announcement, when it was considered safe to return to normal activity, Michael found himself at the White House with the President, Silvia Gutierrez, Sanjay Bhatia, and the director of FEMA, along with other members rounding out the emergency task force.

"We are not exactly out of the woods yet." Silvia sat next to Michael on one of the couches in the Oval Office, across from three team members. President Coves sat behind his desk. Michael was overwhelmed by his new position as acting CEO. Interpol was still confining David to Geneva.

"Explain to me why it is that a month ago everyone on Earth was going to die, and now everyone should be fine." Coves' elbows rested on the desk, his fingers interlocked.

"Well, Mr. President," Sanjay said, "the current thinking is that without telomerase, which is what Sinsen activates in the body, the immune system will once again be able to regulate tumors effectively. One way to think about it is that Sinsen gave tumor cells a bulletproof vest against the tumor suppressors naturally found in the body."

"And within a month this bulletproof vest will go away?"

"Yes, because telomerase is an enzyme that needs to be present daily to be effective. All traces of Sinsen should dissipate within a month." Sanjay looked to Silvia, who nodded in agreement.

"Then why are we not out of the woods?" Coves asked, sitting back in his chair.

"We still have a flu pandemic. That hasn't changed," Silvia said. Michael was glad to hear her point out that the flu, at least, had nothing to do with Aseso or him.

"There is always some sort of pandemic. Coordinate with the Red Cross and hand out some pamphlets or something," Coves said, dismissive of Silvia's concerns.

"We'll get right on that," Silvia responded.

"Now, Mr. Jeffs. The issue I see facing us is how we're going to clean up this entire mess."

"You can count on my and Dr. Oaks's continued cooperation," Michael said.

"Damn straight I'm going to count on your continued cooperation. When Dr. Oaks gets his ass back here, there is going to be hell to pay."

"I can assure you that no one at Aseso knew any of this would happen." Michael felt sweat forming on his brow. His stomach sank.

"You gentlemen ran that company with complete reckless abandon. The public safety was never the slightest consideration."

"As I recall, Mr. President, only a month ago you wanted to sell America's oil to have us distribute Sinsen to the public." Michael knew he was speaking dangerously.

"No. That's not true. I was initiating preliminary discussions to get to the bottom of the whole Sinsen thing. I was skeptical since day one. I knew something like this would happen. I am going to hang David Oaks."

"On what charge? He didn't know this would happen. What law did he break?"

"I have an army of lawyers to figure that out for me, and when they do...." Coves' phone rang. "Yes," Coves answered the phone sharply, clearly annoyed by the interruption. He listened for a moment.

"What do you mean, he's gone?" This time, Coves' voice conveyed shock. He turned his back to the rest of the room and looked out onto the garden through his office windows as if to search for someone with his own eyes. Everyone exchanged glances. The response from the other end of the line was brief.

"Was he abducted, or did he flee?" Now everyone in the room was staring at the back of Coves' head. His hand clenched the phone. This time, the response was much longer.

"Well then, find out, goddamn it!" Cove slammed the phone down. Turning to fully face the room, he stared directly at Michael. "Where is David Oaks?"

65

New York. Three Months Later.

Michael had no idea where David was. Nobody did. It was the day before Interpol was scheduled to fly him back to the United States for questioning. The routine for that day was to be the same as for every other day that month: a black Mercedes from Interpol would shuttle him from his hotel to the WHO's headquarters.

The day he disappeared, David, as usual, had walked downstairs from his hotel room, entered the lobby, greeted the doormen, walked outside, and entered a waiting black Mercedes. The car provided by Interpol would show up at the hotel eight minutes later. The cars and the uniforms of the guards and drivers were identical.

The largest manhunt in history ensued. Nobody knew if David had fled or been abducted. There were plenty of theories. Numerous death threats had originated from around the globe. Families of countless victims wanted revenge. Religious extremists viewed him as evil. Political groups blamed him for the wars that were to be fought in his name. Dr. Tanaka's enemies were his as well.

Perhaps the Chinese had assisted in his escape, as the Americans had helped German scientists escape during World War II. Perhaps mobsters wanted to extract the whereabouts of money David must surely have hidden somewhere. Perhaps ambitious businessmen wanted to invent a safer Sinsen and launch themselves into the market. Although David had cooperated fully with the WHO in researching Sinsen's effects, he had refused to disclose the secret behind the genetic engineering of the plants. This information was still extremely valuable.

The media, which had once been obsessed with David's personal life, was now obsessed with his whereabouts.

"Where is David Oaks?"

Joanna Hochberg laughed. She hadn't expected this to be the first question of the television interview. "Everyone asks me that, as if somehow I should know. I'm just as curious as everyone else."

Two months after David's disappearance, the world had regained some semblance of its pre-Aseso self. Society had begun to pick up the pieces and move on. The flu pandemic had abated; evidence of Sinsen's Dragon Flu effects had completely disappeared. Everyone wanted to know how the world could have been brought to the brink of destruction. How could the political leaders have allowed this to happen? How could society have allowed this to happen? Joanna had quickly become the media's most sought-after commentator. Not only was she intimately familiar with the history of Aseso; she had also, everyone knew, been intimately involved with David.

"I had to ask," the host said apologetically. "But let's get to the heart of the matter. Dr. Hochberg, you have been at the forefront of the Aseso story from the beginning. You were the first to go on record suggesting that anti-aging supplements actually worked, and you also predicted catastrophe. What do you see now?"

"I think too much has been made of my predicting a catastrophe. When I first used the word, I was referring to a Malthusian Catastrophe, in which the resources of the world could not support an explosion in human population. At first, I naively believed that such a scenario was possible. Looking back, I see that it could never have happened."

"Why do you say that?"

"There is a very famous experiment that has been repeated many times, involving mice. Fifty mice are placed in a cage where they can move around comfortably and eat all they want. The experimenters provide enough food to sustain one hundred mice.

Theoretically, after reproduction to more than one hundred, they would go hungry. The objective of the experiment is to see at what number the population of mice will plateau. Some predicted one hundred and ten, others one hundred and twenty—under the assumption that at some point after one hundred, cannibalism would begin."

"Interesting. Did the population plateau at exactly one hundred?"

"No. In fact, repeated experiments showed that the population always leveled off at around eighty. Somehow, it seems that the mice anticipated the un-sustainability of their situation. Eventually, overcrowding and hunger would have become unbearable, and so the mice prevented this by killing off some of their own before that happened."

"And how do you relate that to what is happening now?"

"Thomas Malthus predicted that hunger and overcrowding would lead to the end of civilization as population growth far exceeded the rate of increase of natural resource availability. What he failed to realize, as I failed to realize, was that humans would see this coming from miles away and would destroy some number of themselves—through war or otherwise—far in advance of a Malthusian Catastrophe ever happening."

"I see your point," said the host, "but a war wasn't the end of the story here. A deadly disease seemed to have prevented the Malthusian Catastrophe."

"That, as it turns out, was a piece of good luck. We now know that total deaths from the flu pandemic will be relatively small compared to what might have happened if the world had gone to war. And the number of flu deaths is even less significant when you compare it to what might have happened if all of the earth's resources had continued to be diverted to support the immortality of the wealthy few. As far as catastrophes go, we seem to have lucked out."

"That is a very optimistic way of looking at what happened. I am not sure many people would agree with you. A lesser catastrophe is still a catastrophe."

"You only have to look at the facts. We were headed for either World War Three or the eventual destruction of humanity by starvation. Every once in a while, something bad has to happen to force people to pause and think about how much worse things could have been."

"There is some logic to that. But I still have one last burning question."

"What is that?"

"Where is David Oaks?" the host repeated, laughing.

PART FIVE

THE NINTH YEAR

66

Seattle. The Ninth Year. December.

A year after the Dragon Flu Crisis, the world settled back into a normal rhythm. The avian flu had been successfully contained, and its Dragon Flu effects dissipated. Sinsen had been recalled in every country where it had been distributed. The rebuilding of what had been destroyed by Aseso's activities required an undertaking of historic proportions. Millions of people who had lost their jobs during the Aseso era were hired to put things back together. The savings rate rose and inflation declined as people once again became aware of their mortality and rushed to modify their economic behavior. Land was once again available to plant crops for food, fuel, and animal feed. Governments held a special international session to establish a commission to ensure that the near-catastrophe created by Aseso would never occur again.

Michael stayed on as acting CEO of Aseso in David's absence, working with authorities everywhere to dismantle the organization and deal with the many employees, suppliers, customers, and creditors. He repeatedly visited Washington, working with President Coves' administration to make sure everything possible was being done to mitigate the potential damage. When asked, he honestly replied that he had no idea where David was. None of the many investigations into the disappearance had resulted in any true leads as to David's whereabouts. Several organizations took credit for a kidnapping, but no evidence was ever produced to substantiate those claims.

Just after the second anniversary of the crisis, Michael and Caroline returned to Seattle with Gregor and little Jacqueline. They bought a beautiful house in the Maple Leaf area, close to where Caroline grew up. From their porch, they could see the Olympic and Cascade Mountains. The house was spacious enough for them to raise a big family comfortably. Michael and Caroline spent hours playing with the children in their large backyard. They were very happy.

Mrs. Klein declined their invitation to move to Seattle with them, preferring to spend her final years in the city where she had grown up. She stayed on in an apartment Michael had bought for her under the pretense that it was an investment. He never charged Mrs. Klein anything for living there.

Brad accepted a position in Coves' administration as a political appointee in the Treasury Department. His position as Undersecretary for Domestic Finance afforded him an office that was a two-minute walk from the White House. Jason returned to Chicago, his home town, to attend business school.

"How did it go today?" Caroline was baking cookies in the kitchen when Michael walked in with Gregor.

"Great. This kid is going to be an Olympic champion." Michael had just returned from the indoor pool where Gregor took his swimming lessons.

"Good. Can you help our Olympic champion get washed up and ready for dinner? My parents are going to be here any minute."

"Okay. Hey, champ," Michael said to Gregor as he picked him up, "you heard the boss; let's get you upstairs."

"Don't make too much noise. I just put Jackie down for her nap," Caroline continued as she opened the oven. "Oh, by the way, a package came for you. I put it on your desk in the office."

"Thanks, babe. We'll be down in a bit."

Michael took Gregor upstairs and helped him with his bath. Afterwards he laid out some clothes for him before heading into his study. He turned on the news to catch up on the day's events.

Sitting down at his desk, Michael took out a pair of scissors and opened the top of the thick bubble envelope he found there. It had been sent to him from an address in Chicago. From inside the package he pulled out a slightly smaller package that had been shipped to a post office box in Chicago from an address in New York. This, he thought, was somewhat odd. He cut open the smaller envelope only to find another one, this time from an address in London. Now this was getting silly. Inside was yet another envelope, which had been shipped from an address in Hong Kong. Finally, inside the letter from Hong Kong, there was a last envelope with a return address in Laos. Michael sat staring at the last envelope as his mind raced.

"Hey, Michael, can you bring Gregor down? My parents are here," Caroline called from downstairs.

"I'll be down in a minute," Michael yelled back, holding the envelope in his hand; his heart beating faster. He held it up to the light so that the writing on the letter inside became almost legible. He could not make out what it said, but it was a note in English written in familiar handwriting. He picked up the scissors again and placed one of the blades underneath the flap. Just before squeezing down, he heard Gregor call out to him from the doorway.

"Daddy."

He looked towards the door and saw his future looking back at him. He sat motionless, taken aback by the sight of his own son.

"I'll be right there, champ," he said after a moment.

Michael laid the scissors down and smiled. He took a last look at the envelope, let out a deep breath, and walked over to the corner of the room where the electric shredder sat above a wastepaper basket.

He thought to himself, just before putting the envelope down into the teeth of the machine: *Fool me once....*

ABOUT THE AUTHOR

Ernesto Robles was born in San Francisco, California. He received a Bachelor of Arts from the University of California, Santa Barbara, Master of Science from the University of Texas and a Masters in Business Administration from the University of Chicago.

Before writing *The Malthusian Catastrophe* he spent the majority of his career as a Washington D.C. based economist and New York based investment banker.

This is his first novel.

Made in the USA
Charleston, SC
02 May 2010